Andrew Crofts is one of Britain's most successful ghost-writers. Millions have read his books without realising. Through his work he comes into contact with spies and mercenaries, billionaires and slaves, rock stars and actors, courtesans and fraudsters, gangsters and gurus, and sinners and saints of every kind, and he has told many of their stories in his catalogue of fascinating, and very varied, books. He has also written a selection of manuals and guides on writing and marketing. This is his first work of original fiction published under his own name.

Andrew Crofts

maisie's amazing maids

HOUSE OF
STRATUS

This edition published in 2001 by House of Stratus, an imprint of Stratus Holdings plc, 24c Old Burlington Street, London, W1X 1RL, UK.

www.houseofstratus.com

Typeset, printed and bound by House of Stratus.

A catalogue record for this book is available from the British Library.

ISBN 1-84232-416-0

*This book is dedicated to Susan, Alex, Amy, Olivia and Jessica,
with all my love.*

CHAPTER ONE

The two handwritten envelopes for Joe were almost drowning in the sea of other people's discarded junk mail. The calling cards of plumbers, taxi firms and carpet cleaning services washed across the hall table, eventually spilling onto the floor like coins in an arcade slot machine. No one ever seemed to clear them up.

His stomach gave a dreadful lurch of recognition at the handwriting on one of the envelopes, but the other looked less ominous, and rather intriguing. It was addressed to him, 'care of BBC Radio 4', in a childish scrawl. Some kind producer's assistant had scribbled a forwarding address on what little space was left so that the small, cheap envelope was almost completely covered in illegible writing. Joe was impressed by the skills of the British postal system in being able to decipher and deliver such a mess.

He scuffled back to his room along the worn lino of the long corridor, the heels of his shoes flattened to serve as slippers. Climbing back into the still warm bed he opened the mystery letter first, postponing the other one for as long as possible. Inside was a neatly folded piece of expensive notepaper, with an Eaton Square address printed discreetly at the top. The message was ill written, in capital letters.

DEAR MISTER TYE, I HEARD YOU ON THE RADIO AND YOU SOUND A KIND AMERICAN WHO WILL HELP A GIRL IN TROUBLE. I AM FROM MANILA. I AM A PRISONER IN

*LONDON AND A VICTIM OF TORTURE. THEY HAVE STOLEN
MY BEAUTIFUL NEW BREASTS. PLEASE TELL MY STORY
FOR ME AND HELP ME TO ESCAPE FROM THESE BAD
PEOPLE. PLEASE DO NOT TELL ANYONE THAT I HAVE
SENT THIS LETTER. PLEASE FIND A WAY TO SAVE ME AND
WE WILL WRITE MY STORY TOGETHER AND I WILL BE
YOUR WILLING SERVANT.
YOURS IN HOPE, DORIS*

Joe read it several times. He was used to receiving letters like
this, cries for help from suffering people desperately searching
for some way to pour everything out into a book. It was always
hard to tell the genuine ones from the fantasists, the ones who
really had something of interest to say from the ones who
simply wanted their stories to be heard. This one seemed more
interesting than most. There had been a lot of publicity about
the smuggling of people across borders into Europe and
America, and it would be interesting to listen to someone
who had actually experienced it. And anyone who had been
tortured was always worth talking to.

As he read, Joe's mind had already moved on to the
unopened envelope that lay on the bed beside him. He took
some deep breaths to try to calm his fears of what might be
concealed inside. His ex-wife's handwriting was instantly
recognisable. He had been receiving numerous letters from her
recently and they never brought good news, always some new
legal or financial requirement, some new piece of pain. They
reminded him how much he was missing Hugo and how much
he still hurt inside. They reminded him of what had been
spoiled and could never be repaired. They usually left him with
a queasy feeling in his stomach for days after reading them.

Finally accepting that no amount of procrastination would
quell the fears now, he sucked in a last lungful of air, as if
preparing himself for a deep dive, and tore it open. The nausea
rose up in a wave as a bill for three and a half thousand pounds

dropped onto the bedclothes, with a brief, breezy letter attached.

Dear Joe,
Hope all is well with you. This needs to be paid before the start of term. Hugo sends his love – very excited about new school.
Love, Fliss.

Joe stared at the invoice in horror. He had had no idea that Fliss had expected him to pay the bills when she announced that Hugo needed to go to a "decent" school. He had imagined his ex-father-in-law would have taken care of it from some mysterious trust or other. Surely, that was how old landed families operated in England? Did she imagine Joe could conjure up this kind of money from nowhere? Or did she merely want to shame him into making some sort of contribution?

If shame was Fliss' intention she was certainly hitting her mark. He felt deeply inadequate for not being able to support his son in the expected manner – and this was on top of the feeling of inadequacy he already felt for not having been able to dissuade Fliss from leaving him.

The obvious thing would be to ring and tell her that private education was out of the question until he got himself back on his feet. He simply didn't have the money for it at the moment. In a year's time he might be in a better position. But he couldn't face admitting to failure quite that easily. He would just have to find the money.

For as long as he could remember there had always been money in his account and there had never been that many bills to be met. Suddenly everything had spiralled out of control. He had to stop the rot quickly. He had been making big money in the past few years. There was no reason he couldn't get his career moving again now that the initial trauma of the divorce was behind him and the lawyers had all been paid. He decided he would ring Adele, his agent, and chase up some work. It was time to restart his life.

Heading back past the closed doors of his fellow flatmates, Joe felt his spirits rise a little. He would get something going with this call, stir Adele into action, take control of the situation like a young boy's father should. He felt ready to get back to work, to put his mind to a good, meaty project or two.

'Hi, Adele!' He felt a comforting surge of warmth at the sound of her New York tones on the other end of the line. Whenever he heard her it reminded him how English his own voice had become over the years. 'How's it going?'

'Great Joe, how are you? So good to hear from you. What've you been doing?'

'Oh, this and that, you know. Listen, Adele, have you had any news on the Marion Ray book?'

'Yeah.' He couldn't tell from her tone what might be coming next. 'Marion really likes you. She truly wants to do the project. It's just a question of her finding the time.'

'Has she given any idea when she might be free?' Joe groped desperately for some straws of hope.

'Last time I spoke to her people on the Coast they said she was just going into production on a new project. But once that's out of the way she really wants to do the book with you. So what are you working on in the meantime?'

Adele was obviously trying to change the subject and he couldn't really blame her. They had had roughly the same conversation about Marion Ray every month for a year now. It was inevitable. The woman was one of the most enduring stars in the world. Her name might not be above the title on her movies these days, but she could still fill a stadium when she gave one of her rare concerts. Persuading such a notoriously temperamental star to write an autobiography was bound to be an uphill struggle. Doing the actual job would be hard too – it always was with the big names – but it would be worth it.

'Did any more money come through from the SAS book?'
Joe changed the subject himself.

'I don't know. I'll check it out with accounts and get them to
send through whatever's owing. You got money troubles?'

'Divorce is never cheap.'

'Tell me about it.'

He wanted to keep the conversation going to avoid going
back to being alone with his morning post, to keep the illusion
of busyness up for a little longer. He remembered the letter he
had received that morning.

'I got a letter this morning from a Filipino girl who reckons
she's been white-slaved over here and wants me to save her.' He
gave a hollow laugh, as if expecting Adele to dismiss the idea.

'Could be good,' Adele said, her mind already wandering
onto another call she had to make as soon as she got Joe off
the line.

'She says they've stolen her breasts,' he added, focusing his
mind more fully on the subject.

'Yeah? This sex slave trade is pretty topical at the moment.
Maybe you should at least meet her.'

'Yeah?'

'Sure, why not? It could be a good article if not a book.'

'Right.' Joe didn't like the idea of going back to selling
articles. He couldn't envisage keeping a boy at a British prep
school on the scrapings of freelance journalism. He decided to
end the conversation before his spirits sank any lower. 'Well, if
you could chase up any money for me,' he ended lamely. 'And
I'd be happy to meet Marion Ray again if you think it would
help.'

'Let me put it to her people. I'm due to go over to the States
in a week or two. Drop in for a cup of coffee if you're in the
West End.'

'Okay.' He hung up, wondering how Adele managed to be so
successful in a country that wasn't even her own. She had only
been in England five years and she seemed more at home and

5

confident than most of the London agents who had been there all their lives.

Joe sat slumped in the chair, staring at the communal ashtray on top of the out-of-date directories. It was piled high with the discarded tea-bags and cigarette ends of a hundred futile calls. His reverie was broken sharply by the phone ringing at his elbow.

'Yes?' He snatched it up with a start.

'Joe-boy?' He recognised the East London rasp immediately.

'Hi, Len.' He was pleased to hear from the old gangster and enjoyed the frisson of intimidation Len's voice still sent through him, even after all this time.

'Having some friends round for a barbecue at the house this evening,' Len wheezed. 'Cordelia would like you to come.'

'That would be great.'

'There'll be some interesting people for you to meet too, people with good stories to tell – and celebrities. You might pick up a bit of business.'

'Okay.' Joe felt his spirits lift again.

Going to Len's for the evening was just the sort of distraction he needed. Meeting some new people would take his mind off his troubles, stop him sitting around in the flat brooding, and any chance to meet potential new subjects was worth it.

Len's house was in a spotless, genteel suburb at the far eastern end of the London underground system. Joe had grown to know the route well in the weeks that he had spent going out there to listen to Len's memories when they were writing the book. He had always looked forward to the meetings with a mixture of enjoyment and trepidation. With Len you could never quite tell whether you would be treated with a smile or a snarl. That was what gave him the edge, and had made him successful, both as a gangster and as a minor media celebrity.

When he arrived at the house Joe could hear music coming from the garden. The front door was open and the two

Dobermans followed his progress across the wide open spaces of the sitting room towards the patio without raising their heads. They weren't going to waste their energy unnecessarily on a hot evening.

Cordelia danced, bare-footed and mini-skirted, across the patio when she saw Joe arriving. He was clutching a six-pack and feeling self-conscious. His discomfort increased as she snuggled her body, which only a year before had seemed innocently childlike, against his and pulled him into the crowd of guests on the lawn. One or two of the faces wore the strange familiarity of the television screen; a chat show host here, a comedian turned quiz show master there, all of them smiling promiscuously around in stark contrast to the deadpan faces of Len and his closer associates.

Len's intimate friends might once have been animated young men but now they wore impenetrable masks. Many of them had been constructed by surgeons' knives and stitching techniques, then perfected at all-night poker games in smoky bars. Cordelia moved amongst the gnarled and battered old men and carefully painted women like a shimmering reaffirmation of life.

'Joe-boy!' Len held out his arms, his face immobile despite a smile which made his lips disappear around his shiny white false teeth. He wore a butcher's apron over his shorts and held a vicious, blood-stained fork in his hand. 'Glad you could make it. Everyone!' His voice grew no louder but still silenced the chatter of the crowd. 'Meet Joe Tye, my ghost-writer. The man who took my words and spun them into pure gold. You're a bleedin' alchemist, Joe-boy, that's what you are.' There was a chorus of greetings. 'I'm glad you could come,' Len said again, leading him to the drinks table. 'It's nice for Cordelia to have someone her own age here.'

Joe smiled awkwardly and decided not to point out that he was twenty years older than the girl who was pouring him a Pimm's and pressing it into his hand. He felt absurdly flattered, both by Len's words and by Cordelia's attentions. Just at that moment he was hungry for flattery and didn't intend to do anything to risk ending it. The drink rattled with ice and fruit and he drank it thirstily.

The food seemed to take forever to cook and Joe was on his third Pimm's by the time he sat down with a plateful of charred meat and salad. He was beginning to feel more at home. Cordelia was helping to serve other guests and the table around him filled up with expressionless faces.

'So, you're the ghost-writer then,' a man tearing into a spare rib said. 'Who you writing for now you've finished Len?'

'Well,' Joe hated these sorts of conversations. He preferred asking questions to answering them. 'I've got a few projects in the pipeline.'

'Like who?' His interrogator obviously didn't intend to let him off the hook.

'Well, Marion Ray is thinking of doing a book...'

'Oh yeah? I like her. She's what I call a real star,' another face announced, biting into a hamburger, the bloody sauce dripping unwiped down the parched riverbeds of his scarred chin.

'And I've been approached by a Filipino girl who seems to have been brought over here as some kind of sex slave.'

'You want to watch those oriental birds,' another set of masticating jaws announced.

'What's wrong with them?' Len joined them with a plateload of food for himself, having handed the barbecue over to a well-known television chef who was happily showing off his skills to a group of admirers. 'I heard they know a few tricks.'

'Never trust a man who has to go over there to find a woman,' the first man growled.

'What you talking about?' Len sounded aggressive but the other man seemed unconcerned.

'Look at that Mike Martin and his bird,' he replied, as if that proved his case.

'What about them?'

'Cold piece of work she is. Wouldn't want to turn my back on her.'

'Should make a good couple then,' Len grumbled, gnawing on a rib.

'He's something to do with the government isn't he?' Joe asked innocently. 'Raises money for them or something.'

There was a rumble of laughter around him as if he had said something risibly naïve.

'You should do a book on him,' Len told Joe and they all wheezed with laughter again.

'End up face down in a canal if you tried,' one of them chuckled. 'I doubt he wants his fancy new friends to have their noses rubbed in his past.'

'How's he made so much money, then?' someone else asked.

'In the City,' Len said. 'All legit now.'

'They're a bunch of bleeding crooks in that City,' the scarred chin said and there were mutters of agreement.

'Where does he operate from?' Joe asked.

'Down south somewhere,' Len said.

'Wimbledon,' another added. 'House like a fortress overlooking the Common.'

'Handy for the tennis,' someone said.

'And he has an oriental wife?' Joe asked.

'Maisie's her name,' one of them said. 'I think she comes from Manila or Hong Kong or Bangkok or somewhere. He found her in a massage parlour or something.'

'They all have such English names,' Joe said, more to himself than anyone else. 'It's kind of bizarre.'

'She's as dangerous as him,' the scarred chin added, as if Joe hadn't spoken.

'I heard that,' Len agreed. 'Rumour has it she killed several men on the job in the East, just for their passports.'

They all laughed and the conversation changed as Cordelia slipped onto Joe's lap and put her arms round his neck. She had obviously been at the Pimm's jug herself. Joe could smell the fruit on her sweetly scented breath. He felt his colour rising again and an overwhelming urge to hug her. Len appeared not to notice his daughter's behaviour.

'That agent of yours,' Len said. 'Adele is it?'

'Yes.'

'When's she going to be parting with some more money then?'

'It takes a while to earn out an advance as big as that one,' Joe said. 'And we've had all the serialisation money from the newspapers. There may not be any more money for a year or more. There may not be any more at all if we don't sell enough copies.'

'What about film rights?' another man asked. 'Old Len's life would make a great movie.'

'That would be good,' Joe agreed, aware of uncomfortable stirrings in his lap where Cordelia was squirming around.

'Shouldn't she get off her arse and do some selling?' Len enquired without a smile. 'Isn't that what we pay her a percentage for?'

'I'm sure she's doing all she can,' Joe said weakly. 'She's a very good agent.'

Len looked unconvinced as he picked stubborn chunks of meat from between his teeth.

CHAPTER TWO

The next morning Joe had no post at all and a wave of depression threatened to sink him. How was he ever going to get his life restarted if no new work came in? Sitting in bed he read through the letter from the mysterious Doris again. He had thought about her proposition a great deal on the way back from Len's the night before and he was beginning to like the idea. He still couldn't tell if the girl had enough of a story to make a book, but the only way to find out would be to meet her. It might never earn him a penny, but at least it was a possibility.

The address at the top of the notepaper which Doris had used to write to him said Eaton Square. He knew the square because he had been there to visit an aunt of Fliss' soon after they arrived in London. The aunt had been crumblingly old and the house had been dark and damp, but very grand. The aunt had died shortly afterwards and he and Fliss had spotted the house, newly done up, being advertised in *Country Life* for four million pounds, leasehold.

These places, he knew, were serious pieces of real estate. Len had also regaled him with tales of the Belgravia area from when he was an energetic young cat burglar, jumping from roof to roof in his pursuit of ladies' jewels and portable pictures and silver. Len had become quite misty-eyed as he remembered the days when even the thieves saw themselves as 'gentlemen'.

As Joe made his way down the hallway of the flat the door to his landlord's room opened, letting out a cloud of stale cigarette smoke. Angus poked his thin, once beautiful head out, and coughed.

'Morning Joseph,' he boomed in a voice that many years before had been trained to reach the back stalls and balconies of any theatre. 'Don't forget. Today is rent day.'

'I'm just on my way to the bank now,' Joe lied. 'Unless you'd prefer a cheque…'

'No, no,' the old actor waved the offer aside as if he was being magnanimous. 'Cash will be fine.'

'I'll see you later then,' Joe said, quickly letting himself out before Angus could ask him if he had any work on. When he returned that evening he would pretend to have forgotten to go to the bank and would write a cheque anyway. That would take a day or two to clear, in which time he would hopefully have managed to raise some money from somewhere.

He didn't want to lose his room. He doubted if he would be able to find anything else as central which he could even hope to afford. The thought of moving out from the centre of London filled him with horror. If he was in the suburbs he would be stranded without a car, and there was no way he could afford to equip himself with one of those. He couldn't understand how he had fallen so easily into his own special sort of poverty trap – a man of his age and experience. Just a year earlier it had all seemed to be going so well.

To save the tube fare he walked from Earls Court across Chelsea to Sloane Square. It was a hot day and by the time he arrived at the towering Eaton Square front door he felt uncomfortably sweaty and crumpled. If the notepaper had had a phone number on it he would have called first.

On the way over he had been planning what he would say. He would pretend that he had met the girl somewhere, walking in Hyde Park maybe, and was calling as a potential suitor. He would ask for her to be allowed out for a coffee with him. If her employers were above board they couldn't complain about that. If they raised objections and he could get close enough to the girl, he would slip her a note of his telephone number and address so that she could contact him direct. His heartbeat quickened as he approached the immaculately scrubbed front steps. He was always uncomfortable perpetrating even the smallest deception.

The door opened to his ring, revealing a cool, tranquil interior of high ceilings and polished floors, guarded by a butler in shirtsleeves and apron.

'I'm sorry to bother you,' Joe said, horribly aware of just how unpressed his clothes were. 'I'm trying to find Doris.'

The man's face remained impassive. 'If you would like to come in and wait, I will fetch Mrs Montgomery. What name shall I say?'

'Weston,' he plucked a name from the air. 'John Weston.' Joe stepped into the hall. As the butler shut the heavy front door the last sounds of the outside world were abruptly cut off and the steady tick of a nearby grandfather clock took over. Two small children appeared on the stairs, their attention attracted by the bell. They sat down on the steps to watch him, like the first members of an audience settling down for a show, full of anticipation for whatever entertainment might be to come.

Their mother emerged from downstairs. Joe assumed it was the kitchen area, as it had been in Fliss' aunt's house. Mrs Montgomery was the type of Englishwoman he had grown accustomed to during the last twelve years. Most of Fliss' school-friends had had the same air of easy superiority about them. They had always made him feel that they were charmed to meet an American, but thought Fliss terribly brave to have married a writer with no private income.

'Mr Weston is it?' she asked with a practised smile which suggested she was reserving judgement as to whether she was pleased to meet him.

'Yes,' he said, holding out his hand. 'I'm sorry to come unannounced. I was looking for Doris.'

'Doris?' She shook his hand and gave him a puzzled look. A young woman who appeared to be a nanny had joined the children on the staircase. Although she didn't sit down with her charges, she seemed to be listening to the conversation in the hall. 'I'm afraid I don't know anyone of that name.'

'She's a Filipino,' Joe said. 'She told me she was working at this address.'

'I'm afraid she made a mistake,' Mrs Montgomery gave a pleasant little laugh. 'She must have got the wrong number or the wrong street name. It often happens. People come here when they actually want Eaton Row or Eaton Terrace.'

For a second Joe thought of getting out the headed writing paper to show her that he had the right address, but thought better of it. She didn't look like the sort of woman who would take kindly to the idea of some strange girl using her personal notepaper. He guessed the girl must have stolen it from somewhere, or else the letter was a hoax. Either way he didn't want to cause the Montgomery family any unnecessary worry. He felt like an intruder in their calm, orderly lives.

He wasn't terribly surprised. So many potential stories turned out to be wild-goose chases. He had learnt long ago that it was better to cut your losses quickly rather than wasting time following up dud leads. He would give this one up and try to think of something else to work on.

'You're right,' he said. 'She must have got it wrong. I'm sorry to have disturbed you.'

'That's quite all right.' She moved him towards the door. 'I'm sorry you have been disappointed. Was she very pretty?'

'Pretty?' Joe decided still to go along with the idea that he had a personal interest in the girl. It was the easiest way out. 'Yes, she was. Never mind.' He put on what he hoped looked like a brave smile as she ushered him out into the street and the locks on the door snapped shut behind him.

Realising that he was feeling thirsty, he wished he had asked for a glass of water to save himself the price of a drink. It was too late to go back now. He sauntered to the end of the road, wondering where the nearest place would be where he could get a Coke, when a girl ran out of the side street and collided into him.

Once he had recovered from the surprise he recognised her as the nanny he had seen on the stairs with the children. She must have left the house by a back entrance and run round to catch him. When she spoke she had a heavy Scandinavian accent.

'I am sorry,' she said, stepping back and catching her breath. She had a wide, honest face with the palest of blue eyes. He noticed that she had strong, capable hands, almost like a man's. 'This Doris. I know her.'

'You know her?' Joe was startled. He had been quite ready to believe the highly respectable-looking Mrs Montgomery.

'Yes. I cannot talk now. I must get back before she sees I am away from the children. If you want I can meet you tonight at eight o'clock, when the children are in bed. Yes? You would like that?'

'Yes, of course. Where would you like to meet?'

She looked confused for a moment, unable to think of a suitable meeting place in a city which was not her own. 'You know Sloane Square?' she said, eventually, obviously keen to make the arrangement and get away. Joe nodded. 'I will meet you in the middle of the square, under the trees. There are benches. At eight o'clock. I may be delayed a few minutes, not many. Don't come to the house asking for me. I will come.'

With that she turned and ran back down the side street. He saw her take the first turning back round to the house. He liked the idea of having a mysterious rendezvous with a strange girl. He wished he had fancied her.

The phone started to ring the moment Joe opened the front door of the flat. Anxious not to bring Angus out of his room any sooner than was necessary, he snatched up the receiver to silence it.

'Hello?'

'Hi, Dad,' chirped the voice at the other end.

'Hey, Big Man, how are you?' His heart jumped at the sound of his son's voice and then sank as he thought of the days that had passed since he last saw him.

'I'm okay,' the boy replied, his words tumbling over one another in their hurry to get out. 'We're in London and Mum's going to some boring dinner party tonight and she's going to be out till late and she wants you to have me.' He heard Fliss shouting some correction in the background. 'And I really want to come, because the babysitter is going to be really boring.' There was another shout from Fliss. 'And I want to see you. I've got this great new game. It's brilliant! Mum wants to talk to you.'

Joe heard Fliss say, 'For God's sake, Hugo,' in the background. And then she was on the line. 'I did not say that. He said he really wanted to see you tonight and I told him to ring you and see what you were doing.'

'Right, okay.' Joe didn't want to say that he had just made a date to meet a blonde Scandinavian nanny. He never wanted to miss any time that he was offered with Hugo, in case it wasn't offered again. 'That would be great. What time can he come?'

'He can come over after lunch, and then we'll pick him up tomorrow, on our way to the country.'

'Sure.' How he hated it when she referred to herself and the polo player as 'we'. 'Whatever.'

'Okay. See you in a couple of hours.' The phone went dead in his hand.

'Did you manage to get to the bank, my dear?' Angus' voice boomed out behind him, making him jump. Angus must just have washed his long hair and it flopped over his eyes. He tossed his head back to clear his vision.

'Ah, Angus,' Joe gave a laugh which he knew must sound nervous. 'I'm sorry. Something came up and put it right out of my mind. I'll write you a cheque, now.' He pulled a cheque-book out of his pocket and scribbled a cheque under Angus' watchful eyes. 'There you go.' He handed it across casually and went to sort his room out before Hugo arrived.

'Joe,' Angus' voice rolled down the corridor behind him, bouncing mellifluously off the aged, stained paintwork on the walls. 'You've forgotten to sign it.'

'Have I?' Joe opened his eyes wide in mock horror at such an oversight. 'I'm sorry, Angus. I have a lot on my mind.' He made his way back, taking his pen out and signing with a flourish.

'Joe,' Angus' tone changed to an almost fatherly level. 'If you are short of money at any time you just have to tell me.' He put his hand on Joe's shoulder and squeezed. A mixture of tobacco smoke, stale shirts and aftershave assailed Joe's nostrils. 'I'm sure there would always be some way round the problem.'

'Thanks Angus.' Joe decided to pretend he had missed the innuendo in his landlord's suggestion. 'You're a pal.'

He gave Angus a manly slap on the back and hurried back to his room, leaving the old actor pushing his hair out of his eyes and studying the cheque carefully.

Joe was still vacuuming up the last shreds of evidence of his biscuit-eating bachelor habits, when there was a tap on his bedroom door and Fliss poked her head in. He had intended to keep her at the front door, but he must have missed the doorbell because of the Hoover and someone else had let her in. He felt himself blushing at the modesty of his accommodation. He was worried she wouldn't think it appropriate for Hugo to spend too much time there. Her face didn't seem to register either approval or disapproval. In fact, she didn't show any interest in the surroundings at all.

He was surprised by how blonde her hair had become since he last saw her. He guessed that it was the polo player's influence. It also looked as if she had been under the sunlamp.

Hugo hurtled into the room past his mother and threw his arms around Joe's waist, knocking the wind out of him with the strength of his hug. Joe, taken by surprise, found himself propelled backwards onto the bed by the force of his son's affection. The Hoover gave an excited scream as it escaped from his grip. Fliss switched it off at the wall.

Joe struggled to his feet, embarrassed to have been toppled off balance so easily. He was worried Hugo might feel uncomfortable at the accident. The boy appeared unbothered and continued to jump around the room like an excited puppy, while Fliss and Joe made polite conversation about the contents of their son's overnight bag.

'I got your note yesterday,' Joe said. 'It'll take me a little while to get the money together.' He couldn't bring himself to say that he did not think it was remotely fair that she should suddenly spring private school fees on him when they had never discussed it before.

'Okay.' She smiled forgivingly. 'He doesn't go back for a few days. I just thought I should send it through to you as soon as possible. The letter had been at the house in London for a week or two but we've been away.'

A few minutes later she was gone and Joe and Hugo were left alone.

'We've got an important assignment tonight,' Joe said, conspiratorially.

'What do you mean?' The boy's blue eyes lit up.

'We have to meet a mysterious blonde foreign lady in a public place. She has information for a story I might be writing.'

'Is she your girlfriend?' The expression on Hugo's face suggested that he hoped the answer to this would be negative.

'No,' Joe laughed.

'Is she a spy?'

'Who knows. We'll have to find out.'

'Cool!'

At eight o'clock Joe was sitting on a bench in the middle of Sloane Square. The traffic roared around him as people headed out for dinner or home from late working habits. Hugo had jumped on the next bench and was standing holding out his arms like a tightrope walker.

Joe's attention was divided between watching his son's antics and waiting for the nanny to appear from the far end of the square. He didn't see the old man until he had sat down beside him with a thump which made the seat jolt beneath him.

Joe's new neighbour leant close to his face, emitting a cloud of Special Brew through his grimy beard. 'They're all bloody bastards!' he confided.

'Are they?' Joe was anxious not to create a scene in front of Hugo. His priority was to get rid of the man before he could frighten his son. He was also anxious that if the nanny saw him talking to someone else she might lose her nerve and go home.

'They're all bloody bastards,' the man repeated. As Joe stared into his face he realised that beneath the grime the tramp was probably not much older than him. For a split second he wondered if this man had been leading a perfectly normal life just a few years before and had been dealt one cruel blow by life, which had brought him down to living on the street. Perhaps he had lost his job, or his wife had walked out on him.

'Who are?' Joe asked.

'All of them,' the tramp said firmly. 'Is this your laddie?' He pointed at Hugo, who, realising something more interesting was afoot, had given up the tightrope act and climbed across on to the bench with his father.

'Yeah,' Joe said. 'My name's Joe. This is Hugo.'

The tramp shook their hands solemnly. His grip was uncomfortably strong. 'Your father is a gentleman,' he told Hugo. Hugo laughed. The tramp held up a blackened finger to silence him. 'There's not many of the bastards will give me the time of day any more.' He leant in close to Joe's face again. 'Could you spare me the price of a newspaper, do you suppose?'

'Sure,' Joe reached into his pocket and handed over a fifty pence coin. The old man stood up unsteadily and saluted. Joe could see the nanny crossing the road from the corner of Sloane Street. 'You'll have to excuse us. We're meeting someone. Nice to meet you.' He grabbed Hugo's hand and walked briskly to the curb to intercept the girl as she made her way through the traffic. 'Hello,' he said when she reached them. 'You made it.'

'Yes,' she replied, matter-of-factly, as if unable to understand why he would have doubted that she would.

'Shall we go somewhere for a coffee?'

'No. I do not have much time. They think I am in the laundry room with the children's clothes. The mother is reading them bedtime stories. We can talk here.'

From the corner of his eye Joe could see the tramp weaving towards them again.

'Okay,' he said, gesturing towards a bench. 'Do you want to sit down? This is my son, Hugo.'

'How do you do, Hugo?' She shook the boy by the hand and they walked to the bench. It took the tramp a few seconds to realign himself to follow them.

'This man,' he told the nanny when he finally caught up with them, 'is a bloody gentleman. Not like those bastards.'

The girl looked him straight in the eye, appearing not even to notice the smell which he gave off. 'Please,' she said. 'This is a private conversation. You go away and leave us alone now.'

For a few moments the man swayed like a tree in the breeze as he took in her words. Then, with another salute, he turned smartly around, marched half a dozen steps and tripped over the flapping soles of his boots, sending a cloud of pedestrian pigeons into the air as he hit the ground.

'There was a Doris at the house,' the girl said, taking advantage of the fact that Hugo was laughing too much at the man's antics to concentrate on anything she might be saying. 'She was a Filipino. A maid, but they treated her more like a slave. Working all the time. No days off. I was sorry for her. She was a nice girl. Stupid, but kind to the children.'

'Where is she now?' Joe asked.

'I don't know. She vanished. One morning the butler was asking for her because he wanted something scrubbed or polished. We were all searching for her but no one could find her. Mrs Montgomery told us she had been stealing or something, so good riddance. They told me that I should not mention her to anyone. To forget that I knew her. She talked about loyalty to the family and discretion.' The girl rolled her eyes. 'Then she told me I would have to do all Doris' work now.'

'She ran away?'

'Maybe. But where would she go with no references? She was too stupid to get any other sort of job and she was frightened of everything. She was ugly too, so she couldn't have found a boyfriend. Maybe she was taken by someone.'

'Taken by whom?' Joe was momentarily disappointed by the news that Doris was ugly. A pretty face would have been an asset for selling a book about sex slavery.

'There was a man.' The girl glanced around her, apparently nervous for the first time since her arrival in the square. 'He came to the house a few times to see her.' She shivered at the memory. 'He was disgusting.'

'Who did she say he was?'

'She said he was just a friend, but I knew she was frightened of him.'

'What was his name?'

'She said he was called Max and once he called on the telephone. She was asleep and he told me to get her to ring him when she woke. I wrote down the telephone number, but when she woke she told me she already had the number. So it was still in my pocket.' She passed over a crumpled piece of paper with an out-of-London number and the name Max scrawled on it.

'Do you have an address for him?' Joe asked.

'If I had an address I would give it to you.' She looked at him as if he was as stupid as the girl.

'Doris is a strange name for a Filipino, don't you think?'

'She was the first one I ever met. I don't know what names they have.'

'She said someone had stolen her breasts. What did she mean?'

The nanny shrugged. 'She was stupid. I think she had an operation. I never wanted to ask her too many questions. She was confused all the time. It made me cross to try to have a conversation with her.'

Joe imagined that this dour woman had little in common with any of the people she was working with below stairs.

'Why are you working as a nanny?' he asked. 'You don't seem the type.'

'I am waiting to go to university. It is good to travel to foreign countries.'

The tramp was back on his feet and restoring his spirits from the beer can which had, magically, remained unspilled in his grip throughout his encounter with the pavement. Hugo was watching him with an absorbed look on his face.

'Why did your employer deny Doris' existence to me?' Joe asked the girl.

'Perhaps she is stupid too. The children would tell you about her if you asked. They liked her. She used to sing American songs to them.' She stood up, obviously ready to go.

'Why did you want to tell me all this?' Joe asked.

'It is the right thing to do.' She seemed surprised that he even needed to ask. 'She was my friend. I think she might need someone to help her.'

Joe gave her a piece of paper with his telephone number and address on it. 'Will you call me if you find out anything else? Or if Doris comes back.'

'Sure,' she shrugged and walked away without saying goodbye.

Joe returned his attention to the tramp, who was trying to persuade Hugo to have a sip from his beer can. 'Come on Hugo,' he called and the boy skipped over to join him.

'Good night,' they both said in unison and the tramp gave them a final salute, remaining like a statue until they had crossed the road and disappeared behind the shops.

They walked back to Earls Court, stopping in Gloucester Road for a pizza, most of which found its way down the front of Hugo's jumper. Joe thought that the exercise might tire his son out, but the boy was still talking non-stop when they finally arrived back at the flat in Bramham Gardens.

Annie, a model having some difficulty getting her career started, was on the telephone as they walked in. She covered the mouthpiece when she saw Joe.

'A girl came round to see you,' she told him. 'Said she was a friend of yours. I showed her into your room. Hope that was all right.'

'Is she your girlfriend?' Hugo asked loudly as Annie went back to talking on the phone.

'No, she's one of my flatmates. I told you, I haven't got a girlfriend.'

'Who's this girl in your room then?'

'I have no idea.'

As Joe opened his bedroom door Hugo pushed past him. Cordelia quickly pulled Joe's duvet up to cover her nakedness, but not quickly enough to stop the pose which she had been preparing for Joe being imprinted indelibly on his eight-year-old son's memory. Her hair, which had been the colour of honey a few days before, had turned a metallic pink.

CHAPTER THREE

The musical bleeping entered Joe's dreams and then brought him uncomfortably to a confused state of wakefulness. His eyes remained closed. He knew it wasn't his alarm clock – it was completely the wrong sound for that, and it wasn't loud enough to be a fire or smoke alarm. Even if there was such a thing in the flat! He couldn't understand why his back and neck ached so much or why his bed felt so hard. He opened his eyes and the sliver of light which came through the closed curtains was enough to show him that he wasn't in his bed.

Slowly, as the bleeping continued to drill into his brain, he realised he was lying on the floor, in a sleeping bag, and his memory started to return at a dizzying speed. The noise seemed to be coming from near the bed. He crawled out of the sleeping bag and fumbled his way towards it. His hands came in contact with something soft and furry, making him cry out in shock. He realised it was Cordelia's shoulder bag. The beeping was emanating from inside. He wondered if he should wake her to ask her permission to go in after the offending sound, but decided not to bother. He dived in amongst a clutter of small objects and crumpled tissues. His hand came in contact with a mobile phone. He pulled it out and pressed the answer button.

'Hello?' he enquired tentatively, his voice low so as not to disturb the two sleeping children, neither of whom showed any sign of stirring.

'Who the fuck is that?' Len demanded to know.

For a second Joe thought about hanging up, but then realised that would be futile. Better to brazen it out.

'Hi, Len,' he said, as cheerily as he could manage. 'It's Joe Tye.'

'What the hell are you doing at Rita's?' Len rasped.

'I'm not at Rita's.' Joe had never met Len's ex-wife, but he had heard enough about her from Len to feel that he was on first name terms with her. 'I'm at home.'

'Have I dialled the wrong bloody number? I wanted to talk to Cordelia.' Len was now confused and Joe knew he needed to come clean if he didn't want to risk sounding as if he had a guilty conscience.

'No. She's here. She turned up last night. I think she and Rita had a row. She's still asleep. Do you want me to wake her?'

'No,' Len sounded disinterested in the details. 'Get her to ring me when she wakes up. Tell her I've got a little job for her if she wants to earn some pocket money.'

'Okay. I will.' Joe hung up with a sigh of relief. He had no idea whether Len wasn't worried that his sixteen-year-old daughter had spent the night with a man old enough to be her father, or whether he trusted Joe, or whether it simply didn't occur to him that anything would happen.

He replaced the phone in the bag and pulled on a pair of trousers and a jumper. He could see Cordelia's face in the shaft of light, her pink hair spread out across the pillow. There was no question she was a beautiful child.

He could also make out the top of Hugo's head in the other sleeping bag, his hair sticking out in every direction. Joe left the room quietly. Apart from a few snuffling noises from the sleeping bag, neither of them showed any sign of waking.

Annie was in the kitchen, the room opposite Joe's, wearing only a T-shirt, which covered nothing of her endless legs, and a pair of dark glasses to hide the fact that her mascara had spread in the night. She was eating a fried breakfast and reading *Vogue*.

Joe had just opened his mouth to say good morning when the doorbell rang.

Panic seemed to grip Annie as she heard Angus letting someone in the front door and conducting them down towards the kitchen. The panic spread to Joe as he realised that the visitor was Fliss and she was heading for his room in search of Hugo.

He sprang out into the corridor to intercept her. He was quite capable of imagining how she would react to finding a beautiful sixteen-year-old girl in his bed with her eight-year-old son asleep on the floor.

'Hi. You're early,' he said cheerily.

Fliss looked at his dishevelled state and then at her watch. 'It's eleven o'clock.'

'Is it that late?' Joe said, with what he hoped sounded like a carefree laugh. 'Hugo's still asleep. Come into the kitchen for a coffee while I get him sorted out.' He heard Annie give a squeak of horror at the thought of being seen by another woman in her morning disarray.

For a moment it looked as though Fliss wasn't going to allow herself to be deflected from finding her son but at the last moment she swerved into the kitchen, visibly startled by the sight of Annie with a final dripping forkful of fried egg halfway to her mouth as she scurried towards the bin to try to dispose of the evidence of a heavy cholesterol habit.

'This is Annie, one of my flatmates,' Joe said quickly. 'She'll make you a cup of coffee while I get Hugo up.'

Fliss gave the stained state of the kitchen a distasteful look and Joe managed to dodge out of the room as Annie emitted a half-strangled bleat of outrage. Both Cordelia and Hugo were still fast asleep, oblivious to whatever was going on in other parts of the flat. After a long game of Monopoly, borrowed from the accountant down the corridor, neither of them had got to sleep much before one o'clock – a fact which Joe hoped Hugo wouldn't impart to his mother. Discovering Cordelia in the room had distracted Hugo from his disappointment that his father didn't have a computer set up on which he could play his new games.

Joe had been impressed with the way in which Cordelia had adapted her act from potential seducer to Hugo's big sister as the evening wore on. When the time came to end the game it had seemed perfectly natural that she should have the bed while the 'men' used the sleeping bags on the floor.

Joe realised that Fliss was unlikely to see the situation in quite the same light, but could think of no way of explaining it away to her without asking his son to lie – and that was not something he was prepared to do. He was still more than a little concerned that once Len had had time to think about the situation there might be some uncomfortable questions to answer from him as well. He was just going to have to tough it out and hope for the best.

He unzipped the sleeping bag around his son, trying to be as quiet as possible. The two bags were among the few things that he had been able to claim as his when he was collecting up his worldly possessions to separate from Fliss. The first one had travelled several times round the world with him. The second he had bought for Fliss when they first met in Thailand. She hadn't put up any argument when he insisted on keeping them. They obviously held less sentimental value for her, a fact that had hurt him more than he would have expected.

He could hear Fliss' voice carrying clearly through the wall from the kitchen as she patronised Annie. He lifted Hugo into a sitting position in the hope of being able to pull his clothes onto him before he woke fully. The boy's eyes popped wide open. He beamed at his father.

'Morning, Dad,' he said loudly, throwing his arms around Joe's neck and toppling him off balance so that they both ended up sprawled on the floor. Joe could feel the warmth of his son's newly wakened body and was suddenly aware of all the mornings that he wasn't around for in Hugo's life. For a flashing moment Joe hated Fliss for what she had stolen from him.

'What're you two doing?' Cordelia asked from the bed.

'Don't worry,' Joe said, putting a finger over his son's lips. 'Go back to sleep. I'm just getting Hugo up for his mother. You stay there.'

'I need the bathroom,' Cordelia complained.

'You'll have to hold on a few minutes. I'll tell you when the coast is clear.'

Hugo, infected by the air of conspiracy without fully grasping what was going on, stayed quiet as his father gathered up his stuff and shooed him out to the kitchen.

'Good God, Hugo,' Fliss stared in disbelief at her crumpled child as he blinked in the bright light of day and struggled into his trousers. 'What time did you get to bed last night?'

'He's just had a bit of a lie-in, that's all,' Joe jumped in quickly, trying to pull Hugo's fleece over his head and smooth his wayward hair down at the same time. Behind him he was aware that Cordelia was coming out of the bedroom and heading for the bathroom. Annie slapped a mug of coffee down in front of Fliss. Several drops landed on Fliss' pale grey jumper and she leaped up as if she had been scalded.

'Come on, Hugo,' she said, nervously. 'I've promised we'll meet Granny for lunch.'

'How is she?' Joe asked, without really caring. He was fairly sure that Fliss' mother had encouraged her daughter to leave him for the polo player. Having left Fliss' father many years before, she had often seemed keen that her daughter should do the same, pointedly singing the praises of a life free from domestic slavery. Not that either of them had ever been over-troubled by housework. Joe had always hated going to visit his mother-in-law in the stately Onslow Gardens flat which Fliss' father had been forced to buy her after their separation and which was so filled with priceless ornaments that Hugo had had to remain strapped to a chair whenever he had been included in the invitation.

'She's fine,' Fliss said, taking over the grooming job from Joe as Hugo wriggled and protested beneath her attentions. Within three minutes they were walking down the corridor, leaving the coffee untasted on the kitchen table. Just as they passed the bathroom the door opened.

''Bye Cordy,' Hugo called out cheerfully. 'See you soon.'

'See you, Hugs,' she laughed. 'Don't go buying too many of those houses in Mayfair now, will you.'

'We played Monopoly,' Joe heard Hugo explaining to his mother as they went out. 'I won.'

'Did you, dear?' Fliss replied, absent-mindedly. 'That's nice.'

When Joe returned to the room Cordelia was back in bed. She looked at him mischievously as he tried to find the right tone of voice in which to remonstrate with her for letting herself into his bed uninvited the previous evening. He couldn't think how to phrase it.

'Len phoned while you were asleep,' he said instead. 'He wants you to call him. He says he has a job for you.'

'Pass the phone then.' She indicated her bag, which had been moved onto the faded green armchair at the end of the bed. The gesture made the duvet fall away to show that she had shed the T-shirt that he had lent her as a nightie. She made no effort to cover herself. Joe tossed the bag onto the bed and sat down in the chair which Angus had bought from a house clearance deposit somewhere south of the river, and which still smelled of other people's dust.

'Len,' she told the phone and it dialled automatically. 'Hi, it's me. Yeah...yeah...okay, I'll be there.'

She snapped the phone shut and climbed out of bed, completely unconcerned about her naked body, apparently confident of its flawlessness.

'Are you going?' Joe enquired, unable to take his eyes off her.

'Yeah. My dad wants me to meet a man about some business.'

'Where have you got to meet him?'

'The Metropole Hotel.'

'I don't know it,' Joe confessed, intrigued to know what sort of business a sixteen-year-old girl might be conducting in a London hotel on behalf of her father.

'It's up the Edgware Road. Mostly full of Arabs, I think.'

'Is it an Arab you're meeting?' he asked, but she seemed not to have heard. 'Listen, Cordelia, about yesterday…'

'What about it?' She seemed to be preoccupied with the job of getting herself dressed. She ran a brush roughly through her hair and it sprang glossily back into place with all the ease of extreme youth.

'Well,' Joe cleared his throat, trying not to sound like a schoolteacher. 'It was great to see you, but it might be better if you just gave me a ring before coming round in future. Just to check that I'm not about to walk in with my son, or my great aunt, or the Queen Mother and find you naked in bed.'

Cordelia giggled as she wriggled into her shoes. 'Don't be so stuffy, Joe-boy. It didn't seem to bother Hugo.'

'No,' he agreed. 'But all the same.'

'Whatever you say, mate.' She kissed him on the mouth and he was shocked by just how soft her lips were. 'Must dash now.' And she was gone, leaving him sitting in the armchair like a deflated balloon.

He heard the front door slam shut and the flat suddenly fell silent apart from the distant sounds of Annie splashing around in the bathroom. For a few minutes Joe didn't move, lost in thought as he tried to digest everything that had happened. The silence began to bear down on him and made him feel lonely. He wished Cordelia hadn't gone. He wished he hadn't sounded off like such an old fart. He needed something to distract his attention from the long empty day that stretched ahead. He couldn't phone Adele again. There was no point. It would make him sound too desperate. So he might as well do a bit of follow-up work on the missing Doris mystery.

Pulling himself out of his sloth he went in search of the piece of paper which the nanny had given him, with the number on it. Finding it, he ambled down the long, dark corridor, past all the closed doors. He dialled the operator.

'I have a telephone number,' he said when she answered, 'but I need to know which area the code is for.'

'What is the code, sir?' she enquired.

'01273.'

'That is the Brighton area, sir.'

'If I give you the number, are you allowed to tell me the address?'

'No sir. I'm afraid we can't do that.'

'Okay. Thank you.' He put the receiver down and became lost in thought again. A few minutes later he had a plan and dialled the number. 'Hi. This is parcel delivery service,' he said when a girl's voice answered. 'I have a delivery for a Mr Max but there is a mistake on the address. Can you tell me the correct number.'

'Number forty-two,' the girl said. Her voice sounded slightly slurred, as if he had woken her up.

'Number forty-two...?' Joe held his breath and listened intently.

'Ditchling Avenue,' she finished his sentence for him.

'Thank you Ma'am. Sorry to have disturbed you.' He hung up quickly, before she could ask him any questions. He was startled to find that his heart was beating faster than normal. The perpetration of even such a small deception left him almost breathless from the adrenaline rush. He wrote the address down and went in search of his book of maps. He was pretty sure that he had been to Brighton with Fliss early on in their marriage, but he was a little hazy as to where exactly it was in relation to London.

CHAPTER FOUR

The moment he walked out of Brighton station Joe remembered the last time he had been there. It had been soon after he had come to England with Fliss, probably before they got married. She had wanted him to meet one of her closest friends from school, whose father had set her up with a little clothes shop somewhere in the town. He couldn't remember the woman's name but he remembered how surprised she had been that Fliss should want to marry an American hippie she had found wandering around in northern Thailand; a man who appeared to have virtually no idea what he wanted to do with his life and absolutely no private income. The woman had called it 'wonderfully romantic', but obviously meant 'ridiculously short-sighted'.

She hadn't been the only one who had thought Fliss had made a big mistake. But in the following years Joe had been proud of how well the marriage had worked, and also of how well he had done as a writer. His income had grown to be easily enough to meet all their living expenses, although their home had been provided by Fliss' family. Now, of course, he wished he had put a little of that income aside. But saving had never been a priority when he was married to a woman whose family had all the capital they could ever need. So, whenever a big cheque came in from a publisher or newspaper, he and Fliss would go off to the Caribbean with Hugo for a few weeks, or Fliss would refresh her wardrobe or change her car.

Ultimately, of course, Fliss' friend had been proved right. Fliss had left him for someone even richer than her father and now Joe was having to readjust to a life without the backing of homes that had been in the family for centuries. What had seemed like a good living when they were together now seemed decidedly inadequate when he had to furnish himself both with somewhere to live and a lawyer to plead his case. And all this at the same time as supporting Hugo – a responsibility he had no desire to hand over to his Argentinian replacement.

The emotional upheaval had stopped him working effectively for six months and he was now feeling the effects in his income. The cheques simply weren't arriving with the regularity he had grown used to.

Everyone told him that it would take him a year or two to get back onto his feet, both emotionally and financially. He was willing to accept that they were right, but that didn't make his change in circumstances any more comfortable. He could hardly remember what Fliss' friend in the Brighton dress shop had looked like now, but that didn't stop him feeling a surge of resentment towards her.

He had bought a street map of the town at the station bookstall and managed to locate Ditchling Avenue. It was going to be at least half an hour's walk, but it was a pleasant, sunny afternoon and he was in no hurry. He strolled through the crowded, narrow streets, where shoppers from the suburbs mixed with the locals, and was immediately intrigued by the way the locals' bodies and faces seemed to have been pierced in every conceivable combination of places, their hair shaved to the scalp or plaited into dreadlocks as solid as old rope.

The previous year he would have felt himself to be one of the shoppers, a tourist in this alternative world, but that afternoon, with a bank account sliding into the red, he felt more part of the scruffy world of the local cafés. Their clientele lounged around with their mongrel dogs at their feet and their home-rolled cigarettes in their nicotine-stained fingers. A smell of beer and cheap vegetarian cooking filled the air.

After the several lanes of traffic converged at the bottom of the hill, the scenery gradually changed to shabby residential streets, all of which looked as if they had once been smart and some of which were starting to be so once more. The roads began to lead him steeply upwards again, something the map hadn't prepared him for, and he became aware of the heat of the sun. He kept changing sides of the road to stay in the shade, unable to resist looking in through the ground floor windows of the houses he passed. He could see, past the endless fireplaces and varied furnishings, and through a variety of French windows, out to the small gardens beyond, some as neat as magazine illustrations, others stacked like junk yards.

Ditchling Avenue was one of the grander roads. The tall, red-brick houses must originally have been built for professional Victorian families who might have expected to have the help of one or two servants to keep their smartly tiled doorsteps freshly scrubbed. Some of them looked as if they were still occupied by people aware of the importance of investing in property. Others appeared to have been split carelessly into flats or filled with people renting individual rooms. Many of the windows were open to the street and music drifted out on the warm, lazy air.

Joe knew he was on the right side of the road for number forty-two because the numbers were descending in even pairs as he went. On the other side he could see a parade of local shops approaching. A small supermarket was flanked by a workman's café and a launderette offered service washes in large red letters across the window.

As he passed number forty-eight he could see that there were a group of people standing around on the steps of the house which he calculated would be number forty-two. Two of them looked West Indian, with matted dreadlocks hanging halfway down their backs, their muscular arms appearing to be trying to escape through their torn T-shirts.

The man talking to them was white, although the density of tattoos covering his face, arms and neck made him appear somewhat darker. His head was shaved, perhaps to provide more space for the artwork. The effect was somewhere between the graffiti which Joe had often seen on New York telephone booths, and religious engravings on some Middle Eastern shrine. The man's ears and nostrils were encircled with rings, like some revered African tribesman.

The voices of the other men sounded loud and angry, although their body language appeared friendly, possibly even affectionate. Joe knew better than to let them catch him staring and once he had confirmed to himself that it was the right house, he crossed the road and went into the café without breaking his stride, giving the impression that it had been his intended destination all along. The small, newly decorated room was empty. He ordered a sandwich and coffee from the ponytailed Italian man behind the counter, deliberately not looking outside. He made his way to a seat in the window once the man had taken his money and served him the food.

When Joe did finally glance casually across the road the front steps of number forty-two were deserted. He looked quickly up and down the street but could see no one. There were windows open in the house, but all of them had net curtains inside, and security bars outside. The bars somehow didn't seem to fit with the rest of the house. They looked newly installed and expensive, while the rest of the house looked uncared for and dirty.

A previous customer had left a newspaper on the table and Joe started to read it, glancing up every few minutes. He sat there for an hour before he had to order another coffee. No one else came into the café, but several people went to the house. Sometimes the tattooed man would come outside to talk to them, sometimes they would be allowed to pass through the door. Some reappeared, while others remained inside.

Nearly two hours after Joe first sat down, a gate at the side of the house opened and an oriental girl came out. She was slight and seemed almost dwarfed by the two bulging bin liners she was carrying. They were light enough for her to be able to hold one in each hand without dragging them on the ground, but obviously heavy enough to be a burden. She hurried across the road with strange little shuffling steps, as if anxious to get rid of them, and disappeared from his line of vision. Joe rose and went outside. The café owner appeared not to notice his departure.

The girl was nowhere to be seen on the pavement. Joe felt his heart beating faster than was comfortable. Could this be the elusive Doris? He forced himself to stroll casually along the pavement. He glanced across the road towards the house and saw that the tattooed man had come out and was sitting on the steps, lighting a cigarette. Joe didn't break his pace. He turned smartly into the little supermarket.

Just as he went in through the doors the girl came out of the launderette next door without the bags she had been carrying. She turned into the store, picking up a wire basket as she went.

Joe walked behind one of the displays to give himself a moment to compose his thoughts, but she came round faster than he had expected, staring hard at the shelves. She wore a puzzled look, as if unable to find the product she was after. She was very beautiful which surprised him. The nanny had told him Doris was plain. There was no time to hesitate.

'Excuse me,' he said, making her jump back nervously. 'Are you Doris?'

'Yes,' she said, obviously doubtful about telling a strange man her name. 'Who are you?'

He put his hand out and smiled in a way which he hoped looked reassuring. 'Joe Tye. The ghost-writer. You wrote to me after hearing me on the radio. Do you remember?'

She didn't take his hand, just stared at him hard. 'I think you have made a mistake,' she said. 'You must be thinking of someone else.'

'You are from the Philippines?' Joe persisted.

'Yes. But I live here now.'

'And something happened to your breasts?' He only realised how personal the remark sounded after it had come out. His horror was compounded by the realisation that the slight little girl he was talking to actually had a surprisingly large bust. He now understood why she had looked so comical as she bustled across the street with the black sacks; her top half had been jiggling uncontrollably in her T-shirt as she took her tiny steps. Although she was thrusting them forward proudly, the breasts did not seem to be part of her. Her expression darkened with embarrassment at his remark, but he couldn't think of any way to make his words sound better.

For a second she looked as if she was going to hit him, then she laughed, showing a perfect row of bright, white teeth. Her laughter was interrupted by the sound of a man's voice asking for cigarettes at the till on the other side of the display. She suddenly looked frightened and pushed Joe away.

'Is that Max?' Joe asked in a whisper.

She nodded and hurried to the till with a loaf of bread and a packet of cornflakes in her basket. Joe picked up a pack of biscuits and sauntered after her. The man with the tattoos was paying for the cigarettes. An air of menace hung around him like body odour. He looked like someone who had very little to lose in life and everything to fight for.

Max ignored the girl as she joined the queue behind him and she, in turn, ignored Joe. All Joe could see was the man's back. He studied the tattoos which the skimpy black vest showed off. He noticed, to his surprise, that the name 'Doris' was twined across one of the hairy shoulders in a complicated design of vine leaves and hearts. The way it was integrated into the other pictures suggested that it was not a new addition to

37

the artwork, but the girl didn't look old enough to have predated the elaborate carvings on Max's skin.

Both Max and Doris paid for their purchases and left. As Max turned, Joe caught a glimpse of his face. His lips were parted in a sneer and Joe could see that his front teeth had been filed to sharp points. Joe watched over the shoulder of the boy on the till as the odd couple crossed the road back towards the house. Max walked up the steps to the front door and Doris went through the side gate. Just as she was about to close the gate she shot an anxious look back towards the supermarket, and then disappeared.

Joe had to decide what to do. He bought a local evening paper to give himself a little time before strolling out into the street, pretending to be looking for something in the small ads. He wandered back into the café and asked for a cup of tea. The Italian made no sign of recognising him. An old couple were sitting at the table he had occupied before. He sat opposite them, still able to see the house. He thought, once or twice, that he had seen one of the grubby net curtains twitch, as if someone was peeking out. The old couple left and he began to feel conspicuous.

He walked out into the street, passed the supermarket and went into the launderette. A couple of women in overalls and bedroom slippers were busily folding sheets.

'Hi,' he said. 'I'm from number forty-two. Did an oriental girl drop some laundry in earlier?'

'Doris?' one of them replied.

'Yes,' he said.

'It won't be ready for another twenty minutes,' she said. 'I told her when to come back.'

'Oh, no problem,' Joe dismissed her worries with a wave of his hand. 'It was just on the off chance. I wasn't sure what time she brought it over.'

He walked purposefully out of the shop and along the street until he was obscured from the house by the mighty trunks of several of the avenue's trees. He stopped and leant against one of them, looking back along the pavement towards the fronts of the shops. Half an hour later his patience was rewarded and Doris appeared briefly in his line of vision before disappearing into the launderette. He walked briskly back, pausing as soon as he could see the door, and then taking a last spurt when he saw her fighting to get it open with her hands full of plastic sacks. He met her in the middle of the pavement. She looked startled to see him again and her eyes immediately darted to the front door opposite.

'It's okay,' he said. 'Don't be afraid. Can I give you my address and number? If you decide you want to go ahead with it just call me, or drop me another letter. I'd like to hear your story.'

'No,' she said, her voice fierce with fear. 'Go away. They watch me.'

He walked off immediately, not wanting to increase her distress. He hoped that anyone looking out from the house would just have seen a near collision on the pavement and a man apologising for his clumsiness before moving disinterestedly on. He willed himself not to look up at the house. Had he done so he would have seen Max watching the street from the doorstep where he was sitting with another girl, smoking a cigarette.

CHAPTER FIVE

'Hi, Hugo, it's Dad.'

'Hi, Fartface,' Hugo crowed gleefully.

'I'm ringing to wish you luck at the new school.'

'Oh.' Hugo's voice gave away nothing of what he might be feeling. 'Cool.'

'Are you all packed and ready?'

'Mummy's in a real strop,' Hugo announced. 'She says it's ridiculous that she has to put loops and name tags on every single sock.'

'Your mother's doing that?' Joe found the image of Fliss sewing socks hard to conjure up.

'No,' Hugo admitted, 'Nanny Harris is doing it. But Mum's still in a strop.'

Now Joe had a clearer picture of the scene that must be going on around his son's school trunk. 'I've got a new phone number,' he said. 'Have you got a pen?'

'I'll remember it,' Hugo promised.

'Get a pen, just in case,' Joe advised.

'Okay.' He vanished for a moment and then his voice was back on the line. 'Have you bought a mobile then?'

'Yes. I'll have it with me all the time. So you can call me whenever you want.'

'Cool. I thought you were broke.'

'It's a pay as you go thing.'

'Oh. What's the number then?'

'Have you got some paper?'

'No.'

'What are you going to write it on then?'

'My knee. I haven't got any trousers on because Nanny Harris has put everything in the wash.'

After he had hung up Joe sat looking at the phone for a few minutes, as if trying to will himself down the airwaves and into the house where his son was being prepared for one of the biggest days of his life. He wanted to be there, but at the same time he knew he had to allow Fliss and Paolo, the polo man, to get on with their lives without him. It would not be healthy for Hugo always to have his father hanging around the place like a spare part. It would be better for him to know that his father had his own, separate life. He hoped Hugo saw him as a romantic, exciting figure, enjoying endless heady adventures. It was how he wanted to see himself.

There was a tap on his bedroom door and Annie let herself in before he had time to say anything.

'I need to borrow a jacket,' she announced. 'It's for an audition.' She pulled back the curtain on the makeshift wardrobe that Angus had built a few years before and started sorting through Joe's clothes. She was wearing nothing except her underwear and Joe stared for a few moments at her figure before putting the phone down and getting up off the bed.

'You've got a mobile!' Annie shrieked. 'Brilliant. That'll be really useful.'

'Sorry,' he said. 'It's a hotline to Hugo – and my work.'

'I'll pay for any calls,' she said, indignantly.

'Just choose a jacket, Annie. There aren't that many.'

'I've got to look like I've just had it off with the boss at the office party, and I've pulled his jacket on over my undies.'

'What are they advertising?'

'Underwear that you would not be ashamed to show to your boss.'

'Good God!' Joe grimaced.

Annie looked a little crestfallen. 'Don't be like that. It's a good job. The campaign is going in all the glossies. They're even planning to use it on posters. It's good money for one day's work.'

'Hey, listen, I'm not knocking it. If someone offered to pay me to be photographed in a G-string I would be at the studio before they had even hung up the phone.'

He liked Annie, although he didn't know much about her. He had tried questioning her about her background one evening in the kitchen when they had both been a little drunk, but she had been evasive, keener to talk about her dreams of fame, fortune and future social ascendancy than her past. He had discovered that her family lived in a suburb of west London somewhere, but they never phoned her or came to visit. As far as he knew, Annie made no attempt to keep in touch with them either. He could fully sympathise with that. He couldn't remember the last time he had spoken to his parents. He had a nagging suspicion he should have written to tell them about the divorce. He kidded himself that he was trying to spare them from pain for as long as he could, but he knew that wasn't true. He just didn't want to admit to them he had failed. He didn't want to have to discuss any part of his life with them, let alone something as painful as that.

Annie seemed equally comfortable to be free of her family. She was inventing a life for herself and her past didn't fit into the picture she was painting. She spent most of her nights at the sort of clubs where she hoped she would meet rich and influential men who would be able to help her with her ambitions. On the nights when she didn't come home, Joe assumed she was test-driving them. None of them seemed to have passed the test yet, but she wasn't allowing that to dim her optimism.

Annie pulled the jacket off a pinstriped suit which he had bought when he married Fliss and only ever used for official functions like weddings and going to see his solicitor.

'This will be great!' she said. 'Just the sort of old-fashioned thing a boss would wear. What's that?' She spotted a magazine lying on the bed and picked it up, slipping into the jacket as she flicked through it. '*The Lady*? Are you developing new and strange interests, Joe?'

'It's research, for a story I'm thinking of writing.'

'On what, knitting patterns?'

'White slavery.'

Annie gave him a puzzled look and stared back at the sedate pages of the magazine. 'It looks like there is more about cookery and flower arranging here.'

'Look in the small ads.'

She flicked to the back of the magazine. 'Nannies and housekeepers,' she read. 'Butlers and au pairs. Well, I suppose it's a sort of slavery.'

Joe laughed. 'Apparently, according the newsagent, it's where all the grand people hire their staff from. But I think the magazine staff may be unaware of just what some of their advertisers are actually selling.'

'Working for the tabloids now, are you?'

'It might come to that.'

'Thanks for the jacket.' She kissed his lips. He raised his hands to hold her shoulders but she had already pulled back. Annie couldn't afford to waste her best assets on a man who had to live in a bedsit, however attractive she might find him.

Once she had disappeared with the jacket Joe climbed back onto the bed and thumbed through the classified pages of the magazine more carefully, studying each ad in turn.

'Yeah!' he hissed a few minutes later, feeling his heart missing a beat. The ad was a little larger than those surrounding it on the page, but still discreet enough not to appear out of place. *Maisie's Amazing Maids*, it read, *internationally trained household staff – a full employment service provided.* There followed a telephone number. He had remembered the names 'Mike and Maisie' from his

43

conversation with Len and his friends. There couldn't be that many 'Maisies' in the business. The connection was strong enough to be worth following up.

Joe stared at the ad for at least ten minutes, preparing himself to dial, almost like an actor girding himself to make an entrance onto the stage. When he was finally ready he lifted the phone and punched in the number.

The line connected and rang six or seven times. He was about to hang up when someone lifted it. There was a pause and then an oriental woman's voice said: 'Maisie speaking, how may I help you?'

'Hi. My name's John Weston. I'm answering your advertisement in *The Lady* magazine.'

'Good morning, Mr Weston. How can I help you?' Her voice was without character or inflection, like a computer.

'I've just arrived from New York. I'm planning to set up a home in London and I need a housekeeper.'

'Thank you for calling us, Mr Weston,' Maisie said. 'We have many good women on our books.'

'I'm a bachelor, so I'm kinda irregular in my habits.' Joe was beginning to enjoy himself, getting into his stride. 'I'm looking for someone who'd be able to provide a broad range of services, if you understand what I mean.'

'All our girls are internationally trained to give good service to their employers,' Maisie replied without missing a beat.

'Could I have a word, old boy?' Angus' tousled head had appeared round the door.

Suddenly thrown at having to think of two things at once, Joe gestured frantically at the phone to indicate he was busy.

'Ah,' Angus raised a finger to his lips to indicate he understood, and then tiptoed into the room, closing the door behind him.

Joe tried to think what he was going to say next but failed. 'Excuse me,' he said into the phone, and pressed the mute button. 'I'm just in the middle of something here, Angus. Can I come down to your room in a few minutes?'

'Of course, of course, sorry. Stupid of me.' Angus beat a retreat, closing the door behind him.

'Hi.' Joe went back to the phone. 'Sorry about that.'

'I have a very nice lady. Very well trained. She would like to meet you,' Maisie said, having had a few seconds to prepare her sales patter. 'Please give me your address.'

'The house is not quite ready yet, the builders are in. Can I arrange to interview her at a hotel around the corner?'

'Certainly, Mr Weston. Which hotel do you want to meet in?'

'Do you know the Lanesborough? It's on Hyde Park Corner, just at the end of Knightsbridge.' Joe thought that would be the sort of hotel that would seem suitable to Maisie. If she thought it was 'around the corner' from his house he would have put himself in the right area for someone who could afford to pay for staff. He was right.

'Yes, I know the Lanesborough, Mr Weston,' she purred. 'When would you like me introduce you to the lady?'

Joe made an arrangement to meet them in the hotel bar that evening and hung up. His hand was shaking from the nervous strain of giving a performance. He sat, thinking about the situation for a few moments and then remembered Angus' visit. He sighed. Did that mean the cheque had bounced already? He had expected to get at least a few more days grace before he had to deal with that one.

He decided to make one more phone call before going to face the music. He dialled the Brighton number, preparing himself to hang up if anything went wrong.

'Yes?' It was a woman's voice, but it didn't sound like a Filipino accent.

'Hi. Is this the right number for Doris?'

'Yes.'

'Is she there?'

'Hold on.'

He could feel his heart beating in his chest as the woman dropped the phone and he heard her shouting around the house. Please God Max didn't pick it up and ask who he was. He doubted if Doris received many phone calls.

'Hello?' a small, shy voice said.

'Doris?'

'Yes. Who is this speaking please?'

'It's Joe, the American guy who talked to you in the supermarket.'

'Oh, yes,' she said nervously. 'I remember you.'

'Do you have a pen and paper?'

'No.'

'Can you get one?'

'Just a minute.' She disappeared for what seemed like an age and then returned. 'I have a pen and paper.'

'I would like you to write down my mobile phone number,' he said. 'Even if you don't want to do the book, if you ever need help or a friend to talk to, I want you to call me. I'll have the phone with me all the time. It doesn't matter what time it is. It could be the middle of the night if you want.'

'You want me to call you?' She was clearly puzzled. He decided he needed to make his motivations appear less mysterious. She seemed determined not to remember that she had written to him about a possible book.

'I like you,' he said. 'I think you are very beautiful. I would like to see more of you.' She giggled at this, and he could tell that she was convinced by his words. She now understood what he was after. 'If you ever decide you would like to see me or talk to me, just call. I would like to be your friend and help you.'

'It is difficult,' she said, suddenly serious again. 'He make me work all the time. He don't like me to have friends.'

'Will you write down my number and ring me if I can ever do anything for you?' he coaxed. 'Please.'

'Okay.'

He dictated the number and then she seemed in a hurry to hang up, as if someone had come into the room.

Joe then made his way along the corridor and tapped on Angus' door. It opened under the pressure of his knuckles. Angus was wearing a rather grubby quilted dressing gown and a cravat, but the Noel Coward image stopped with his bare, hairy calves and black socks. One toe poked out, luminously white against the worn nylon, the nail jagged and uncut.

'Ah, dear boy,' Angus boomed. 'Sorry about barging in like that. Most thoughtless.'

'Don't worry about it.'

'Needed to ask you for a reference.'

'Of course I'll give you a reference.' Joe heaved a sigh of relief that it wasn't about the cheque. 'But are you sure I'm the right person? Wouldn't it be better if it was your bank manager or your doctor or someone?'

'No, no,' Angus let out a bellow of laughter and put his bony arm around Joe's shoulders, steering him into one of the worn leather armchairs. 'Not a reference for me. A reference for someone who wants to take a room here. She says she's a friend of yours. Pretty little thing.'

'A friend of mine?'

'Cordelia Jones. Name ring a bell?'

'Cordelia wants to rent a room here?'

'Apparently. Would that be a problem for you?'

'Um,' Joe's mind was racing. Why would Cordelia want to move into a flat in Earls Court? And what's more, wouldn't Len object to his daughter moving out?

'She seems a little young,' Angus said. 'I wondered if you knew anything about her financial situation?'

'No. I know her father. He's pretty well off. At least I think he is.'

'What line of business is he in?' Angus enquired, putting on his most clubbable voice.

47

'Well, crime mainly. Although I think he has a few straight businesses as well.'

'Ah,' Angus stroked his chin thoughtfully. 'Then she probably is all right for money. She offered me the deposit in cash.' He produced a thick wad of notes from his dressing-gown pocket. 'I thought it a bit strange. A little girl like that carrying so much money.'

'Yes.' Joe was puzzled. 'So, you accepted her deposit then?'

'I could always give it back if you thought it wiser. You know my views on women tenants. They nearly always cause trouble, but they do at least clean the bathroom.'

'There is always that,' Joe agreed. He knew that by 'cause trouble', Angus meant they were usually the ones who complained about the dirt that had been building up in the communal areas for a good few years. 'Have you got a spare room then?'

'The drummer is moving out, thank God. He's going on tour with some girl group. It's the last time I'll ever have a musician in the flat, I can tell you.'

'Cordelia would certainly be quieter than him,' Joe agreed.

'But you think she'd be all right? For the rent I mean?'

Joe felt a twinge of guilt at the man's trust in him when Joe's own rent cheque was about to bounce straight out of Angus' account. 'Yes,' he said. 'I think she would be all right for the rent.'

'And it won't cause any problems for you, her moving in?'

'Problems?'

'Of a personal nature,' Angus averted his eyes. 'You know…'

'Oh, a *personal* nature,' Joe laughed. 'No, I think I can handle it. She's a good kid.'

That evening Joe dressed in his best Ralph Lauren outfit, the one he never wore normally, just so that he would have something in the wardrobe that wasn't frayed or worn when he needed to impress someone. He wanted to look the part of a wealthy American setting up home in Belgravia. He intended to give Maisie the idea that he might be a good target for whatever scam she was involved in with these girls. It felt good to be dressed in clean, expensive clothes for a change. He felt a twinge of regret that he couldn't afford to buy himself anything new, but banished it quickly from his mind.

The Lanesborough looked like an English stately home, as imagined by a Hollywood set designer. There were marble floors and Persian rugs, mighty pillars and painted ceilings, gigantic flower arrangements and clusters of impossibly comfortable sofas everywhere. Uniformed flunkies moved discreetly from guest to guest, ensuring that their every need was instantly catered for.

The bar had the air of a grand gentleman's club in St James's, but was actually far too polished and perfect to be the real thing. There would be no elderly generals snoozing behind their newspapers here, Joe thought, as he looked around, just eager young businessmen and newly wealthy women coming in from shopping.

There was no one there who looked as if they might be waiting for him, so he settled himself into a corner and asked for a mineral water from one of the waiters. The man vanished and reappeared a few minutes later with a large cut glass tumbler clinking with ice and a small bowl of lemon slices. The bubbles were still jumping from the surface of the drink as he placed it in front of Joe, alongside a plate of dainty canapés.

Maisie arrived exactly two minutes after the designated time. She looked completely relaxed in the surroundings, as if she spent most of her time in five-star hotels. Joe knew just enough about fashion to tell that everything she was wearing was expensive. Her shiny dress was patterned with Roman busts, the silk clinging to her pencil thin body like a sheath. She carried a small brown bag decorated with some designer's initials, and her very high heels appeared equally costly.

Her face looked Thai, with high, sloping cheekbones below tiny, almond-shaped eyes. Her hair was pulled back from her face into a tight ponytail. It was as if some invisible hand was trying to lift her from the floor by her hair as she walked across to him, her perfect mouth unsmiling, her hand held out for him to shake, the fingers tipped with scarlet talons so huge they must have been false.

Joe stood up politely and found himself towering above her. His hand enveloped hers and he immediately loosened his grip for fear of crushing the fragile bones.

Another girl walked behind Maisie. She was probably twenty years younger and a complete world away from the confidence of her mentor.

'Mister Weston,' Maisie said as she folded herself neatly into a winged leather armchair and indicated for the girl to sit next to him on the sofa. 'I am Maisie and this is Doris.'

This was Doris? It certainly wasn't the Doris he had met in Brighton. Was this the Doris who had contacted him from Eaton Square? If so, that would explain why the one in Brighton had seemed not to have any idea what he was talking about.

Joe held his hand out for Doris as he sat back down beside her and she did not raise her eyes from the floor as she shook it. Her hand was also small, but not as delicate as Maisie's, and a stronger grip. It was a hand that he could imagine doing physical work. Doris said nothing, although her lips moved as if there were words she wanted to say.

Joe studied her. She was a little plain, as the nanny at Eaton Square had described. He automatically glanced at her chest. She appeared to be trying to cover it, as if embarrassed, hunching forward on the sofa with her arms up, her chin resting on her palms as she studied the carpet. As far as he could see, she had a very full pair of breasts, more than would have been produced by a padded bra if she had had her breasts 'stolen'.

'Doris is a very good girl', Maisie announced.

'I'm sure she is,' Joe replied, uncertain what he could say that wouldn't sound patronising.

A waiter appeared at Maisie's shoulder. 'Can I get you a drink, Madam?' he asked.

'Oh, a drink,' Maisie gave a tiny, delighted clap of her hands at the thought. 'What shall I have?'

'Can I get Madam a nice chilled glass of champagne?' the waiter suggested and Joe's heart gave a little lurch. Would he have enough money to cover this? If he ended up having to count coins out of his various pockets he was going to ruin his image as the smooth American abroad.

'Yes, champagne, and a Coca Cola for my friend.'

Joe could hear a faint ringing somewhere. Someone's phone was cutting into the tranquil murmur of the hotel guests as they gathered for the evening. Only on the third ring did he realise that it was his.

'Excuse me,' he said, pulling it out of his pocket.

'Dad?' Hugo's voice sounded distant and forlorn. 'I'm at school. Mum's gone and I don't like it here. I want to go home.'

Joe felt sick at the sound of his child's unhappiness. He racked his brain for the appropriate thing to say. 'Where are you calling from?' he asked, lamely.

'There's a call box,' Hugo said. 'Outside matron's office. I've only got twenty pence. I want you to come and get me.'

'I can't do that, fella,' Joe said, aware that Maisie was fidgeting irritably at this interruption. 'You've gotta give it a few days. You've gotta be brave. Once you've found some friends and had a few games of football you'll be fine. Just get a good night's sleep tonight and call me again tomorrow. Things will look better in the morning, I promise.'

There was a click and the line went dead. Hugo's money had run out.

'I'm sorry about that.' Joe forced himself not to think of his little son, alone and lost in a school full of echoing corridors and shouting strangers, not knowing whom to trust or where to turn to for comfort. He wished he could have thought of something better to say to the boy than the clichés he had come up with. The waiter brought the women their drinks and Maisie got straight back down to business.

'Doris is a good girl,' she said again. 'She is from Manila where she worked for an English Lord. He was very sad she decided to go, but she wanted to better herself and work for a gentleman in London. She is very anxious to please her employers.' Maisie inclined her head very slightly towards Joe, as if to imply that he was that chosen gentleman.

Joe turned to Doris who hadn't shifted from her crouched position. 'How do you like London so far, Doris?'

'Very nice,' she said, in a whisper.

'It's an exciting town, isn't it?' He wanted to put her at her ease, but he could see that addressing her directly was making her more nervous. She cast confused looks at Maisie, who appeared unbothered.

'When will your house be ready for Doris to move in?' she asked.

'Ah, well, that's a good question,' Joe gave what he hoped was a good-natured chuckle. 'You know what builders are like. Once you get them in it's hard to get them out again.'

'Doris could move in while they are still working. She could get the house cleaned up for you to arrive.'

'I think it's a little too much of a mess for that. It really is still a building site,' Joe said, hurriedly.

'Doris doesn't mind,' Maisie insisted.

'Well, give me a little time to think about it.'

'You want to meet other girls before you make up your mind?' Maisie asked, lighting herself a cigarette which looked incongruously long between her miniature fingers and drew attention to the unnatural size of her nails. 'You can meet more but Doris is best. I pick her for you from all the girls on our books because she is the hardest worker. She is willing to do whatever you ask her. You need new builders? Interior decorators?' She had changed her tack. 'We can handle all that for you. Complete service.'

'That's great,' Joe beamed, his mind still drifting back to Hugo.

'You like her?' Maisie snapped.

'Sure.' Joe looked across at Doris and smiled. It was wasted, her eyes were still on the floor. 'She seems very nice.'

'Ask her any question you like.'

'Do you cook?' Joe asked.

Doris nodded.

'She cooks American style,' Maisie butted in. 'All my girls trained to do steak and chips and hamburgers just as good as stir fry. Cook, clean,' she paused. 'Keep you company. She'll do anything you ask. Very reasonable wages. You want to discuss money now?'

'I was recommended to you by some friends of mine,' Joe shifted the subject. He felt uncomfortable talking in front of the girl about the price which Maisie was going to put on her head. 'The Montgomerys.'

'You want to know her wages?' Maisie was not going to be knocked off course that easily.

'Do you know the Montgomerys?' Nor was Joe.

'Yes.' She sounded impatient. 'I know them. Very good clients.'

'Their girl disappeared, I believe. She was called Doris too.'

'They complaining?' Every sinew in Maisie's exquisite little body had tightened in preparation for a fight. 'They have no cause to complain. I find them another girl if they want one. She was a good worker, and very cheap. Not the agency's fault she disappears. Probably some man, fall in love and not know how to say. They tell you they want new girl?' Her English noticeably slipped as she became more agitated.

'No, they haven't said anything to me.' Joe smiled pleasantly. He felt that for a second he had gained the upper hand. She sounded nervous, defensive even. There was a scent of danger around her, as if she might jump forward and implant her nails in his face if he wasn't careful. 'They are just neighbours of mine, really. I was chatting to them. You know how it is when you first arrive in a new neighbourhood, you want to pick up tips, useful names and addresses.'

'Neighbours, eh?' Maisie relaxed a little. 'They live in Eaton Square. Yes?'

'Yes,' Joe agreed.

'Good address.' She nodded approvingly.

'How old are you?' Joe asked Doris.

'She's young and strong and all her papers in order,' Maisie answered for her. 'You will be very satisfied. You want to talk about wages? You pay deposit of one thousand pounds with agency. Then you pay us one thousand pounds a month. She lives in your house. She is your responsibility to feed. Not a problem, she not eat much.'

'The Montgomerys told me I wouldn't have to pay that much,' Joe bluffed.

Maisie made an annoyed clicking sound at such indiscretion amongst clients. 'They get good deal. Costs go up. Okay. You have Doris one thousand deposit, seven fifty a month. Best deal in town.'

'I don't see why I should pay more than the Montgomerys,' Joe persisted. 'Your costs are your problem, not mine.'

'Okay,' Maisie snapped angrily. 'You pay me five hundred deposit and five hundred a month.'

'Four hundred, and I think I would be more comfortable paying Doris direct,' Joe said, aware that he was being mischievous.

'Not possible,' Maisie said. 'Agency rules. We handle all the money for the staff. It's our policy. We have overheads. Four hundred a month but you pay us.'

'Well, the rates seem very reasonable,' Joe said.

'Best in town. No one can match us. Other agencies cheaper but their girls steal and lie and lazy. Not hard workers.'

'Well, I'll need to think about it. I'm not quite ready to commit.'

'Give us a deposit and then Doris will wait until your house is ready. If not, then someone else will hire her. She's good, strong girl. Someone else will hire her for sure.'

'I'm sure they will. But I'm afraid I'll just have to take that risk,' Joe said. 'Let me think about it and ring you in a week.'

'May be too late,' Maisie's tone was hardening like steel. 'Pay deposit now, no more worries. Doris wait for you to call and tell her you want her. Best service in London, advertised in *The Lady* and *Tatler* and all top magazines. Give me down-payment of four hundred pounds, pay rest later.'

'May I ring you back once I have the house straight?' Joe said. 'Please excuse me,' he stood up. 'I have another appointment.' He held out his hand for Doris. She looked surprised and then took it. Maisie did likewise and held onto his hand tightly, like a child determined to drag a reluctant adult into a playground.

'Don't make a mistake, Mister Weston. Girls as good as Doris are very hard to find. Don't make a mistake and lose her. Give me two hundred and fifty pounds now and pay rest when she starts.'

'I'll call you.' Joe pulled his hand away. He felt a chill running through him as Maisie's impassive face stared up at him. There appeared to be no human being behind the eyes.

He turned abruptly on his heel, unable to think of a more gracious way to end the interview, and walked out of the bar. As he came into the entrance hall he saw a flash of pink hair going past between two men. Both men looked like businessmen with dark suits, sober ties and raincoats over their arms. Both seemed to be making a point of not looking around them as they walked. They were men with a purpose.

It took him a second to register what he had seen and by the time he turned round Cordelia was disappearing around the pillars towards the lifts. He opened his mouth to call out and then thought better of it. He wanted to get out of the building before Maisie caught up with him, and there was something about the two men Cordelia was with that suggested they would not like to be hailed by a complete stranger in a public place. She didn't look as if she was wanting to be rescued.

All these thoughts raced through his brain in just a few seconds and it wasn't until he had reached the street and was walking briskly down Knightsbridge that he realised he had not paid for the drinks. That was not likely to endear him to Maisie, but it was a relief to still have the cash in his pocket. He dived into a pub and bought himself a beer and a burger to celebrate. He didn't want to go back to the flat yet. He wanted to think about his son, even though he knew it would make him unhappy.

CHAPTER SIX

The cheque fluttered out of the envelope and landed in a small pool of coffee on the kitchen table. Joe picked it up and dabbed it dry with his dressing-gown sleeve before reading it. He was deliberately delaying the moment of discovering how much it was for, aware that it would almost certainly be a disappointment, and allowing himself the luxury of a few moments of wild fantasising.

When he did finally focus on them, the figures took his breath away. Adele was sending him over ten thousand pounds. He pulled the rest of the paperwork out of the envelope. It seemed that the book he had done with the SAS corporal had started earning royalties abroad sooner than expected.

For a few minutes the exultation of having money made him forget the knot of depression which had been in his stomach ever since the call from Hugo the previous evening. He was carrying the phone around with him everywhere he went, even into the bathroom, determined to be there to take any other calls his son might make.

'Joe, old man,' Angus interrupted his thoughts. 'Rather embarrassing.'

'Angus,' Joe's mind was racing. 'I am so sorry. My bank has just told me that they've bounced that cheque I gave you. I can't believe they would do such a thing. I am so angry. I have a good mind to change to another bank.'

'I...' Angus tried to interrupt but Joe didn't give him a chance.

'As soon as I'm dressed we'll go down to my branch together and I'll give you the money in cash. I can pay this in at the same time.' He gestured casually at the cheque, giving Angus enough time to register the long row of figures before whipping it away and stuffing it into his pocket.

'Give me five minutes to pull some clothes on and I'll come and collect you.'

He rushed into his room and closed the door, leaving Angus standing in the middle of the kitchen with his mouth open.

'What I was actually going to say,' Angus said, quarter of an hour later, as they were strolling down the Earls Court Road to Joe's bank, 'was that I had a call from your friend's mother.'

'My friend?' Joe's mind was elsewhere.

'Cordelia Jones.'

'Cordelia's mother? She rang you?'

'Yes. Apparently Cordelia gave her my number because she thought my 'posh' voice would put her mother's mind at rest about her moving into the flat.'

'And did it?'

'I don't think so. She threatened to send the police round. Seemed to think I was some sort of pimp, hoping to sell her daughter's services to the entire population of West London.'

'She said that?'

'I can't remember exactly what she said. It was all somewhat of a tirade. I dropped your name in, hoping that would calm her down.'

'And I guess it didn't?'

'If anything it made it worse. She said you were just one of her ex-husband's lackeys. That you were probably sleeping with her daughter already, possibly had been ever since she was fourteen.'

'Oh. Sorry, Angus. I had no idea she would phone you. I've never met the woman. I won't mind if you want to tell Cordelia the deal's off.'

'I suppose I could,' Angus sounded doubtful. 'But I had a little flutter at the bookmakers yesterday and I've rather committed that money she gave me. I wouldn't necessarily want to have to return it.'

'Ah,' Joe nodded his understanding. 'Well, we'll just have to take our chances with Rita, then.'

'Rita?'

'Cordelia's mother.'

'Ah. Is that her name?' Angus looked distinctly worried. 'She sounded remarkably fierce.'

Once the cheque had been banked, a short-term overdraft agreed, and Angus had been paid, Joe went in search of a car. The call from Hugo the previous evening had made him realise how cut off they were from one another. If his son was in a school in the countryside of Sussex, Joe needed to be able to get to him within a couple of hours at least, without having to rely on trains and taxis or car hire firms. He bought himself an early edition of the *Evening Standard* and sat down with a cup of coffee and a felt-tip.

Two hours later he was sitting in a prim Chelsea kitchen, writing out a cheque to a rich man's wife who wanted to get rid of her Fiat Panda quickly in order to raise the money for a holiday with a girlfriend. The car was ten years old but had lived all its life in a locked garage and looked as if it had just been driven out of the showroom. Joe felt pleased with himself. The woman seemed to be totally confident that his cheque wouldn't bounce and waved happily as he drove the car away, having insured it through her broker – apparently a family friend. Once you have money in your pocket, Joe thought, things just start to fall into place.

He set off down the King's Road with the window down, watching the girls go by as the traffic chugged forward at less than a walking pace. When the phone rang in his pocket it made his stomach lurch. He dreaded hearing whatever Hugo had to say.

What would he do if the boy pleaded to be taken away from the school again? What would be the correct paternal response? He didn't see why Hugo should have to endure the place if it made him unhappy. But shouldn't he at least be encouraged to give it a go? And if he did want to come out, would Fliss ever agree? If she didn't, would he be able to have Hugo live with him, so that he could get him to and from a day school each day?

All these thoughts sped through his mind as he reached into his pocket and pulled out the phone. Fliss' voice took him by surprise. Hugo must have given her the mobile number.

'What the fuck are you playing at?' she demanded. 'I've had the school on the line. You were supposed to pay the fees by the first day of term. Are you determined to ruin your son's life? I've had to lie for you. I said you've been travelling and have only just got back to London. You've got to sort it out.'

For a moment he considered telling her that Hugo had called, but then thought better of it. He would use the fees as a reason to drive down to the school. He would be able to see Hugo and decide what needed to be done. If he said anything to Fliss about Hugo being unhappy she would take it as a criticism of the way she was bringing him up and would go on the attack. He needed to find out the situation for himself before he started a war.

'I'll take the cheque in personally today,' he said. 'Sorry. I've had a few things on my mind.'

'Pity one of them wasn't your son,' she snapped and hung up.

Joe swung the car down a side street and headed back towards Earls Court to fetch a map and the necessary paperwork. He felt faintly sick, partly with anger at Fliss' tone, and partly with guilt at having let his son down.

The boys were filing out from lunch as he walked into the school office and asked to see the bursar. He tried to spot

Hugo, but they all looked frighteningly alike in their uniforms and passed too quickly for him to be sure what he had seen.

The building must once have been a stately home. He guessed it had been built by some Victorian merchant, keen to show off his new wealth. Every feature of the place, from the gargoyles curling out over the giant, studded oak front doors, to the dark panelling and tall, tightly latticed windows, seemed to have been designed to overawe an unprepared visitor. If it had this effect on him, he thought, what effect would it have on a small child leaving home for the first time?

'Do you have an appointment?' the secretary asked, peering over her glasses, from which a gold chain hung down round her neck. Joe felt her eyes looking him up and down. He wished he had changed into something a bit smarter than the baggy shirt and trousers which he had pulled on when he got up that morning. He also wished that he had checked his hair in a mirror before coming in from the car. He had a feeling that it was sticking out at some odd angles. Sometimes he just couldn't believe that he was old enough to be taken seriously as a father.

'I'm afraid not,' he said. 'My name's Joe Tye. My son, Hugo, started here this term and I've only just arrived back in the country from a trip. I've brought the payment.'

'Oh, right.' The woman relaxed as she realised he wasn't there to complain or make work for her. 'I can take that from you. Would you like a receipt?'

'No, no,' he assured her. 'That'll be fine. Is there any chance of seeing Hugo for a couple of seconds, do you think? Having been away...'

Through the windows he could see boys coming out onto the sweeping green lawns, some of them stopping to play games, others making their way to the woods beyond. The woman stiffened again and looked as if she was going to find a problem with that. She then seemed to recognise the look of pleading in his eyes and softened once more.

'Let's see if we can find him,' she said.

She led him out of the office and through a set of French windows onto a terrace. Weeds were pushing up the ancient paving stones and the building towered behind them, grey and grim.

'Anthony,' she called to a large boy who seemed to be starting to grow a moustache. 'There's a new boy called Hugo Tye. Do you know him?'

'The new boys are doing football trials,' the boy grunted. 'They're in the changing rooms.'

'Would you take Mr Tye over and see if you can find Hugo for him?'

The boy nodded and started walking. Joe assumed he was meant to follow. He thanked the woman and set off. He thought about trying to make conversation with the boy in front of him, but thought better of it. He had too much on his mind. He couldn't work out whether or not he was making a huge mistake. Would this visit make Hugo even more homesick? He just knew that he couldn't drive away without at least seeing his son.

The changing rooms smelt damp and rotten. The sound of excited little voices filled the fetid air. Anthony waded in amongst them, asking for Hugo. Joe saw his son emerging from a door that he assumed led to the lavatories. He was already changed for the trials, all his kit brand new and far too big for him, making him look like a cartoon as he clopped across the floor in his stiff, new boots, the laces trailing behind him, his shirt tails hanging out, almost obscuring his shorts. Joe felt a rush of emotion and wasn't sure if he was going to be able to stop tears from coming to his eyes. Hugo looked so small and so lost, but at the same time he saw him as an independent being, someone with a life now completely separate from him and Fliss.

Hugo spotted him and, to Joe's relief, broke into a grin. Running to get to his father, he stood on his bootlace and sent himself sprawling forward into a group of his fellows, knocking them all to the floor like skittles in a bowling alley. Joe wanted to wade into the mêlée and haul his son out, but held back, waiting until Hugo extricated himself and came over, followed by some muted abuse.

'Hello,' Hugo said, eventually, hugging his father tightly. 'What are you doing here? I'm doing football trials. We had sausages for lunch. They were so gross but they made us eat them.'

Joe returned the hug. 'I just had to deliver something to the school office,' he explained. 'So I thought I'd say hi.'

'Okay. I've got to go now. I'll ring you on your mobile.'

Hugo ran after the other boys who were making their way out of the door, his laces still trailing behind him, his shirt tail flapping. Just as he was about to disappear from sight he turned and Joe caught his eye. He felt as if he was watching a part of himself going for ever. Aware that other boys were staring at him and giggling, he turned and walked back to the car park.

Climbing into the car, he drove down the winding drive, past the walls of rhododendrons that had been allowed to grow wild, no doubt providing dense undergrowth for mock battles and elaborate camps. This would be a good place to spend a few years of your childhood, Joe told himself. Better than being trapped in the stifling atmosphere of Fliss' Kensington house.

The phone rang as he joined the motorway, piloting the little car into the stream of traffic heading back towards London. Keeping his eyes on the road he wrestled it out of his pocket and struggled to switch it on with one hand. The noise from the engine, as it strained to keep up with the streams of powerful cars racing past, made it hard to hear the pitiful little voice over the airwaves.

'Hello?' it said, trying to work out if there was a human ear listening to it amidst the roar of engine and road noise.

'Hello,' Joe shouted back.

'Joe, the American man?'

'Yes.'

'Doris calling you.'

An articulated lorry ploughed past, rocking the Fiat in the wind of its slipstream as Joe worked out it must be the Brighton Doris.

'Hello, Doris,' he said. 'Sorry about the noise. I'm in the car.'

'Joe. The doctor says I have tumours. He says I have growths the size of chicken eggs. He says I have to have an operation.'

'What doctor?'

'The doctor who looks after me. He says I must have lumps cut out, very quick or the cancer will spread through my whole body and I will die.' She was crying now.

'I'm so sorry, Doris. Is there anything I can do?'

'I'm frightened, Joe. I have no family in England and my friend has gone away.'

There was the sound of shouting in the background, a male voice, then a small scream and the phone went dead.

Straining to keep his eyes and mind on the road, Joe tried to ring the number back. When he raised it to his ear the line was engaged. He hung up, dropping the phone into his lap. He was travelling on the Brighton road, but going in the wrong direction. He needed a slip road that would lead him round to the opposite carriageway. He could imagine what might be happening to the poor girl, could envisage the hideous Max, his face contorted in anger, beating her to the ground. She had called him for help and there was no one else in the world who knew she was in trouble. She was so many thousands of miles away from her home, he couldn't ignore her plea.

The road seemed to grind on northwards forever beneath the struggling engine as he scanned the horizon for a sign telling him he could escape. Nothing came and the milometer kept clicking up, taking him further and further from Brighton. The phone rang again. He picked it up.

'Who's that?' a man's voice snarled into his ear. Joe said nothing, staring at the road ahead, praying for a sign. He was sure it was Max. He must have taken the phone off Doris and pressed redial. 'Just stay the fuck away from her or you're dead!' the voice said and hung up.

A sign appeared ahead of him and he swerved into the left-hand lane. Thirty minutes later he was pulling into the end of Ditchling Avenue. The Panda nosed cautiously down towards number forty-two. There was no sign of anything happening from the outside. It looked like every other house in the street, just a little more run-down and rather more forbidding with its bars and curtains.

Joe parked the car and climbed out, his heart thumping. He wondered if he should make an anonymous call to the police, telling them that he believed a woman was being beaten up inside. He didn't think they would be that interested. They would probably send an officer to investigate, but it would be much too little, much too late. He mustered his courage and sauntered up to the front door. He pressed the bell. It rang loudly inside, as if attached to a fire alarm.

There were some shuffling noises from behind the door and subdued voices. It opened a crack and an English girl's face peered out. She was wearing a large man's fleece and tracksuit bottoms, both of which were covered in food stains. Her face was too thin to be pretty, her eyes too frightened.

'Max isn't here,' she said. 'He's just gone out.'

'I've come to see Doris.' He was about to launch into the explanation which he had been preparing in his mind, about how they were old friends from Manila, but the girl obviously wasn't interested.

'She's with Max.'

'I lent her a book and she said I could have it back if I dropped by.'

'You'll have to come back,' she said, trying to push the door shut.

'If I could just pop into her room,' he held the door with his hand, trying not to look too aggressive and alarm her. 'I'll be two seconds.' He tried his most charming smile. 'You can time me.'

The woman looked at him blearily for a moment and then obviously decided that arguing was too much of an effort.

'Okay.' She stood back and let him walk past. 'Her room is at the top of the stairs. The one with the red door. If Max comes back I've never seen you before.'

'Thanks,' he said, already walking in. 'I'll be as quick as I can.'

As he made his way down the hall to the staircase he glanced into the rooms on either side. Every spare inch of floor was covered in mattresses and sleeping bags that looked as though they had only just been vacated. There was a smell of stale food, cigarette smoke and perspiration. He could hear sounds coming from a room down some back stairs.

When he turned the woman who had let him in had disappeared. She was obviously used to strangers coming and going in the house. There clearly wasn't anything worth stealing. He climbed the stairs, past more rooms in a similar state, and found the red door at the top of the house. The old servants' quarters, he assumed. He gave a light knock and let himself in.

This room in the roof was much neater than the others, and as spartan as a cell in a monastery. A small skylight in a sloping wall let in some daylight. There was a single mattress with an uncovered duvet neatly spread across it and a chair with an alarm clock on it. Beside the clock was a picture of a bunch of girls who looked as if they were part of the same family, presumably taken in Manila. The young girl at the centre of the laughing group looked like the Doris he had met in the shop. A cheap sports bag stood behind the door.

Squatting down he opened the bag. Inside were some neatly folded T-shirts and underclothes and a small notebook covered in fluorescent green fur. He opened the book and saw lists of names and telephone numbers. A piece of paper fell out onto the floor. He unfolded it. At the top was printed the Montgomerys' address in Eaton Square. Below, scrawled in a child's crayon, was the message: *Try ring me evening. Sometimes can answer phone. Give me number. I call you back. We talk.*

He put the book and letter back into the bag and stood up. Looking round the room once more, he decided there was nothing more to see and made his way downstairs. There was no one on the ground floor but he could still hear voices coming from the basement. He made his way down.

There was music playing and a wide-screen television flickered silently in the corner as a game-show host hugged some ecstatic contestants. Several people were sitting around a table drinking mugs of tea. A packet of biscuits lay open in front of them, and they were all munching. Above their heads another television screen showed a quiet street scene.

'Hi,' he said casually. One or two of them looked up. 'Anyone know where Doris has gone?'

'She was sick,' a man in a woolly hat told him. 'Seriously sick. She had to go to the hospital.'

'Any idea which hospital?'

They all looked blank.

'You want to wait? Max'll probably bring her back here once she's fixed up,' the girl who had let him in suggested.

'Nah.' Joe didn't fancy the idea of coming face to face with Max, who was bound to guess that he was the person Doris had called in her moment of distress.

'Did you find your book?' the girl asked.

'Nah,' Joe replied. 'It's not important. I'll come back when she's better.'

The group in the kitchen seemed to accept this as a goodbye and all went back to whatever they had been talking about when he came in. The picture on the television above their heads hadn't changed and he realised that the street was Ditchling Avenue. Somewhere on the house there was a hidden camera watching everyone who came anywhere near the front door. He left the room, aware that as far as these people were concerned he was invisible.

As he walked back into the flat in Earls Court, Joe was aware of a disruption only a split second before he was pinned against the wall, his head banged painfully against the door frame and powerful fingers encircling his throat.

'You bastard, I've a good mind to kill you,' his attacker hissed, her spittle spraying his face.

'Come, come, come, come,' Angus fluttered in the background, trying to attract the attacker's attention away from Joe. 'This is no way to sort out any disagreement.'

'I know everything about you.' The woman pushed her face so close to Joe's that he couldn't focus on her. She looked familiar but he couldn't work out why. 'I know how long you've been after her. You should be fucking well locked up!'

'For Christ's sake, Mum, what are you doing?'

Joe saw Cordelia coming out of the room where the drummer used to live and he realised where he had seen this woman before. This was Rita. An older Rita than the one who had featured in the picture section of Len's book, but definitely Rita. In the wedding pictures she had been beautiful. The beauty was still there but it had hardened, set in lipstick and eyeliner and bitterness.

'He's not after me. He's just a bloke who works for Dad,' Cordelia protested. 'He's a nice guy.'

'No one around your father is a nice guy,' Rita snarled.

'He's a writer, Mum. He wrote Dad's book.'

'I know who he is,' Rita tightened her grip on Joe as she remembered the book. His eyes were beginning to bulge. 'I've read the lies he told about me in that fucking book. I've had my lawyers read it too. I'm not letting these lowlifes walk all over me.'

'Muuuum! Do you mind? This is where I live.'

'Cordy!' Rita let go of Joe's throat, allowing air to get through to his lungs once more, throwing her arms around her daughter as Joe gasped for breath. 'Why don't you come and live with me? Your father stole the best years of your life from me and I deserve something. Why live in all this squalor when there's a nice clean house with a bedroom all of your own waiting in Pinner?'

'Squalor?' Angus looked around him, aghast.

There was the sound of a key and the front door opened suddenly, sending Joe flying forwards onto Rita as she hugged her daughter.

'Sorry,' Annie said as she came in. 'Why's everyone standing in the hall?'

'Mum, this is Annie,' Cordelia said. 'Another of my flatmates.'

'Thank God,' Rita said, 'a woman.'

It was nine o'clock in the evening when Joe arrived on the Montgomerys' doorstep and rang the bell. He had his speech ready for the butler and was surprised when the door was opened by a man in evening dress with a napkin in his hand, clearly having just been disturbed at dinner. He looked as though he were master of the house.

'Hi,' Joe said. 'Mr Montgomery?'

'Who are you?' The man looked irritated at being disturbed. Joe could hear the sounds of a dinner party emanating from the dining room.

'My name is John Weston. I'm a friend of Doris. Your Filipino. She asked me to pick up her things.'

'Bloody cheek,' Montgomery huffed. 'You'd better come in. We're in the middle of dinner.'

'Sorry to disturb you.'

Montgomery didn't bother to respond. He marched back to the dining room and boomed across the conversation.

'Elizabeth. There's an American here to pick up that Filipino's belongings.'

'Has Doris left you?' one of the female guests asked loudly.

Joe appeared in the doorway behind Montgomery, just in time to see a look of panic flit through the eyes of the elegant Elizabeth Montgomery as she rose from her chair at the end of the lavish table. His eyes scanned the room. The table was lit by candles which made the cut glass and silver glitter. There was a scent of good food and wine in the warm air and he was fairly sure he recognised one of the men at the table as a senior government minister.

'You sit down and eat, dear. I'll deal with this.' Elizabeth walked straight past Joe. 'Come with me,' she said, not moving her lips. Joe fell into step behind her. 'I'm getting pretty fed up with all this harassment,' she snapped as they started the long climb upstairs.

'Harassment?' Joe pretended to be puzzled. 'I just came to collect Doris' things. I couldn't pick them up on my last visit because you told me I had the wrong house.'

'You know bloody well what I mean.' Her jaw was still clenched tightly as she spoke. 'Ever since I had the temerity to lodge a complaint with the agency about that girl I have had nothing but trouble. First of all they send round a band of goons to take her away, then you turn up. Then that bloody Maisie woman rings me morning, noon and night telling me I need another of her dreadful girls, refusing to take "no" for an answer…'

'What was your complaint against Doris?'

'She was stealing.' Elizabeth Montgomery lowered her voice to a hiss as they passed the children's bedrooms.

'Stealing what?'

'Phone calls. When our itemised bill came in there were endless calls to Brighton, and other places. She'd even been calling home to Manila. She never once asked for permission.

70

God knows it's expensive enough keeping staff without them stealing from you.'

'Would you have allowed her to make the calls if she had asked?'

'There is a perfectly good public telephone around the corner. Or she could get her own mobile and talk herself to death for all I cared. Just not at my expense.'

'So, these goons who came to get her...'

'They were unbelievable. They barged into the house like some sort of SAS hit squad. There was one, covered in tattoos, who was terrifying. Thank God Nanny had taken the children out. Doris was in her room at the time, doing some sewing, and he ran straight up the stairs, while the others checked the kitchen downstairs. They seemed to know exactly where they were going. One of them stood beside me and made sure I didn't call the police. It was terrifying, I can tell you. I could hear that gorilla laying into Doris, shouting and swearing. It sounded like he was throwing her around the room.'

'What was he shouting?'

'Something about her planning to escape and leading the others on.'

'Did she say anything?'

'Not that I heard. When he came down he was dragging her by the scruff of the neck. She was whimpering like a puppy. It sounded like she was praying. I felt quite sorry for her. Whatever she might have done I didn't think she deserved that sort of treatment. And, as they went out the man stuck his face right into mine and said that, if I knew what was good for me, I wouldn't mention Doris to anyone. Just pretend she never existed.'

'Didn't you think of ringing the police?'

She looked at him as if he were mad. 'These people know where we live,' she said, as if that answered his question.

'And you were hiring Doris illegally?'

She didn't reply.

'Maisie told me that Doris had just disappeared,' he persisted.

'These people lie all the time. It's a way of life to them,' Elizabeth spat.

They had reached the top of the house. She opened a door into a room very similar to the one he had discovered in Brighton, only smaller and darker. There didn't appear to be a window of any sort.

'Did you tell your husband?' Joe asked as he looked around the sparse room. There was a camp bed and a tiny chest of drawers which filled almost all the floor space.

'My husband is a very busy man,' she said, imperiously. 'He does not have time for the details of our domestic arrangements. He leaves me to run the house in the way I think best.'

'Doesn't sound like you're doing a very good job.' Joe was surprised by how angry he felt as he stood in the meagre little room and imagined the poor frightened girl being dragged out of it by Max.

'It's not easy running a house like this,' Elizabeth said and there was just the slightest hint of a tremor in her voice. 'Decent staff are almost impossible to find. And when you do find them, they want the world on a plate.'

'Maisie's Amazing Maids must have seemed too good to be true,' Joe said, sarcastically. 'Slave labour at rock-bottom prices.'

'Well, I shall never use them again,' she said, recovering her composure. 'Here.' She handed him a sports bag almost identical to the one he had found in Brighton. 'They left this. Anything of hers which we found I put in there.'

'Thank you.' Joe took the bag and started to walk downstairs.

'I trust this will be the last we hear of the whole matter.' Elizabeth's voice rang out after him. He didn't bother to reply. Downstairs, the dinner party was back in full swing as he let himself out of the grand front door.

CHAPTER SEVEN

'Hi, Jo-Jo.'

It had been a long time since Fliss had called him that. It brought back pleasant memories which dispersed almost as soon as they appeared.

'Hi,' he replied, suspiciously. If Fliss was being nice then it was going to cost him in some way. A feeling of dread at what might come next spread through him.

'Listen, thanks for going down to the school. That was good of you.'

'That's okay.' His suspicions deepened and darkened. He allowed a silence to fall down the airwaves, determined not to allow her any reason to think he was pleased to hear from her.

'Um.' That was always a prelude to something bad. 'I wondered if you could do me the most enormous favour.' Even worse.

'What?'

'Hugo has his first weekend out in a couple of weeks, and Paolo and I just have to be in Paris for a party. It's one of Paolo's sponsors so there is absolutely no getting out of it.'

Joe's heart gave a little leap of joy. Fliss was actually going to hand him Hugo for a whole weekend. He couldn't believe his luck.

'Let me check my diary,' he said, allowing nearly a full minute to elapse before coming back on the line. 'Yeah, I guess I can do that. I'll have to juggle a few things around.'

'You are a love. I'll repay you, honestly. I feel terrible about it.'

'Don't worry. It'll be great to see him. You can party with a clear conscience. Anything else?'

'No.'

'Okay, I gotta go. Bye.'

He hung up before she had a chance to say goodbye. 'Yes!' He punched the air in excitement. Hugo all to himself for an entire weekend. There was a God after all. He peered out of the window of the bus as he put the phone back in his pocket. They were nearly at Piccadilly Circus. He stood up and walked to the platform at the rear, jumping down to the road as the bus slowed for some lights. He had thought about bringing the car up to the West End, but had decided he might want to have more than one drink over lunch with Adele.

He walked through to Regent Street and up to the agency's office. Adele came out to reception to meet him and they made their way down to the street, crossing over and diving into Soho. Although she was nudging fifty, Adele was still a handsome woman. She had a strong, olive-skinned face and thick, straight dark hair which she kept extraordinarily glossy. Her dark-rimmed glasses gave her a severe air, which she was only too happy to play up to, using them as props to intimidate publishers and authors alike. Her clothes were always very simple, and nearly always black. She had an openness and a directness of manner which people responded to.

Once they were seated in the fashionable basement restaurant which Adele was currently favouring, with its original artworks on the walls and computer-connected waiters hurtling from table to table, she asked him how things were going for him.

'Could always do with a bit more money,' he said, with a wry smile.

'Couldn't we all?' Adele agreed, reading the menu as she talked. 'You might be in luck. There's been a sniff at the film rights for Len's book.'

'Yeah? How much?'

'Too early to say. I'll let you know if it comes to anything. What happened with that Filipino girl who contacted you?'

'Well, I was going to talk to you about that...' A waiter arrived and they spent a few minutes ordering. Once he had gone and a bottle of wine had been brought and poured, Joe continued.

'It seems there is more than one of them.'

'I'm sure there are thousands of them,' Adele agreed. 'Everyone wants a Filipino maid these days.'

'No, I mean, more than one Doris.'

'Doris?'

'Doris is the name of the girl who contacted me. But when I went to look for her she had disappeared. I investigated a bit further and so far I have found two more Dorises.'

'They all have the same name?'

'So it seems, and they're all being brought into the country by a woman called Maisie. I think she might be Thai, although she was working in Manila before she came here. It seems that Maisie is shipping these girls over and then renting them out as virtual slaves to wealthy families.

'The Doris who contacted me seems to have wanted to get away, and was in contact with at least one other Doris, possibly more...'

Adele gave a snort of laughter. 'I'm sorry,' she said, 'but a plague of Dorises strikes me as just a little comical.'

'Well, I guess there is a comical side,' Joe said, doubtfully. 'But I think these girls are actually being treated pretty brutally.'

'Of course, yes. I'm sorry.' Adele composed herself. 'Go on.'

'Well, I thought I would keep on trying to track down the original Doris. If I find her, I'll get her story out of her and see if it'll make a book. Just as she suggested.'

'And if you don't find her?'

'If I don't, I think I'll have uncovered enough background material to write the book anyway, based on a fictitious Doris, a sort of amalgam of all of them. Or I could try writing it with one of the other Dorises I have managed to find. Starting with a childhood in some remote Philippine village, how she got recruited and smuggled into the country, and then how she was treated by the rich folks who bought her services. It could be like a modern-day Dickens.'

'Modest enough ambition,' Adele laughed.

'They all seem to be having plastic surgery as well, to enhance their breasts,' Joe continued, lost in his own story-telling. 'I think it probably isn't being done very well. Whatever they're doing to them is going wrong because the first Doris said they had "stolen her beautiful new breasts", which I guess means she had to have a mastectomy. And the second Doris I met says she has been told she had tumours the size of chicken eggs.'

'In her breasts?'

'She didn't say, but I assume so. It could be a great story. Imagine starting out in life as a simple peasant girl in the Third World, if the Philippines are the Third World, being brought to a strange country, used as a slave and then operated on without having any idea what's going on. Having no one to talk to.'

'So, are these Dorises going into the sex trade as well?'

'I guess the prettier ones are. That would explain why they're giving them boob jobs. Maybe they're getting facelifts as well. If you met this Maisie woman it's not hard to imagine her as a procuress of some sort. I posed as a potential employer and she made it damn clear that the girl I was being offered as a "housekeeper" would be happy to do whatever I wanted.'

'Yuk.'

'Thanks.'

'Nothing personal.'

He stopped talking as their starters were put in front of them.

'Marion Ray is going to be in London next month,' Adele said, once they were eating. 'I thought we might set up a meeting. Are you still keen?'

'Sure. What's she over for?'

'Thinking of making a movie here, apparently. They say she really wants to meet you again. She realises that she's been messing you about. She wants to talk about the project seriously.'

'Great. Just give me the dates. What do you think about the Doris idea?'

'It's good. Topical. Scary. A good women's book.'

'Exactly.'

'When you feel ready, do a synopsis and I'll try it on a few publishers. There's someone else I wanted to talk to you about.'

'I'm listening,' he said, tucking into the food with gusto as Adele talked.

'I've been approached by an ex-policeman. He spent twenty years on the vice squad and then got caught with his trousers down in some massage parlour or other. He's very pissed off and wants to spill the beans on everyone. He's given me a synopsis which is absolutely packed with names. Everyone from cabinet ministers and cardinals to pop stars and television actors. It is an absolute "who's who" in the world of sleaze.'

'Would any publisher dare touch it?'

'I don't know. He says he has all the evidence he needs to back up his accusations. Apparently he's been quietly removing files for years, for just this day.'

'How did he come to you?'

'Through your friend, Len Jones. Apparently they know each other well. He read Len's book and asked his advice. Len gave him my number.'

'So, what's the material he's given you like? Can he write?'

'No. He'll need a ghost.'

'Have you told him?' Joe asked, taking a gulp of wine.

'Yes.'

'How did he take it?'

'He doesn't like the idea of sharing the money, but I pointed out that without a ghost there won't be any money. Better a shared pot than none at all. He said in that case he wanted to have the same ghost as Len. Are you interested?'

'I'd like to meet him,' Joe said.

'Okay. I'll set it up.'

As they continued with their meal the restaurant filled up around them and the noise level grew. When his phone started to ring it took Joe a few seconds to realise what the sound was. When he finally put it to his ear, he could barely hear the weak little voice at the other end.

'It's Doris here,' it said.

'Doris?' he shouted. 'Where are you?'

'Wimpole Clinic. I'm so sad, American Joe. Please help me.'

'I'll come and visit you,' he said and she hung up.

'Doris?' Adele raised an eyebrow.

'Where's the Wimpole Clinic?' Joe asked.

'In Wimpole Street, I guess.'

'Is that far?'

'No. About ten minutes walk.'

Joe stayed for coffee, but his mind was no longer on whatever it was Adele was talking about. He was trying to imagine what sort of reception he could expect at the clinic. There was no reason why Doris shouldn't receive a visit from a friend, but if Max was there he would surely smell a rat. Max would almost certainly know that Doris didn't have any friends in England that he hadn't met. He would guess that Joe was the man she had called in her moment of panic. And what if Maisie was there? How would he explain himself to her?

There was no way out of it. He had promised Doris he would go to her if she needed help. He would just have to take his chances. Adele gave him directions to get to Wimpole Street and, on his way, he bought a bunch of flowers from a stall, picking his way through the discarded boxes and vegetable matter.

The Wimpole Clinic was not obvious to the casual glance. It was just another stately house in the row. Only a discreet brass plate beside the door advertised its existence. Joe tried to open the door but it was locked. On ringing the bell, a middle-aged woman in a smart two-piece suit let him in.

'My friend, Doris, is here,' he said. 'She's from the Philippines.'

'Ah yes, Miss Brown.' The woman smiled and Joe felt a little more relaxed.

'Is she able to have visitors?'

'Oh yes, I think so. Although you probably shouldn't stay too long. I believe she's very tired. I'll get a nurse to take you up.'

She ushered him across the hall to a waiting room. A few minutes later a nurse came in.

'A visitor for Miss Brown?' she asked.

'Yes.'

'Follow me, please.'

They walked up a creaking, polished wooden staircase, past some dark glowering portraits, which Joe guessed must have been bought as a job lot with the house before it was converted into a nursing home. There were one or two pieces of antique furniture dotted along the wide landing, and none of the sterile, brightly lit bustle of a modern, purpose-built hospital.

Just as the nurse reached a door and put her hand on the handle, it burst open and a doctor rushed out. At least, Joe assumed he was a doctor. He certainly had the face of a senior consultant; thick grey eyebrows and neatly combed grey hair, gold-rimmed half-moon spectacles and a ferocious glower. He was wearing a green coat as if he had just come from the operating theatre, but it was gaping open to show a bare chest beneath, with a small gold medallion amidst the tufts of white hair. The coat, and the green trousers beneath, were stained with blood.

'Who the fuck are you?' he enquired in a voice which sounded more like it should belong to a friend of Len's than a West End consultant.

'The gentleman has come to visit Miss Brown,' the nurse said. She didn't seem surprised by the doctor's manner.

'What, that Miss Brown?' he asked, obviously incredulous. He glanced at the flowers. 'How bleedin' romantic.'

With that he strode off and went down the stairs, two at a time, shouting over his shoulder. 'Don't get her excited, laddie. And leave her fucking tits alone.'

'He's a doctor?' Joe asked the nurse as she ushered him into the room.

'Take no notice,' the nurse replied. 'He's the most brilliant surgeon. He likes to shock people, that's all. He does all the stars, gives them implants, facelifts. He's absolutely a genius. Really.'

The room was small, just enough space for a bed and a chair. The decorations must once have been pretty, but were now fading, the floral curtains hanging at a slightly odd angle from a flimsy plastic rail above the window. Outside, there was no view beyond a brick wall.

Doris was lying in the bed watching the door. She smiled when she saw it was Joe. The nurse closed the door behind her. Joe put the flowers down on the table by the bed, which was bare, apart from a water jug and glass, and sat in the chair. There was a telephone attached to the wall beside the bed.

'How are you feeling?' he asked.

'Bad, American Joe. I feel I been run over by big truck.'

Joe smiled and couldn't think of anything else to say.

'The doctor,' she went on. 'He has cut out all the lumps. He says there is no more cancer. He has cut it all away. No more breasts either.'

She pulled back the sheets to show the tight bandaging around her chest.

'You think I still find nice husband in England now?'

'Of course you will,' Joe said. 'You're a very pretty girl.'

She nodded and smiled but he didn't think she believed him.

'Tell me about your friend Doris, in Eaton Square. The one who used to call you on the telephone.'

'She make Max real, real angry,' she said, her brow furrowing at the memory. 'I tell her, stop phoning me because every time it ring I was frightened it would be her and Max would hit me again. He is a bad man. He drinks and takes drugs and it makes him mad.'

'Did she suggest running away together?'

'Sure. She had lots of big plans. I told her, where would we run to? Two poor girls in a foreign country. Where would we go?'

'You could have got away from Max.'

'I would like that.' She smiled. She looked tired. 'He is a bad man. I would like to be away from the hitting. I think he hates women. That's why he hits us all the time. He likes the men, you know what I mean?'

'He's gay?' Joe prompted her.

'Sure. So many men. Every day. They have sex with him to pay their debts, but he still takes their money, if they have any. He screws girls too. He likes orientals. All day. Never closes the door, just does it wherever he feels like it. He hits who he likes and screws who he likes.' She gave a sleepy little giggle. 'One day he will die of a bad disease and many people will be very happy.'

Her eyes were closing.

'You sleep now. I'll come back and see you again tomorrow.'

'Okay American Joe,' she said, without lifting her lids.

Bending down he kissed the top of her head, feeling a strange sense of paternal protectiveness. She seemed as much of a lost child as Hugo did in his grand new school. Even through the hospital smells Joe could detect her personal fragrance. It reminded him of the East and he felt a pang of nostalgia for the exotic excitements of Hong Kong, Bangkok and Manila. He let himself out of the room. Doris didn't open her eyes but a small smile twitched at the side of her lips.

'His name is Rod Miller,' Adele explained over the phone. 'I've told him all about you and he's keen to meet up. There's a pub in Poland Street. Can you make it there for twelve o'clock?'

Ex-detective Rod Miller was younger-looking than Joe had expected. He had imagined that someone who had been in the police force for twenty years would look like an old man, probably running to a paunch. Miller looked more like a soldier, fit and lean. His thinning hair was shaved short, only a little longer than the stubble on his chin. He was wearing jeans and a leather jacket which looked as if it had been on his back throughout his whole career.

'I'm told you know Len Jones,' Joe said once they were sitting over drinks in a corner of the room.

'I've known Len for years.' Rod smiled, as if thinking of a favourite wicked uncle. 'I read your book. Load of bollocks, you realise that don't you? Half the jobs he claims he was involved in he was nowhere near, and the ones we know for certain he did never got a mention.'

'I guess he didn't want to incriminate himself with anything that might lead to a prosecution.'

'I bet he didn't. You did a good job though, great read.'

'Thank you.'

'That's why I asked for you. I can give you a story that'll make Len's book look like Noddy in Toyland. I can tell the truth, you see, even if it means changing a few names here and there.'

For two hours Rod talked about the vice business, naming names and detailing all their various preferences. Joe interjected the odd question, but there was hardly any need. The material simply flowed forth.

As they reached a natural break in the conversation, Joe changed track. 'What do you know about a couple called Mike and Maisie Martin?' he asked.

'Why do you ask?' Rod's face changed to stone, all animation gone. The friendliness had drained from his voice and Joe could imagine just how uncomfortable it would be to be a suspect undergoing questioning.

'They've cropped up in the research for another book I'm writing. I just wondered if you knew anything about them.'

Rod fell silent for a few seconds, as if choosing his words carefully. 'If I could find a way to put Mike Martin away I would die a happy man,' he said. 'We were after him for years. We put away dozens of his henchmen one way or another, but we never got close to him. It was him who stitched me up and forced me to resign.'

'Stitched you up?'

Rod's eyes seemed to bore into Joe's head as he considered whether to confide in him. 'I wouldn't necessarily want this to go into the book.'

'That would be up to you. It's probably better that I know the truth, so that I can judge what to leave out, if you see what I mean.'

Rod nodded his agreement. 'There was this girl,' he said eventually. 'She was new on the scene, just down to London from up North somewhere. She was working in a club which Martin owned a piece of. We raided the club and she got pulled into the net. I could see she wasn't any part of it. She had no idea what was going on. I gave her a break, a chance to get out while she still could. She was very grateful. Kept coming back to thank me, bringing me little presents, you know how it is. She seemed to have a bit of a crush.

'Anyway, I weakened. The temptation was too strong. The next day a videotape of the whole thing landed on my boss' desk. I'd been set up. Apparently she was a couple of years younger than she had told me. It ended my career, ended my marriage.

'When I started asking questions the trail led back to the Martins. I got a bit silly about the whole thing. I got Martin on the phone, told him I was out of the force now and that I was going to come after him. Two days later the girl turned up dead near her home town. She'd been mutilated in a way that linked her murder to a serial killer who had been put away a few years before. Now there's a lobby saying this proves the man in jail is innocent, that the real killer is still on the loose. But I know it was Mike Martin.'

'He ordered the killing?'

'He executed her. Either ordered it or did it himself. I can never prove it, but I know it's true. He thinks nothing of killing people. It's how he maintains his authority. Anyone who crosses him disappears. He doesn't trust anyone.'

'Not even Maisie?'

'Specially not Maisie. She was a hooker in the Far East, running a chain of brothels. They went into business together in some way and he started screwing her. Or it may have been the other way round. For a while I think he must have fallen in love, or at least fallen in helpless lust. She took full advantage of his weak moment. She's as hard as he is. She's just as likely to slice him up if he messes her about as he is to do her.'

'That must keep the relationship sparky.' Thinking back to his meeting with Maisie, Joe had to admit that he could imagine her capable of anything.

'Don't even think of getting involved with them at any level,' Rod said. 'These are not old-fashioned crooks like Len, who restrict themselves to beating up others like themselves. The Martins are the big league, at least he is. He went into the City during the Thatcher era and made a fortune. I mean, big

money. He also made a lot of friends in high places –
politicians, you name it, in all the parties. He's a major
fundraiser for the government. It makes him almost invincible.
He and Maisie will wipe out anyone they even suspect might
threaten their position.'

'But you were willing to let him know you were going to go
after him?' Joe pointed out.

'It wasn't necessarily the most brilliant thing I ever did,' Rod
admitted. 'But I don't have anything much left to lose now. And
Martin knows that. He also knows I'd be as happy to take him
out as he would be to take me. As long as I don't put myself in
any silly positions he won't come after me, not at the moment.
He knows I'm always armed. I'm banking on him thinking it
would cause more trouble than it's worth to try to rub me out.
Hopefully he thinks I'm just another dumb cop. It always pays
to be underestimated by your adversary.'

Joe fell silent and thoughtful for a few moments. 'You said
earlier that you were still in touch with a lot of your old contacts
on the force?'

'All of them. There isn't a policeman in the world who
doesn't know that but for the grace of God he might end up in
the same place as me. Even my boss, when he was firing me,
told me that.'

'So,' Joe was thinking aloud, 'if I wanted to know whether a
particular body had shown up somewhere, you'd be able to
check it out in some way?'

'I could ask around. If a body fitting that description turned
up I could let you know.'

'That's what I need to know. There's this Filipino girl, goes
by the name of Doris, but I doubt that's her real name, who was
working for a family in Eaton Square but she disappeared. I
would be interested to know what's happened to her.'

'Sure. I'll ask around. So what'll happen about my book
idea, then? You interested in helping me?'

'Yeah, I think it could work. The problems would be legal. Who can you safely name without ending up in court? But we could at least get talking to publishers.'

'Sounds all right. What happens first?'

'I'll prepare a synopsis for you to look at. Once you're happy with it, I'll give it to Adele and she can start trying it on publishers. What we want is to get one of them to come up with a decent advance, so that there's some money in the bank while we actually write it. There might be a good newspaper serialisation deal in it as well.'

'Okay,' Rod extended his hand. 'Let's do it.'

CHAPTER EIGHT

Len had booked a table at Langan's, just off Piccadilly. 'It reminds me of the good old days,' he told Joe. 'When we all had money to burn, and Langan was happy to supply the matches. Of course in the end the bloody idiot set light to himself.' Len gave a wheezy laugh as he puffed on a thick cigar and surveyed the menu.

Joe had initially been annoyed at the interruption of Len's command to lunch, and then relieved at being able to forget, at least temporarily, the problems of setting up his computer in his bedroom. The problem was mainly space. He had had to construct an elaborate support system consisting of his bedside table, the coffee table and a cheap kitchen table from a nearby DIY shop, to simultaneously hold the machine, its keyboard and printer, as well as a few pages of notes and a coffee cup.

The next big cheque that Adele sent, he vowed to himself as he wrestled with the instructions for assembling the kitchen table in the few square feet of remaining space on his bedroom floor, would go towards a laptop.

The equipment had been at Fliss' house and he had been forced to speak to Paolo in order to arrange to collect it first thing that morning, because Fliss had gone to the hairdressers. That had started his day off badly. Not that Paolo had been unpleasant, quite the contrary, he was the soul of affability. In fact, Joe got the distinct impression that the man was trying to recruit him as a pal. Perhaps Paolo was hoping to be able to share some tales of woe about the horrors of marriage to Fliss with someone who would understand completely what he was going through. Joe did not feel inclined to fulfil such a role.

Joe had seen pictures of their wedding in *Hello!* magazine. He had tried to force himself not to open the pages but had been unable to resist. The sight of poor old Hugo, dressed up in a polo shirt, jodhpurs and shiny boots in some hideous pastiche of a page boy role, had made him want to scream. He hadn't asked his son anything about the day and Hugo had remained resolutely silent on the subject. Joe liked to think that the boy was acting out of deference to his father's feelings, but he suspected he had actually forgotten the whole thing already – simply wiped it from his memory.

When Joe arrived at the house, Paolo had answered the door himself. He seemed to hover on the brink of putting his arm around Joe's shoulders as he ushered him into the familiar hall, which had been Joe's home for the ten years of his marriage to Fliss. Joe had declined offers of tea and coffee and made excuses about having to hurry because he had deadlines to meet. This was true, although they were self-imposed deadlines and could easily have been broken had he wanted to accept the man's oily hospitality.

As a result of having the coals of his temper stoked by Paolo, and the flames fanned by the practical difficulties of setting the whole thing up once he got back to the flat, Joe had been unable to get any work done at all, either on Rod Miller's or on Doris' synopses. It felt like a wasted morning and he had a feeling that he was now going to waste the afternoon as well, listening to Len telling him stories that should have been in the book but had unaccountably slipped his remarkably selective memory at the time they were writing it.

'Adele says she's had a sniff at the film rights,' Joe said as he read his menu. 'Not that that necessarily means an offer, but it's a start.'

'Michael Caine's a friend of mine,' Len said casually. 'I'll mention it to him.'

'Michael Caine's a friend of yours?' Joe dropped the menu on the table. 'Michael Caine's a friend of yours?' He had no idea whether to believe Len or not.

'Yeah,' Len looked surprised at Joe's surprise. 'Didn't you know? We go back a long way, to when we were kids. Done a lot of charity work together. He half owns this place. We used to come here together for lunch sometimes.'

'You never mentioned that.'

'Well, you don't want to go blabbing about your mates, do you?'

'It is customary when you're writing a book.'

Len grinned. 'Only kidding, mate. You did a great job with what I gave you. You didn't need to be spoon-fed rubbish like "how I stole Michael Caine's girlfriend". You were coming up with a real story.'

'You stole his girlfriend?'

'Nah. Never even met the bloke. But if I had I could have set him up with a nice motor in exchange.' Len let out a guffaw at his own wit and Joe shook his head sorrowfully, as he finally realised that his leg was being pulled and that Len was enjoying every minute of it.

'If it had been true, a story like that could have added twenty grand to the price we got for serialisation,' Joe said, trying to regain some credibility in the conversation.

'Wouldn't have let you put it in, even if it had been true. You can't put a price on friendship, Joe-boy,' Len said, sagely, keen to keep it going for as long as possible. Joe was very relieved when he did finally change the subject. 'Now, what are you planning to eat.'

Joe told the hovering waiter what he wanted and then waited until Len had finished ordering. 'Talking of your past love life,' he said, 'Rita nearly killed me the other day.'

'Rita?' Len look startled. 'You're not doing a book for that stupid cow are you?'

'She seems to be under the impression I have somehow coaxed Cordelia away from home. Did you know she had taken a room in my flat in Earls Court?'

'Rita?'

'No. Cordelia.'

'I was gonna say,' Len gave a guffaw of laughter. 'The amount of maintenance I pay her she should be buying the whole block.'

'Did you know Cordelia was renting a room in my flat?' Joe persisted.

'I knew she was renting a room. She needs an address in West London for a few bits of business. She told me she was doing it through a friend. I didn't ask who it was. Take no notice of Rita, she's always been overprotective of that girl. I told her, "You'll sap her entrepreneurial spirit, you stupid cow. Encourage her to get out there and make a living." She'd have her sitting around the house in a fluffy nightie, painting her nails and watching the shopping channels if she had her way. Stupid cow.'

'What line of business is Cordelia in, then?' Joe asked, trying to make the question sound casual.

'Oh, she does the odd bits and pieces for me. But she's a bright girl. It won't be long before she's running a business of her own. In fact, she probably already is.' He laughed heartily again. 'Children rip you off something chronic. You'll find that out once young Henry gets his hands on your wallet.'

'Hugo,' Joe corrected him. He considered the idea of Hugo planning to rip him off and decided he would be quite pleased to see that much ingenuity in the boy. It would suggest a better chance of survival in the adult world than his current abilities of tripping over shoelaces and dropping food down his front.

'Thanks for recommending Rod Miller to Adele. He's got a good story.'

'Yeah,' Len chuckled as he tested the wine which the waiter had poured for him and nodded his approval. 'It's ninety per cent bollocks, of course, but that still makes him more honest than any other policeman I've ever met.'

'He says more or less the same about you.'

'Bastard,' Len said, affectionately. 'I'd be interested in having a chat with you after you've talked to him. There are a few questions I would be interested to know his answers to.'

'I'll have to respect his confidence once he's a client,' Joe protested.

'Yeah, right. Anyway, if you get a sale remember who made the introduction, won't you? Donations to the old pension fund are always welcome.'

'I'll buy you a return lunch here,' Joe said, hoping he was establishing the fact that he expected Len to pay for today's meal.

'I trust you'll feel you owe me a bit more than a good lunch,' Len growled.

'Let's see if we sell it first,' Joe said, not wanting to bring the meal to an acrimonious halt before he'd even had his starter.

'Of course you will,' Len laughed again, bursting the bubble of tension. 'Greatest ghost-writer in the country, aren't you? Even if you are a yank.'

'So they say.' Joe grinned, despite himself. Several fellow writers had teased him about the title after he had been introduced with it on a radio programme.

'Like calling Charles "greatest heir to the throne", isn't it,' one distinguished biographer had suggested at a subsequent dinner. 'He'd still rather be the king.'

'Greatest leader of the opposition,' a poet tipped to be a future Laureate had added from across the table. 'He'd still rather be Prime Minister.'

Joe had smiled at them and wondered whether he had actually been born with an underdeveloped ambition gland. He'd been quite flattered by the title.

'Rod came round for a drink after meeting you,' Len said and Joe felt a rustle of unease in his stomach. Was he about to hear something unpleasant?

'Oh yes?'

'You impressed him. He said you were asking a few questions about Mike Martin.'

'Oh, yes,' Joe felt the tension release.

'You don't want to get mixed up with him,' Len said.

'Yeah, you told me the other day, at the barbecue.'

'But I'm not sure you believed me, son. If you do get mixed up, don't ever turn your back on him. Unless you're sure he's dead.'

'I wasn't planning on getting that close. Rod seems to be the one in danger of doing that.'

'Rod Miller takes things too bloody personally. We all have reasons to hold grudges against Mike Martin. But there's no point unless you're willing to go to war.'

'What's your grudge?'

'Listen, the book's written now. I don't have to answer any more of your nosy fucking questions.'

'Just making a little bit of conversation over a nice lunch, Len,' Joe said as the waiter laid their starters in front of them.

Len didn't reply and started eating his quails' eggs, spearing each one angrily and appearing to swallow them whole. He didn't speak until the last one had gone, followed by the bed of lettuce they had been nesting on.

'I had a son with my first wife,' he said, wiping his mouth with his napkin.

'Oh shit,' Joe dropped his spoon into his soup in a gesture of despair. 'And I suppose he grew up to be Tom Cruise but you didn't think it was worth putting in the book.'

'Shut up, Joe,' Len snarled and several heads turned at neighbouring tables. 'And listen.'

Joe could see that he was serious and waited while Len gathered his thoughts. The waiter removed their plates, assuming they had both finished. Joe didn't protest. He wanted to know what Len was going to say.

'His name was Frank. He was a good boy. I planned to bring him into the business. I imagined he would take over from me. I didn't imagine I would still be working at this age.' Len paused for a moment. 'When you look at your boy's face, do you see yourself looking back?'

Joe didn't have to think about that one. 'Oh, yes.'

'That's how it was with Frank. He was me, just twenty-five years younger. He made me feel immortal. But when I met Rita, and Frank's mother and I had our bit of trouble, he took it badly. He lost his way. Lost a bit of his respect for me. He started messing around with drugs. I'm as broad-minded as the next man, Joe, you know that. I don't mind people messing about with drugs. It passes the time as well as whisky or watching television or reading the crap they put in the papers each day.

'But he couldn't work for me in the business and mess his brain up. The two things don't go together and I told him. But Frank wanted to give me a hard time, wanted to show the world what a bad father I was. He started hanging around with Mike Martin.

'Martin was nothing like he is today, but you could still see he was someone who was going to get somewhere. Frank knew I didn't like Martin and so he let everyone know he was Martin's right-hand man. He was getting out of control, becoming a liability.

'I might not have liked the man, but I knew Martin had kids and I thought I would be able to appeal to him as one father to another. Know what I mean? We set up a meeting. I was willing to go onto his territory – some poxy club in south London somewhere. He told me I wasn't to bring anyone. I was happy to comply. This was just a chat about my problems with my boy, right? When I got there…'

'One plain Dover Sole,' the waiter appeared beside them with plates of steaming food.

'Here,' Len indicated the table in front of him without looking up.

'And one seafood special.' The waiter placed the plates down with a flourish. Both men sat as if someone had pressed a pause button until the waiter had disappeared, then Len resumed his story as if the food wasn't there.

'When I got there I was taken to this room underneath the club. Like a soundproofed cellar. I was being stupid. I should have left then, but I wanted my boy back.'

Joe nodded, not wanting to interrupt the old man's flow.

'They kept me waiting a few minutes and then Martin came in, followed by Frank. Martin looked the business as usual, so discreet he could have been an adviser to the bloody queen. No flashy little pinkie rings or chunky identity bracelets for him.' Len rattled his own jewellery to make his point. 'Just the immaculate Savile Row suit, the white shirt, the club tie, everything sober, understated. Nothing to attract attention. Everyone's idea of the trusted merchant banker. Know what I mean?'

'I get the picture,' Joe said.

'I could see that Frank was out of his head. He was grinning like a fucking idiot and his eyes were darting all over the place. "Frank," I said, "get the fuck out of here. I want to talk to Mr Martin." "Don't talk to my boy, like that, Len," Martin says. "Your boy?" I says. "Yes," he says. "He's not your boy," I says, "and don't ever think he is." "Show him who's boy, you are, Frankie," Martin says and I see Frank pulling out this shooter. He was never a great shot when he was stone-cold sober, that day he couldn't have hit a house if he was standing next to it.

'The bullets went all over the place, but nothing hit me. He was strong and the drugs made him wild. I fought him for the gun and there must have been one shot left because it went off and hit him square in the head, blowing his face to pieces. That face that had been like looking back in a mirror.

'He was that far away from me, Joe,' Len held his hands a foot apart. 'I was so covered in his blood and mess that it looked as if I'd been the one who'd taken the bullet.'

Len stopped and took a drink of water. Joe said nothing, hardly daring to move for fear of disturbing Len's train of thought.

'I knew he was dead,' Len went on. 'So there was no point hanging around. Martin was nowhere to be seen. He must have bolted when the bullets started flying. I ran upstairs and no one tried to stop me. I must have looked a pretty scary sight. Martin can't have told anyone up there what was going on downstairs and no one would have heard anything from that cellar, not with the music they had going and all the rest.

'I guess Martin didn't want to have to do any explaining he didn't have to at that stage in his career. So Frank's body disappeared. Martin knew I wasn't about to go reporting him missing or anything.'

'What about Frank's mother?' Joe asked, surprised to find his voice was cracking.

'She took it badly. Frank was her pride and joy, and suddenly he didn't come to see her any more. I made up a story to make her feel better. Told her Frank had got into a bit of trouble with Martin and had to go abroad while it was sorted out. She'd seen *The Godfather*. She understood. I married Rita and we had Cordelia.'

'So, no one ever knew anything about it?'

'There were people working for Martin who saw me there that night. Someone would have had to do the cleaning up. There must have been whispers. Rod was a young copper then and he was one of the people who came to talk to me, to ask me about Frank. I said I'd heard he'd had to go abroad, but Rod's a bright copper. He worked out what happened, but he kept it to himself. He's a good man.

'So, you see, Joe, one day Martin's going to get what he deserves. But when you're dealing with the devil you don't go rushing in with nothing but a toasting fork in your hand. These days Martin is better connected than the National Grid.'

Len picked up his knife and neatly divided up his Dover sole before forking it into his mouth, his eyes averted from Joe's.

'That story would certainly have put up the serial rights,' Joe said eventually.

'Don't ever joke about it, Joe,' Len growled. 'Because I still don't find it funny. Even after all these years.'

'No, right, sorry. Couldn't think of a suitable response.'

'Don't say anything. Just eat your food.'

Joe did as he was told for a while, although he was barely conscious of even what he was eating let alone how it tasted. Eventually, he said. 'You didn't invite me here to tell me this story, right?'

'You're right.' Len finished his fish with a sigh of satisfaction and sat back in his chair with his glass of wine as the empty plate was removed from in front of him. Joe continued to pick at his shellfish in a half-hearted fashion for a while.

'I've been thinking about my pension scheme. Money doesn't buy what it used to, Joe, and I find I need a lot more than I ever thought I would just to maintain the lifestyle I've grown accustomed to. I still have to support Frank's mother, and Rita, and neither of them come cheap. I'm too old to earn a living ducking and diving now. Let others of this world have all the headaches. I've enjoyed becoming an author, and the pay hasn't been bad, considering the amount of effort.'

Joe was about to point out that most of the effort had been his, but thought better of it.

'I've always been a bit of reader of crime novels. I love 'em, but sometimes the plots are not that brilliant. Know what I mean?'

'I know exactly what you mean,' Joe laughed.

'I've got a million of them,' Len said.

'A million what?'

'Plots. I could tell you stories and you could turn them into books and we could share out the money. That'd put a smile on your bank manager's face. Wouldn't it?'

'I guess it would.'

'Okay, then. So, how do we start?'

Joe had just got back to the flat from the restaurant when his phone rang.

'I've got some information you might find interesting,' Rod said.

'What's that then?'

'Not over the phone. You want to meet for a drink?'

'Sure.'

'Same place?'

'If you like.'

Two hours later he was back in the West End, sitting in Poland Street with a drink, waiting for Rod to arrive, lost in thought.

'Sorry I'm late, mate.' He landed beside Joe, making him jump.

'No problem. What do you want to drink?'

A few minutes later they were sitting over their pints and Rod pulled out a black and white photograph. 'Thought this might interest you.'

Joe stared at it for a moment, trying to make it out. 'What is it?'

'Contents of a skip in Liverpool. Some poor geezer doing a bit of DIY, wheeled his barrow out to the skip and found that.'

Joe stared at the picture again until the shapes began to make sense. It reminded him of the first time he had seen a scan of Hugo before he was born. The nurse and Fliss had seemed to be able to see the shape for what it was. He had had to stare for ages just to make out a leg or an arm, and even then he wasn't sure he had really seen anything more than a passing intestine.

In the picture, amongst the rubble in the skip, and the twisted remains of an old bicycle, he realised he was looking at an upper torso. Once it came into focus it was glaringly obvious.

'See it now?' Rod asked.

'Yes.'

'That clearer?' Rod handed him another picture. This one was a close-up, leaving nothing to the imagination.

'Yes,' Joe said.

'My contact tells me it's the torso of a young woman of Asian origin, probably Chinese or something like that. It was cut with a chainsaw. Arms off, head off, across the middle at the waist. Must have been the most incredible fucking mess.'

Joe sat, silently staring at the picture. Trying to imagine how anyone could ever do such a thing.

'Some sadistic bastard he must have been,' Rod said, tracing a line on the picture with his finger. 'He sliced her bloody tits off before killing her. But then sewed them up again. See the stitch marks? Is that sick or what?'

'That may have happened earlier.'

'What do you mean?' Rod wanted to know.

'She might have had a double mastectomy a few weeks or months before she was killed.'

'A double mastectomy? A girl in her teens or early twenties?'

'It may have been plastic surgery that went wrong, set up an infection or something, and had to be cut away.'

Rod took the picture back and stared at it harder. 'You mean to tell me a trained doctor did that stitching?'

'I think so.'

'I can sew better than that. He'd have done better using Sellotape.'

'I guess he was in a hurry. She probably didn't have anything to pay him with.'

'Bloody hell.' Rod fell silent for a moment. 'So what do you base that theory on, then?'

'If it is the girl I was looking for, she wrote and told me someone had stolen her "new breasts". I then met another Filipino who was having the same operation in a clinic off Harley Street. I met a doctor there who would be quite capable of doing work of that standard.'

'Christ Almighty,' Rod said. 'I knew a lot of these oriental birds had silicone jobs, but I didn't realise that could happen. I've never understood why they do it, anyway. It always feels like they've stuck polystyrene tennis balls inside themselves. Hardly the sexiest thing.'

'It's a cheap method,' Joe said, remembering listening to Fliss and her friends talking at dinner parties about their various experiences under the knives of surgeons – doctors just like the man he'd seen at the Wimpole Clinic. 'When the customer has money to spend, no one would ever know they weren't real.'

Rod nodded thoughtfully. 'That figures,' he said. 'I've met a few of these girls in the Thai massage houses around London. None of them look like anyone has invested much money in them.'

'Are they the sort of places Maisie Martin might be involved with?'

'Yeah, she might be supplying them with girls, I guess. They call them "Thai" but the girls could come from anywhere east of India. None of the punters would have the faintest idea if they were Chinese, Thai, Filipino or anything else. They just want to know that the girls look oriental and take their clothes off to order. Want to go visit one?'

An image of his time travelling around the Far East flitted temptingly across Joe's memory. 'You can't afford to be caught in a place like that, can you?'

'Absolutely nothing to lose any more,' Rod laughed. 'No job and no marriage. Free as a bird.'

'Isn't there a danger of running into the Martins?'

'About as likely as finding Bill Gates serving in your local computer shop. Have you any idea how big time Mike Martin is these days?'

'I've heard.'

'He's hardly likely to be taking tickets at the door of a brothel then, is he?'

'Okay. Let's do it.'

Rod had parked his car, a twenty-year-old BMW, on a pavement round the corner, apparently unconcerned that anyone would complain. No one had.

'I guess I should tell the police what I know about this,' Joe said as they drove out towards the East End, the highly tuned, powerful old engine roaring like an aircraft ready for take-off.

'Waste a lot of your time if you do,' Rod grunted.

'It might help them find the killer.'

'They'd need more than that. Never underestimate the incompetence of any police force. They're underfunded, undermanaged and undermanned. They all take short-cuts and mess up whatever they take on.'

'Jesus. Why would they ever have wanted to get rid of someone as keen on the force as you?'

Rod laughed. 'I never made any secret of my views. The average policeman is no genius, but he's nearly always more competent than his boss. There's no officer class in the force, you see, just plods who've been promoted until they haven't got a fucking clue what's going on around them. The result is chaos. Good at catching speeding drivers and stopping young drunks from beating up old ladies; out of their depth when they come up against people like the Martins.'

'The information I have shouldn't go to waste.'

'It won't,' he grinned. 'Because we've got it.'

Joe decided not to ask any more questions.

Rod parked a few streets away from their destination and led him to a small house in a modest residential road. All the curtains were drawn. Rod rang the bell and the door was opened by a young Italian man.

'Got anyone free to give us a massage?' Rod asked.

'Sure.' The man spread his hands and smiled, like a waiter welcoming them to a restaurant. 'Come and choose your masseuse. All the girls very, very good. Very, very beautiful.'

He led them through into a front room where four young oriental girls sat watching television, three huddled together on a sofa and the fourth curled up in an armchair. They all had on short skirts to show off slim, girlish legs, and clinging tops which were cut low to display identical, proudly raised cleavages.

As Rod and Joe walked in, the girls leapt to their feet and ran chattering towards them, laughing and pawing at them like children. They tugged their jackets off and pulled them down onto the sofa. One brought them drinks and they all talked at once.

'You want massage?'

'You want very good time?'

'Which of us you like best?'

'You like my breasts?'

'You want all of us?'

'We give hand massage, Thai massage, any massage you want.'

'You want to see my tits? They so beautiful.'

Joe felt a little hand rummaging in his lap and more fingers working on the tensions which he suddenly realised he had in the back of his neck. Rod seemed completely relaxed, treating the girls like the children they had so recently been, unembarrassed and unashamed of his own obvious enjoyment.

Upstairs in a bedroom that had been converted to double as a bathroom, Joe lay in the warm, soapy bathwater. One of the girls was turning down the sheets on the bed, another had removed her clothes and was climbing into the bath on top of

101

him to rub her naked body against his in the manner sold around the world as a 'Thai massage'. Water surged over the sides and flowed onto the floor, but she didn't seem bothered. The bath was standing in a sealed, tiled area, the excess water being channelled into a drain.

Her breasts stood out as firmly from her delicate rib cage as they had when encased in a bra. Joe cupped them in his hands. Rod was exactly right – polystyrene tennis balls.

CHAPTER NINE

'Is this your new car, Dad?' Hugo asked as they came out into the school car park. 'Cool. Hey!' He shouted at a passing group of boys. 'This is my Dad's new car. It's a Fiat. It's red.'

Joe watched the other boys smirking and wanted to hit them for it. He loved Hugo so much for his innocent enthusiasm, and feared for his guileless honesty at the hands of his fellows.

'Climb in, Big Guy,' he said, with forced joviality, and Hugo didn't need a second telling.

By the time Joe had crammed his son's weekend case into the back and climbed in himself, Hugo had already studied every dial on the dashboard and found the instruction book in the glove compartment. He had a thousand questions and he wanted his father to know all the answers. Joe did his best as he reversed the car out from between two towering four-wheel-drive show jeeps. He joined the impressive queue of BMWs, Mercedes and people-movers as they snaked their way out between the shrubberies, carrying hordes of boys away for the weekend. Most of the drivers were women. He guessed all the other fathers had proper jobs which kept them at their offices on Friday afternoons.

The questions kept firing out as they drew onto the motorway and then Hugo spotted the mobile phone sticking out of his father's pocket and a new wave of enthusiasm hit him. He lurched across, knocking Joe's arm on the steering wheel, making the car swerve and bringing furious hooting from the next lane. He snatched the phone and returned to his seat triumphantly as Joe waved his apologies to the other drivers.

'Never interfere with someone driving a car, Hugo,' Joe said, as sternly as he could manage, given that his throat seemed to have closed up in terror.

'Wow! Cool!' Hugo started to press buttons on the phone like a touch-typist.

'Be careful,' Joe said, trying to keep the panic from his voice as a cacophony of different ringing tones filled the car. 'I get a lot of work calls on that. It's very important not to break it.'

'I won't break it. Just changing your ring. Can I send a message to Ben?'

'Who's Ben?'

'My friend.'

'He has a mobile?'

'Yeah, in his father's car.'

'You know the number?'

'Yeah.' Hugo had already given up waiting for permission and was punching his message in.

'You know your friend's father's mobile number?' Joe was having trouble getting his head round such an idea. He had trouble even remembering his own.

'Sure. He knows yours too.'

'Oh, great. Tell him to call some time.'

'Okay.'

'That was a joke.'

'Yeah? Cool.'

Joe decided that if the phone kept Hugo occupied and quiet for the rest of the drive it would be worth risking missing a few calls. He concentrated on the road ahead.

A few minutes later a high velocity electronic version of 'Bat Out Of Hell', trilled through the car, causing Joe's heart to miss a beat and the car to swerve dangerously near the curb.

'Hi,' Hugo answered it. 'Cool. It's Ben,' he told his father. 'He says he's on the same stretch of road.' He went back to his friend. 'Red Fiat Panda, really cool... I'm looking.' He hung up and sat forward in his seat, squinting at the road all around.

'What are you looking for?' Joe asked.

'Ben. Look for a silver Discovery with a personalised number plate.'

'How do you know he's on the road?' Joe asked.

'He lives in London.'

The phone exploded into song again and Hugo picked it up. 'Hi...Hugo...who's that?...Hi... He's my Dad... Yes, he's here.' He passed the phone across.

'Who is it?'

'Some woman. Is she your girlfriend?'

'Hello?' Joe wedged the phone to his ear as he drove and Hugo went back to looking for Ben.

'Good news about Rod Miller,' Adele's voice came down the airwaves. 'I've had an offer from Satellite Books.'

'How much?'

'A hundred thousand.'

'A hundred thousand pounds?' Joe thought he must have heard wrong.

'Yeah, excluding serial. They think they can get round the libel problems. I've talked to a couple of newspapers and I think we can get another hundred thousand from them for serialisation.'

'Are you accepting the Satellite offer?'

'Not yet. I'll use it as a floor and talk to a couple more. See if I can get them bidding. Hugo sounds cute.'

'He is.'

'Talk to you later.'

'Okay. Good work.' He hung up and put the phone back in his pocket.

'A hundred thousand pounds?' Hugo enquired. 'Is someone going to pay you a hundred thousand pounds?'

'Maybe,' Joe said. 'But not all in one go.'

'Wow. Cool. How much did this car cost?'

'A lot less.'

'Could we buy a Discovery?'

Joe laughed. 'You are such a good man,' he said. 'This car is so not cool. Am I right?'

Hugo gave a rueful grin. 'Sort of.'

'Next time I turn up at the school,' Joe said, 'I'll have something worth calling your friends over for. I promise.'

'Cool. Can I ring Ben and tell him?'

'No. See if you can get the radio working. I can't.'

'Okay.' Hugo pulled out the book and set to work as Joe drove on and tried to digest the news from Adele.

As they came onto Vauxhall Bridge the phone went off in Joe's pocket, making him swerve again as he fumbled to get it out.

'A hundred and fifty but we have to give them an answer now.' Adele said.

'Holding back serial rights?' Joe pulled the car over to the side and put the hazard lights on so he could concentrate.

'Holding back serial rights.'

'Why have you stopped?' Hugo asked, and suddenly succeeded in getting the radio working, without realising he had it at full volume.

'What in God's name was that?' Adele wanted to know.

'That cute kid you talked to earlier,' Joe said, switching off the radio. 'Have you talked to Rod?'

'No reply from his home phone. I don't have his mobile number.'

'I do. Give me five minutes, Adele. I'll try to reach him and come back with an answer.'

As the traffic roared angrily past on the bridge, rocking the little car back and forth in its slipstream, he rummaged through his pocket for his diary. He found Rod's number and dialled. Rod answered immediately. It was obvious from the background noise that he was in a pub.

'Adele's had an offer from a publisher of a hundred and fifty grand, not including the newspaper rights,' he said, without bothering to introduce himself. 'The newspaper might pay another hundred, so we would have a guaranteed quarter of a million before we got started. What do you think?'

'What do you think? You're the expert in these things.'

'I think it's a good offer. I think we should say yes.'

'Then say yes, and we'll have a meal to celebrate.'

'I'll get back to you in half an hour or so.'

'Okay.'

He rang Adele's number. 'We think you should accept the offer,' he said. 'I'll talk to you later, when I get home.'

'Someone is going to pay you a hundred and fifty thousand pounds to write a book?' Hugo asked as Joe pulled back out into the traffic.

'I have to share it with another man, a policeman.'

'Cool. Can I tell Ben?'

'Not yet. It's bad luck to tell anyone until the deal is all signed up. Things can always go wrong, and often do.'

'Who lives in this room then?' Hugo enquired as they walked down the corridor towards Joe's bedroom.

'Annie.'

'And this one?'

'Cordelia.'

'Cordelia has moved in?'

'Yes.'

'Cool. What about this one?'

'A guy called Gerry.'

'Who's he?'

'He's an accountant. He's out at work a lot.'

'What does an accountant do?'

As Joe rummaged through his brain, trying to work out how to explain what accountants did, he opened his bedroom door and ushered Hugo in.

'Wow! Cool!' Hugo exclaimed as he walked in and saw the computer equipment perched precariously on its nest of tables. 'Are you on the Internet?'

'Not at the moment,' Joe said, dialling Rod's number. 'Hi,' he said as Hugo set about switching everything on. 'Shall we go for a Chinese or something to celebrate?'

'That would be great,' Rod said.

'Okay. I'll organise something and call you back.' He hung up and dialled Adele's number as Hugo sat down in front of the screen, his mouth hanging open, his eyes wide. 'Hi, I'm home now. Listen, I didn't really get a chance to say well done. This is a brilliant deal.'

'Couldn't have done it without your brilliant synopsis,' Adele said.

'Is this the policeman's story?' Hugo asked as he brought up the synopsis on the screen. 'Wow. Cool.'

'Do you want to go for a celebratory Chinese with us tonight?' Joe asked.

'That would be great,' Adele replied.

'Okay. I'll ring you later with the arrangements.'

'Hey, Hugo,' Cordelia said, sticking her head round the door. 'I thought I heard your voice. How're you doing?'

'Okay, thanks,' Hugo replied. 'Dad, what's a transsexual vice ring?'

'Bloody hell Hugs,' Cordelia said. 'What you got there?'

She bent down to look over his shoulder.

'I think you should close that down and find something else,' Joe said.

'Don't be so stuffy,' Cordelia said, reading avidly with the boy.

'Dad's doing a book with a policeman and the publisher is going to pay him a hundred and fifty thousand pounds,' Hugo informed her. 'But he has to share it with the policeman.'

'That would be a bit handy,' Cordelia said.

'It's not all signed yet,' Joe said hurriedly. 'Things could still go wrong.'

'We're going out for a Chinese meal to celebrate,' Hugo said. 'Can you come? Can Cordelia come, Dad?'

'Yes, of course,' Joe said. 'But she might have other plans.'

'I have,' she said, 'but not till later. I'd love to.'

'Can we invite your other flatmates?' Hugo asked.

'Sure,' Joe sighed. 'Why not?'

'Cool.' Hugo leapt away from the screen and disappeared out the door.

'I'd better make a booking,' Joe muttered, rummaging through a box full of scraps of paper and business cards. He found the one he wanted, a restaurant in Gerrard Street, at the heart of London's Chinatown. He booked a table for ten people. He could always adjust the numbers nearer the time.

'I've got a car for the evening, with a driver,' Cordelia said. 'I could give you a lift up the West End. You'd have to find your own way back though. I have to go on out to the airport to meet a late flight.'

'Who are you meeting?' Joe asked, his mind only half on what she was saying as he dialled Rod's number again.

'Just some business contacts of Dad's.'

'They all want to come,' Hugo announced, bursting back into the room just as Joe got through to Rod.

At seven o'clock everyone in the flat was milling around in the kitchen. Cordelia had told them she would give them all a lift. Joe was beginning to wonder what sort of car it was to fit six passengers and a driver. Angus had dug an evening suit out from the back of his deepest and darkest wardrobe and looked as if he might be planning to play in an orchestra. The accountant, a rather pallid young man with a bad skin condition who had only just arrived back from work to be accosted by Hugo with an invitation, was wearing his normal workday suit. He had taken his tie off to show that he was preparing to enjoy himself. The poor man did not look comfortable amongst his flatmates. Annie was wearing a dress which showed off every inch of her perfectly honed body.

Joe was trying to decide if he was being irresponsible taking Hugo out for a meal in Soho at his age. Would Fliss be able to make it sound like child abuse in a courtroom? Looking at Hugo now, the boy gave every appearance of having arrived in heaven. He had decided he wanted to wear a tie and he had made a very good effort at brushing his hair, with the help of Cordelia's gel, but it was already beginning to rise up on different areas of his head as he bobbed about amongst the adults, grinning inanely. Joe saw Angus pat him affectionately on the head and then withdraw his hand quickly and wipe the excess gel off on his handkerchief.

'The car's here,' Cordelia announced. She looked ten years older than usual. Her own hair had disappeared beneath a jet black wig which she had teased down in strands around her face, framing eyes which were made huge with dark eyeliner. Her black outfit looked brand new and expensive, as if it had come straight from one of the designer emporiums in Bond Street.

'Wow,' Hugo breathed to his father. 'She is so cool.'

'She sure is,' Joe agreed. 'Especially for a sixteen-year-old.'

'She should be your girlfriend. That would make Mum so mad.'

'I don't think it would. After all, she has Paolo.'

'Paolo is a greasy Dago,' Hugo said, matter-of-factly.

'Hugo!' Joe was shocked and forced himself not to laugh.

'That's what Granddad says. He says Mum was a fool to leave you.'

'Your grandfather doesn't like change. When your mother first brought me home I was a "gold-digging yank". It took me a long time to win him over.'

'Did you find any gold?' Hugo asked, his eyes darting from one person to the next as he talked.

'No,' Joe laughed. 'Granddad thought he was the gold.'

'Oh,' Hugo said, deciding the subject was no longer interesting enough to pursue.

They all made their way down to the road where the car was double-parked and waiting for them. It was a gleaming black stretch limo with darkened windows and a black, uniformed chauffeur holding open the door.

'My dear child,' Angus said as Cordelia escorted him across the pavement. 'All my life I've wanted to be swept away in one of these.'

'Always live your fantasies when you can, mate,' she said. 'You might never get another chance.'

'You are so right, my dear,' he said. 'I just wish this suit was a little less Oxfam and a little more Valentino.'

'You look lovely just as you are,' she assured him as he stepped into the thickly carpeted interior.

As the limo disgorged them at the end of Gerrard Street, Joe saw Rod's BMW parked in the middle of the pedestrianised street, directly outside the restaurant. No one seemed to be taking any notice of it.

'Is this like a carnival?' Hugo wanted to know, pointing up at the oriental arches and street decorations.

'No,' Joe told him. 'It's always like this. This is Chinatown.'

'Cool.'

Cordelia spoke briefly with the driver, who nodded, before getting back into the car and sliding it away. Adele and Rod were already inside the restaurant and the rest of the room was buzzing with customers. Most of them were Chinese, interspersed with people getting something to eat before going to a show in Shaftesbury Avenue or a movie in Leicester Square. Joe couldn't help glancing at the Chinese women's chests. They were all noticeably flat.

'Jesus,' Annie grumbled as she watched him. 'Can you men think about anything else at all?'

Joe grinned sheepishly. 'Shall we have some champagne?' he suggested.

'Absolutely,' Annie said. 'And then tell me everything there is to know about your gorgeous friend in the leather jacket.'

'Rod? He's just a policeman I'm doing a book with.'

'Doesn't look like just a policeman to me,' Annie said. 'Looks decidedly dangerous to me.' She slid across to introduce herself to Rod.

'Why do you have to go early?' Hugo asked Cordelia once they were sitting down and eating.

'I have to pick someone up from the airport.'

'Can I come too?' he asked, gazing up at her with adoring eyes, and dropping a well-sauced lump of duck into his lap. 'I really like airports.' He looked at the empty pancake in his hand with a puzzled expression before shoving it into his mouth anyway.

'No, you can't,' Joe interrupted quickly, a vision of Fliss and her solicitor flickering through his mind once more.

'Can I have more lemon chicken, then?' He fished the duck out of his lap and pushed it into his mouth after the pancake. Some of it popped back out.

At half past ten the chauffeur arrived at the restaurant door and waited silently. Cordelia disappeared out into the night with him without saying a word to anyone. As Joe watched her go he felt a slight shiver of apprehension on her behalf pass through him. Hugo had disappeared under the table in search of lost napkins, which he was busy trying to turn into replicas of the rose shapes they had been when fresh in the place settings. Joe decided it was time to get the boy home to bed.

The following day Joe suggested to Hugo they should go to the zoo together. It sounded like the sort of thing that responsible divorced fathers did with their sons in London. He was a little disappointed by the coolness of his son's reaction.

'Couldn't we go to a cybercafé and go on the Internet?' Hugo wanted to know.

'Maybe afterwards,' Joe said. 'It's a famous zoo, really, you'll enjoy it.'

Once they arrived at the zoo in Regent's Park their roles reversed. Hugo immediately became desperate to see every single animal, bird and insect on display, moving from area to area at the speed of light. Joe followed behind, his spirits sinking lower and lower with each sad, imprisoned creature they stared at.

'A friend of mine is in hospital not far from here,' Joe said after three hours of touring cages, when they had come to rest in a café. 'Shall we go and visit her?'

'Is she a girlfriend?' Hugo asked as he pushed a handful of chips into his mouth and the ketchup slid unnoticed down his chin onto the front of his fleece.

'She's a friend and she's a girl, if that's what you mean.' Joe tried to mop the ketchup off with a handful of napkins as Hugo pushed him away absent-mindedly.

'What's wrong with her?' Hugo asked through his half-chewed mouthful. 'Why's she in hospital?'

'She had a little operation.'

'What sort of operation?'

'To remove some growths.'

'From where?'

'From her chest. You ask a lot of questions.'

'That's what Mum says.' Hugo refilled his still brimming mouth.

'Well you should do,' Joe said, having another go with the napkins. 'It's good to want to know about things. Don't let grown-ups put you off.'

'I won't,' he said, sucking the last piece of moisture from his milkshake to try to help the food down.

'How are things going at school, then?' Joe asked casually as they strolled across the park behind the zoo, with the wolves pacing along beside them in their enclosure.

'Okay,' Hugo said, his eyes flicking from one passer-by to another, giving each one a friendly smile and a greeting.

'No one being horrible?'

'A few people.'

Joe felt his heart sink. 'A few people are being unkind?'

'Yeah.' Hugo seemed keen to move on from a subject which promised to be painful. But Joe wasn't ready to move on.

'What sort of horrible?'

'Names. Stuff like that.'

'They don't hit you or anything?'

'Sometimes.' Hugo laughed as he watched two dogs rolling on the grass in a mock battle.

'What sort of names do you get called?' Joe persisted as the dogs raced off and Hugo grinned appreciatively at their owner.

'They say I'm a boff.'

'A boff?'

'Boffin.'

'And that's bad?'

'I don't like it. They mean it to be horrible. And they say I'm gay.'

'What do they mean by that?'

'Sad.'

'Oh.' Joe thought for a few minutes as his son watched some children flying kites. Hugo made some friendly comments to them but they ignored him.

'You've got friends, though, haven't you?' Joe persisted as they moved on.

'Not really.'

Tears threatened to come to Joe's eyes. He blinked them back. 'What about Ben?'

'He's okay. But everyone hates him. He really is a boff.'

'You never say that to him, do you?'

'Of course not.'

'So are you happy at the school, overall?'

'Not really.'

'Would you like me to talk to Mummy about looking for somewhere better?'

The boy fell silent for a moment and Joe wasn't sure if he had heard him. 'I think,' Hugo said eventually, 'that I would probably have the same trouble anywhere. I think, perhaps I'm not really a school sort of a person.'

Having dwelt long enough on such a painful subject, Hugo ran off to watch a game of football going on ahead of them. Joe didn't rush to catch up. He was lost in thought.

Coming out of the park, Hugo seemed to have forgotten the subject and was prattling happily once more, firing off questions and hardly ever stopping long enough for his father to give any answers. Joe bought a bunch of flowers to make himself feel more like an authentic hospital visitor.

'Can I have one of those?' Hugo asked as they passed a small newsagents.

'One of what?' Joe asked.

'These.' He pointed to a London street map.

'It's only a map,' Joe said. 'Wouldn't you rather have a comic or a magazine?'

'I like maps,' Hugo said. 'They're interesting. I could plot our route.'

'Okay.'

They bought the *A to Z* and Hugo proceeded to direct them to Wimpole Street, via several interesting short-cuts.

'I wish Cordelia had come back to the flat after she met her friends,' Hugo said as they made their way back up a cul-de-sac which he had accidentally directed them into. 'Then she could have come to the zoo with us. She's so cool.'

'Yes, she is,' Joe agreed and they both fell into silent contemplation for a while.

'Where do you think she went with them?' Hugo asked as they came into Wimpole Street.

'With who?'

'Her friends from the airport.'

'I've no idea,' Joe said. 'Here we are.'

'This is a hospital?' Hugo looked up at the grubby brick townhouse. 'It doesn't look like one. Where are all the ambulances?'

'Well, it's more like a sort of nursing home, really, where they do operations as well.' He rang the bell and one of the nurses opened the door. 'We've come to visit Miss Brown.'

'Miss Brown has checked out,' the girl said, with a charming smile.

'Are you sure?' Joe was shocked. Doris had looked a long way from being well enough to get out of bed when he had seen her two days before.

'Quite sure. She left yesterday.'

'Okay. Thank you.'

As Joe walked back down the street, lost in thought, Hugo danced around his legs. 'What are you going to do with them?' he said, pointing to the flowers.

'I don't know,' Joe said. 'Why?'

'Can I give them to Cordelia?'

'Yes, I guess so. If she's there.'

'Come on,' Hugo said, pulling out his book of maps. 'I'll lead you somewhere.'

CHAPTER TEN

'I've had a flicker of interest in the Doris book from Helen at Piper,' Adele said. 'She'd like to talk to you about it. She would also like to talk to Doris.'

'I told you,' Joe said. 'I haven't exactly got a Doris at the moment.'

'I know,' Adele said. 'But I didn't think I could exactly explain that. It would be better coming from you, face to face.'

'All right. When shall I meet her?'

'She says she could fit you in this afternoon if you would like to go to the office and make a pitch.'

'That quick? She must be interested.'

'Yeah, I think she is. She knows your work. She knows you're reliable. But I don't think she'll be offering the same sort of money as you're getting from Satellite.'

'Okay. I think I might not tell her I haven't got a Doris. I'm pretty sure I'll be able to find one eventually. I thought I'd got one already, but she's disappeared again.'

'Whatever you think is the best approach.'

'What time should I be there?'

He was pleased to be given a meeting to go to. He had been working at the computer all morning, trying desperately to distract himself from the picture in his mind of his little son being swallowed up in a crowd of other boys, and swept through the great dark doors of his school. Joe had hardly been able to sleep at all for the whole night after taking Hugo back.

He had been wrestling with the idea of ringing Fliss and asking her if she didn't think Hugo would be happier at a day school in London somewhere. But the thought of talking to Fliss about anything was very depressing. He knew she would take it as a personal criticism, and in a way she would be right. He was also pretty sure she would have a lot of good educational reasons why Hugo should stay at a boarding school, reasons which he wouldn't be equipped to argue with. All he knew was that it didn't feel right to be sending a small boy off to somewhere that was making him unhappy.

Helen, an editor at Piper, had bought a couple of books from him before. He liked her and looked forward to the meeting. The Doris story was one he felt confident he could sell, although the absence of a flesh-and-blood Doris was going to be a problem. When he arrived at Helen's office he was surprised to find several other people waiting for him. There was a woman from marketing, another from publicity and a man from sales. Helen, who looked at least seven months pregnant, was as pretty as he remembered her, and as incisive.

'So, when can we meet her?' she asked once the introductions had been made and the refreshments dispensed.

'Doris?' Joe said. He had been thinking over his strategy on the way there and was ready to play his cards a little closer to his chest than usual. 'She's very nervous about meeting anyone at the moment.'

'I'm not surprised,' the woman from marketing said. 'After all she's been through. Your synopsis made it all sound very traumatic.'

'Good,' Joe said. 'I mean, thank you.'

'We would ideally want her to be able to promote the book herself,' the woman from publicity joined in. 'What do you think the chances are that she would be up to that?'

'I think once she has actually been through the whole story with me, and once she knows that it really is going to be a genuine book from a serious publisher,' Joe paused to let his compliment take effect, 'then I think she'll be happy to do whatever promotion is necessary. At the moment she only knows she has been betrayed by everyone she trusted. She was betrayed by her parents who sold her, by the people she was sold to, by the people who were supposed to be looking after her, doctors and employers. Everyone has used and abused her and she's still very nervous. Girls she has known have ended up dead because they talked to the wrong people.'

'It's a good story,' Helen said, glancing through Joe's synopsis, which was lying on the desk in front of her. 'It really needs to be told.'

'How on earth have you managed to win her confidence?' the woman from marketing asked.

'Joe can be very persuasive,' Helen said, smiling enigmatically. 'All sorts of people you would never imagine would talk to anyone end up telling him their most intimate secrets.'

'What I need to know is whether Doris would be able to tell her story to the media,' the man from sales said. 'It may be a great story but people will only buy into it if it can be personalised.'

'It will be very personal,' Joe assured him.

'We really want to make an offer on this, Joe,' Helen said. 'But it's hard for us to be able to evaluate it without meeting her, or at least seeing some pictures.'

'You see, if she is good on the television and radio, then we'll do much better than if she's tongue-tied and hiding away somewhere,' the publicity woman added.

'How much are you hoping for?' Helen asked.

'You'd need to talk to Adele about that,' Joe said. 'Doris needs money to live and I need money so I can get out to the Philippines and see where she comes from, trace her journey through Manila to England. I need to be able to see what she saw in order to write about it clearly, in her own voice.'

119

By the end of the meeting he knew they were going to be making an offer to Adele, and he also knew he was going to have to find himself a Doris who would be willing to claim the book as her own story.

Helen must have put a call straight through to the agency because Adele was on the phone to him an hour later.

'She's willing to offer fifteen thousand. I could probably get more if I shopped around, but it's difficult until you actually have a girl to attach the story to. It needs to be a publisher who already knows you and trusts you.'

'I think we should take the offer. If I can get it right it's a book that will earn some royalties. I just need enough money to get started on the research. It's an important story. These girls need someone to speak up for them.'

'I agree. How do we split the money if we don't know who the girl is going to be?' Adele asked.

'Just send me my half and hold the other half back until I've got the right girl.'

There was no sign of life in Ditchling Avenue as he parked his car the following morning. He walked briskly to the café, ordered a coffee and Danish pastry, and sat down in the window to watch the silent house opposite. Two coffees later, still nothing had happened. When there were no other customers in the café to overhear, he pulled out his phone and dialled the number. A woman's voice answered.

'Can I speak to Doris?' he enquired.

'Hang on.' The woman must have covered the mouthpiece, although not completely. Joe could hear a mumbled conversation.

'Someone wants to speak to Doris.'

'Who is it?'

'The same guy, I guess.'

'Tell him she's not here. Let Max handle it.'

Joe was staring intently at the house as he listened, trying to imagine which curtained window they might be behind. Could it be that this Doris was dead now, too? Another mutilated torso in a skip somewhere?

The table holding Joe's empty coffee cup and plate suddenly flew into the air, knocking the phone from his hand and throwing his chair backwards. His head hit the wall with a painful crack, disorientating him. A powerful hand gripped him round the throat and another clamped him between the legs and he was lifted, agonisingly, into an upright position.

'Come on now, take this outside,' the café owner was saying in the background, unable to believe what was happening before his eyes, in broad daylight.

'Shut the fuck up,' Max hissed at him, and the man shrank back behind his counter.

Letting go of Joe's crotch, Max picked up a wine bottle which had been standing on another table with a flower in it. He smashed the bottle down against the edge of the table, freeing a stream of stale water which drenched Joe's trouser leg. He pressed the jagged end into Joe's Adam's apple, making him gag and drawing blood.

'You stay away from my girl,' Max snarled, showing Joe his filed, yellow fangs. 'Otherwise I'm going to cut you into the tiniest fucking pieces imaginable. Do you understand?'

Joe was unable to move or speak. He was having trouble breathing, hardly daring to take a breath for fear of forcing his throat further onto the razor edge of the broken glass.

'Do you understand?' Max screamed, his sour-smelling spittle spraying over Joe's face.

'Yes,' Joe managed to squeak.

Max let go. 'That's a good boy. Don't let me see you around here again.' He tossed the broken bottle into a corner and sauntered towards the door. It was something about the arrogance of his gait which pushed Joe over the edge. Max obviously thought he had frightened his opponent so thoroughly there was no danger in turning his back. Joe grabbed the chair which had been knocked over in the fight and, with every ounce of strength he could muster, brought the metal leg down onto the bald, patterned head in front of him. Max did not utter a sound. He merely slid to the ground as the blood began to flow and merge with the spilled water.

'If I were you, mate,' the man behind the counter said. 'I would make myself scarce. I know this guy. You wouldn't want to be here when he wakes up.'

Joe nodded and scooped up his phone. 'Thanks. Can you give me five minutes before you ring for an ambulance?'

'Sure.'

Joe ran out across the street. A car came to a squealing halt a few feet away from him and the driver hit the horn angrily. Joe kept going. He bounded up the steps to number forty-two, rang the bell and banged on the door. One of the women he had seen in the kitchen on a previous visit opened it.

'Where's Doris?' Joe asked, in a voice which gave her no option but to reply.

The woman shook her head as if trying to clear it. She glanced over Joe's shoulder, as if to check there wasn't anyone coming. 'Max locked her in her room, and then ran out of the house when he spotted you.' She seemed quite happy to help Joe, as if she too had been waiting for someone to free her from Max's tyrannical rule.

Joe went up the stairs two at a time, driven by adrenaline. The red door was secured by a large bolt. It looked as if it had been newly screwed on, by someone who was not worried about the niceties of interior decoration. Joe pulled it back and threw open the door. The room was just as he had seen it before. There was no sign of Doris.

The little skylight was open and a light breeze wafted in, making the air fresher than in the rest of the house. Climbing on the bed Joe pushed his head through the window. There were roofs in all directions, but no sign of Doris. She could have been anywhere by then, there was no point in going out onto the roof after her.

Joe was keen to get away before the police arrived at the café. He ran back down through the house. All the other inmates had disappeared.

Coming out into the street he could see the café owner was on the phone. He ran to his car and climbed in. The Fiat took three attempts to start and then it lurched out into the traffic. Joe didn't mind which direction he went in, as long as it was away from Ditchling Avenue.

'Hi, American Joe,' Doris said, sitting up on the back seat.

Joe screamed, nearly running straight into an oncoming car. 'Jesus Christ! How did you get there?'

'You forgot to lock car door.' She smiled sweetly. 'Very careless. Many cars stolen every day in Brighton.'

'How did you know it was my car?'

'Saw you arrive on camera. Max very angry.'

'How did he recognise me?'

'One of girls saw and said you were the man who had come to house to see me. He guessed you were who I rang on the phone. He was very angry. He locked me in my room. So I climb out over the roof.'

'How did you get off the roof?'

'Very difficult. Had to get into tree from gutter. Nearly fell down. Had to drop my things.' She held up her battered little bag of possessions.

'Where are you going to go now?' Joe asked.

'I come and live with you? I'll be your servant. I don't think American Joe will beat me like Max.'

'I don't really need a servant, Doris. Even if I wanted one.' Her face fell at his words. 'Do you have no one else you can go and stay with?'

'Don't know anyone else in England.'

'Okay. We'll go back to my flat and work out what to do.'

On the main road out of Brighton they both realised they were hungry. Joe drew off the dual carriageway at a sign for services and they spotted a pub. As they drew into the car park they realised it had a Chinese restaurant behind it.

The restaurant obviously did more trade in the evenings than at lunchtimes. A couple of travelling businessmen sat in one corner, talking in hushed tones. Joe indicated to the waiter that they wanted to sit as far away as possible. They chose a table next to a tank full of giant carp. Joe ordered him and Doris a set meal. He noticed that Doris winced and clutched her chest every so often. She seemed determined to overcome the pain, not to allow it to be an embarrassment.

'I only live in one room,' he explained as they waited for the food to arrive. 'There isn't any space for you.'

'I cook for you. I clean for you. I shop for you. I do all your chores for you. Wash your socks and your underpants.' She put her hand over her mouth to try to stem her own giggles. She seemed quite confident that she would be able to wear him down, that everything was going to be all right, now that she had her own personal guardian angel.

'I'm sure you would do all these things, Doris. The problem is where you would stay. There are no spare rooms in the flat.'

'I just need piece of floor. I don't need bed. Or I sleep in your bed, American Joe, and serve you there as well.' She giggled again. This time at his obvious embarrassment at the suggestion. 'You not like my idea?'

'It sounds great, Doris. But maybe not that practical.'

'You have girlfriend?'

'No.'

'You not like girls?' She seemed surprised but not shocked.

'Yes,' he laughed. 'I like girls.'

'Well, then?'

'I have a better suggestion of what we might be able to do.'

'Why you not have girlfriend, handsome guy like you?' she asked.

'I just got divorced.' Joe was keen to get off such personal areas.

'You fall off horse you should get right back on. Otherwise you be walking for rest of your life.'

'Where'd you get that from? Your grandmother's knee?'

'Clint Eastwood movie, I think. Or maybe, John Wayne.'

Their food started to arrive and from the speed with which Doris laid into it, Joe guessed that she hadn't eaten properly for some time.

'I write books,' Joe said after a while. 'That was why your friend in Eaton Square contacted me.'

'Doris?'

'Yes. She wanted me to write her life story for her.'

'You gonna do it?'

'I can't find her. I think it's possible she's been killed.'

Doris didn't look up for a moment, just kept ladling rice into her mouth as if she hadn't heard.

'Do you think that's possible?' Joe persisted. 'Might the people who brought you to England have killed her?'

'Max could kill anyone.'

'What about Maisie Martin and her husband? Have you had anything to do with them?'

She shook her head. 'Heard of Maisie. She find jobs for my friends. Max says he want to keep me because I was the best servant he ever had. So, you not going to write Doris' story, then?'

'How about if I was to write yours?'

'Make me famous?' She gave a broad smile, her eyes sparkling. 'On all the television shows?'

'Perhaps.'

'Make lots of money?'

'Make a bit. Anything I received for the story I would give you half. In exchange you tell me all about yourself – truthfully. You tell me about your parents and family, about your life in Manila and how you ended up in London.'

'I tell you my story.' She seemed to be trying to get the whole idea straight in her head. 'And you turn it into a book with a picture of me on the cover?'

'That would be it, pretty much.'

'I live with you while I tell you life story?'

'We'll sort something out.'

'Deal, American Joe.' She held out her hand with a flashing smile which Joe could imagine warming the hearts of the Piper publicity team.

The moment they stepped into Joe's room, Doris started putting things straight.

'You have clean bedclothes?' she asked, fingering the sheets on the bed suspiciously.

'No,' Joe said. 'I just take them down to the launderette every so often.'

'I take them for you.'

'No!'

Doris jumped at the abruptness of his tone, like a dog which was used to being beaten by its master. She shrank back from him and waited for his next order.

'No,' he said, more gently. 'You are not to be my servant. You are my friend.'

'Okay,' she said, moving towards the bed and kicking off her shoes.

'Doris.' He took her by the shoulders and held her still. 'Just a friend. Not a lover. Just a friend.'

A look of hurt puzzlement flitted across her face. She looked down at her flat chest and sighed. 'Is it because Doris has no boobs now? I can still please you. Pleasure guaranteed.'

'It's nothing to do with that,' Joe assured her. 'I think you're very beautiful.'

Doris' face brightened again.

'Come on,' Joe said. 'I'll make you a cup of tea and we'll get to know each other better.'

Annie and Cordelia were both in the kitchen. It looked as if they had been deep in conversation. Annie was sitting at the table. She had her hair up in curlers and was in the middle of doing her make-up in the mirror. Cordelia was painting her nails alternately black and white. Joe made the introductions and forced Doris to sit down with them as she started to attack the stains on the top of the cooker with a grubby looking pan-scourer from the sink.

The girls talked as Joe made everyone tea and coffee. Eventually Annie asked Doris where she was staying.

'Well,' Joe interrupted. 'That's kind of a problem. She doesn't have anywhere at the moment. I guess she can sleep on my floor until we think of something.'

He noticed that Annie gave Cordelia what he could only have described as a 'knowing' look and Cordelia seemed to stiffen.

'A bit cramped for that, isn't it?' she said.

'It's been done before,' Joe replied. 'Hugo and I managed it when you were staying.'

'I think we can do better than that for Doris,' Cordelia said. 'At least on a temporary basis. I have the use of a flat up in the West End. It's for Dad's foreign business contacts to stay when they're in London, but there's no one there at the moment.' She turned to Doris. 'You'd have to get out on the nights it was needed, but that isn't that often. You could come here and use my room on those nights. I often don't get back here anyway.'

'You very kind.' Doris grinned happily. 'I clean and tidy your flat and your room, scrub them top to bottom.'

'You should be resting, not trying to clean the whole of London,' Joe said, putting a mug down in front of her.

'I'm okay,' Doris waved his protest aside.

'Have you been ill?' Annie asked.

'Doris had an operation last week,' Joe said. 'She should be resting.'

127

'I had lumps in my breasts,' Doris said, matter-of-factly. 'The doctor cut them out.'

'Christ Almighty!' Cordelia said.

'Were they benign?' Annie asked, mascara brush halfway up to her eye.

'Oh, sure. All better now. But no big tits any more.' Doris gave a tinkling laugh, partly at her own wit and partly at the amazed look on the two English girls' faces.

Cordelia was serious about her offer of accommodation. A couple of hours later she and Doris climbed into Joe's car and they headed up towards the West End.

'You've got to get some better wheels than this, Joe, mate,' Cordelia grumbled as she perched uncomfortably in the passenger seat. 'This is not going to do your credibility any good at all. It's a bleeding old grandma's car.'

'I know,' Joe agreed. 'It was an emergency purchase. Once I've got some money through from the publishers I'll get something a bit less embarrassing.'

'You should talk to Dad,' she said. 'He's got lots of contacts in the motor trade. He could fix you up with a nice little BMW convertible or something. Hugo'd love that.'

'I'll talk to him,' Joe promised.

'I should hope so.'

The block of flats which she led them to in Gloucester Place was like a cross between a medieval fortress and an old-fashioned cruise liner. A uniformed porter sat behind a magnificent wooden reception desk and gave a small salute as Cordelia swept in.

'Hello Bernie,' she said. 'This is Doris. She's going to be staying in the flat for a few days. Make sure she's okay, won't you.'

'I will, Miss Jones,' he assured her, and Joe thought he detected a hint of a blush on the old man's cheeks.

'Dad said to say hi, Bernie,' Cordelia said. 'He wanted to know if you're happy with the job.'

'Very happy, tell him,' Bernie said, half standing up and inclining his head respectfully at the mention of Len.

'Brill. See you later,' Cordelia called back cheerfully as they got into the lift.

'My God, Cordelia,' Joe exclaimed as she threw open the door to the apartment. 'Why do you come slumming in Earls Court when you could be here?'

'I like seeing you,' she said and then thought better of it. 'This is for clients really. But I don't see why Doris shouldn't use it in her hour of need.'

Joe wandered across the polished wooden floor to wide French windows that led out onto a balcony, looking across the rooftops to the trees of Regent's Park. Cordelia led Doris through to the bedroom, showing her where all the light switches were as she went, like a hotel busboy. Joe followed them, stunned by the luxury of the place, which Cordelia and Doris both seemed to take so for granted.

'What sort of clients does Len entertain here?' he asked as he saw the massive master bed. 'Presidents?'

'Don't show yourself up, Joe-boy,' Cordelia sniffed, and led Doris on to the bathroom.

Once the tour was over, Cordelia handed a key to Doris. 'All right, Joe. You can take us both out for a pizza and then it looks to me as if Doris here could do with some shut-eye.'

Later that night, as they drove back to Earls Court, Joe put forward a suggestion that had been growing in his mind.

'If that apartment is empty all the time,' he said. 'Do you think I could use it during the day to interview people?'

'What sort of people?'

'Well, Doris for one, and Rod Miller.'

'Oh yeah, 'course you can. Dad's always had a soft spot for Rod.' She put her hand on his thigh and squeezed it affectionately. 'You're a mystery to me, Joe-boy,' she said.

'In what way?'

'How come you haven't jumped on me yet? I've talked to Annie and she says you haven't jumped on her either, and you didn't seem to be in a hurry to crawl between the sheets with Doris. You can't be gay, because of Hugo, unless you've had a change of heart. Is that it? Is Angus the new love of your life?' She let out a raucous bellow of laughter.

'I guess I'm still a little raw from my marriage break-up,' Joe said. 'Nothing personal to any of you.'

'Oh, well,' she sighed, 'as soon as you feel less raw, you just give me a shout.'

Joe concentrated hard on his driving.

CHAPTER ELEVEN

Joe and Rod had already been talking for two hours when Fliss'
call interrupted them. They had spread themselves out on the
sofas in the Gloucester Place living room and Doris had been
ferrying coffee and biscuits in to them from the kitchen. She
seemed to be in seventh heaven, humming to herself as she
polished and scrubbed already gleaming surfaces, and cleared
out already immaculate cupboards. The tape recorder was
running and Rod's memories were flowing like water.

Joe was not pleased to hear Fliss' voice at any time, but
particularly when he was working.

'He's disappeared,' she said.

'Who's disappeared?' Joe asked, praying she might be
talking about Paolo, but already fearing the truth.

'Hugo's disappeared. They were on a field trip or something
in Brighton and he vanished.'

'Oh, shit.'

'The police are co-ordinating the search from the school
because they reckon that's where someone will phone if they
find him.'

'I'll go straight there. Do you need a lift or anything?'

'No. Paolo will fly me down in the helicopter. It'll be quicker.
Do you want us to pick you up from somewhere?'

'No. It would take too long to arrange. I'll meet you there.'

He hung up and swore. The thought of Paolo swooping to
the rescue of his son at the controls of a helicopter was almost

more than he could stand. He forced himself to think positively. If it got Fliss there quicker it was worth it.

'My son's gone missing in Brighton,' he told Rod.

'Brighton?' Doris had appeared in the doorway to the kitchen, drying her hands on a tea towel, fear in her face. 'Max?'

'Max?' Joe remembered the last time he had seen Max, felled and bleeding. God knows how angry he would have been when he came round. But how would he ever make a connection between an American who was showing an interest in Doris and a small English prep-school boy?

'I don't think so,' he said. 'He's probably just wandered off.'

'Brighton bad place to wander,' she said.

'I'll have to go down there,' he said to Rod, packing his stuff into his case as he stood up, his hands working on automatic pilot as his brain rushed to cope with all the thoughts and fears attacking it simultaneously.

'I'll drive you,' Rod said.

'No. It's okay. I've got a car.'

'I've seen your car,' Rod said. 'I'll drive you. You're not in a good state to drive anyway. Come on.'

'Good luck,' Doris called at their departing backs. 'Find him safe.'

Joe was glad that Rod had insisted on driving. He wanted his mind free to go over every possible scenario of what might happen next. Rod drove like a policeman in a chase scene, with his foot flat on the floor, weaving and pushing his way through the traffic. Other cars just seemed to give way before the force of his personality and the mighty roar of his engine. The speedometer hardly ever seemed to drop below sixty, even as they dodged their way through south London. Joe kept seeing helicopters overhead and imagining that they were carrying Fliss and Paolo. He pictured them blowing up and falling out of the sky in a fireball. Then he erased the thought. He didn't want to deprive Hugo of his mother.

'Most kids who get lost are found within a few hours,' Rod said. 'They only want a bit of freedom and then someone spots them. Maybe he just lost the group.'

'That's possible,' Joe said. 'He does live in a world of his own. But he's not happy at this school. He might want to run away.'

'What do you keep him there for, then?'

'I'm not sure,' Joe admitted. 'I've been kind of steamrollered into it.'

'It's a private school, right?'

'Right.'

'And you're the one paying the bills?'

'Right.'

'Then take him out if he's not happy.'

'I did ask him and he said he wasn't sure he would be any happier anywhere else. Said he didn't think he was a "school type of boy", or something.'

'Sounds like a pretty self-aware kid,' Rod said, his eyes fixed on the road as he swerved past someone hogging the fast lane.

'Sometimes.'

'We'll find him. Don't worry.'

Joe nodded and went back to staring at the sky.

The police at the school seemed to recognise Rod as one of their own, even without knowing who he was. It was something about the confidence with which he walked into their midst in the headmaster's sitting-room, the way he phrased the questions, firing them out like rounds of ammunition. They all knew they were dealing with someone who had been in these sorts of situations before. A professional.

Joe could see Paolo's helicopter parked on the lawn outside, surrounded by an admiring group of boys. The man himself was sitting with Fliss, his arm around her shoulders, a theatrical expression of anxiety on his handsome, tanned face. Fliss looked pale and seemed to be shaking. She was smoking and her coffee cup was rattling in the saucer as she held it on her lap.

'He just vanished,' the headmaster was saying. 'The teachers were herding them into the Regent's Palace and when they counted heads, ready to go on the tour, they were one short. It seems he must have decided to take himself off on some sort of adventure.'

'Have you any idea why your son might do this, Mr Tye?' a policeman asked.

'He was being bullied,' Joe said.

'Oh, I don't think so,' the headmaster, an elderly man with an overly groomed nautical beard, who Joe took an instant dislike to, spluttered. 'We don't allow that here. We're very hot on it.'

'Well, that's what he told me.'

'Children can sometimes be very oversensitive, looking for attention, playing on the guilty consciences of the parents…' the headmaster was blustering on.

'You asked me why he might go off. That is the best reason I can think of,' Joe snapped.

'He never told me he was being bullied,' Fliss said and Joe could hear a catch in her voice. She was exercising every ounce of self-control not to fall to pieces.

'Perhaps he didn't have an opportunity to tell you,' Joe suggested.

'We've got him,' a policeman on a telephone shouted over the general noise. 'A boy answering his description has been picked up on the pier. They're bringing him in.'

Paolo let go of Fliss in order to applaud and she collapsed forward, sobbing into her hands. The headmaster rescued her coffee cup just before it toppled. Joe wished he could put his arm round her. He wished they could be a united front on this, for Hugo's sake. It would be so good for the boy to find both his parents waiting for him together. Rod must have been thinking something similar.

'That your machine?' he asked Paolo, gesturing towards the lawn.

'Yes,' Paolo nodded proudly.

'Very nice. Would you give me a lift back to London? I'll leave Joe here with my car keys and he can run your wife back once they've seen the boy.'

Paolo looked unsure about the suggestion, but Rod was already lifting him out of the sofa.

'I think it would be best, don't you?'

Paolo shot a look at Fliss, who nodded, through her tears. 'You go ahead, darling,' she said. 'I'll be back home as soon as we've seen Hugo.'

'See you later, mate,' Rod said as he made his way past Joe with Paolo. 'Told you it'd be okay, didn't I?'

'You did. Thanks for all your help. I'll ring you this evening and we'll do some more work tomorrow.'

As the helicopter took off in a storm of noise, and the various school and police officials busied themselves with other tasks, Joe and Fliss were left alone, in silence, each considering the enormity of their relief.

'I suppose you think this is my fault,' Fliss said eventually.

'I didn't say that.'

'You don't have to. I know your opinion about boarding schools.'

'Is that why you didn't ask for my opinion before enrolling him?'

'Yes, I suppose so. Is he really being bullied?'

'So he says.'

'He wouldn't lie.'

'No.'

They fell silent for a few moments.

'What do you think I should do?' Fliss asked eventually. 'There isn't a decent day school within reach of the house in the country.'

'Isn't there a day school in London he can go to?'

'Have you any idea how competitive the decent schools in London are?' she asked, her voice on the edge of hysteria. 'He probably wouldn't get in.'

'Don't you think he might need some special-needs coaching? There must be little schools which specialise in that.'

'I thought if we could just get him through this place he could go to Eton, like Daddy, and no one would notice how different he is once he was there. Daddy had quite a good time at school.'

'That was sixty years ago. Things change.'

'I know. It's hard to make these decisions on your own.'

'You have Paolo.' He knew he should have resisted saying that, but it was too late.

'Oh God, he's no use. He only got into Millfield because his father gave them a string of polo ponies or something. He thinks a place like this will build Hugo's character.'

'Maybe it will.'

'I know I should have talked to you about it,' she said. 'But you're so prickly with me these days. And what with you being American and everything…'

He allowed that one to hang in the air as Hugo was ushered into their presence by a woman police officer. He looked remarkably cheerful and had a large pink panther under his arm.

'What's that?' Fliss asked, once she had disengaged herself from him.

'I won it. On the pier,' Hugo said proudly. 'One of those grab things.'

'No one ever wins with those,' Fliss protested.

'I did. Hi, Dad.'

'Hi, son. What happened?'

'I don't know. I sort of got lost.'

'You lost yourself on purpose, didn't you?'

'Sort of. Did you two come down together?'

'Why did you do it, Hugo?' Fliss asked.

'I was fed up. They were keeping on and on at me. I needed a break. I meant to rejoin the group at the end of the tour of the palace. I didn't think Sir would notice. I bought myself a map.' He fished it out of his pocket to show them. 'So I could find my way back. But then I lost track of the time. The pier is so cool. Did you come in the Fiat?'

'No,' Joe said. 'I borrowed a friend's car. Rod. Do you remember him?'

'The policeman? Yeah. That car he had at the restaurant? The BMW?'

'Yeah.'

'Cool.'

'Promise us you'll never do this again, darling,' Fliss pleaded. 'It's very dangerous for a little boy like you to be wandering around on his own.'

'I know, but I was okay. I was being careful.'

'Do you promise?'

Hugo looked uncomfortable. 'They go on at me all the time.'

'Listen,' Joe said. 'Mummy and I have been talking about schools. If you still haven't settled down by the end of term we'll have a look around for somewhere in London.'

'It's okay. You don't have to,' Hugo said. 'They would probably hate me there as well.'

'No one hates you, darling,' Fliss said and Joe knew she was on the verge of crying, because he was. 'Little boys just like to pick on people. It's not that they hate you.'

'Oh.' Hugo put his Pink Panther down and stood between them, holding their hands.

'He didn't actually promise not to do it again,' Joe said as they drove back to London a few hours later. 'Did you notice?'

'Yes. In a way I quite like it that he shows so much spunk.'

'That headmaster is an idiot,' Joe said. 'He hadn't the faintest idea what to say to Hugo in front of us.'

They lapsed into silence for a few minutes.

'A friend of mine has just got back from Thailand,' Fliss broke the silence. 'She says we wouldn't recognise it. The place has been ruined by tourists.'

'People always say that about places they've enjoyed. I bet it's still pretty magical.'

'It was magical, wasn't it?'

They fell silent once more, both of them remembering their first meeting. It had been in a village on the northern borders of the country, an area which was then still only for the more hardened travellers. Joe had been back-packing around the Far East for six months by that stage and had almost run out of money. Fliss was travelling with a schoolfriend.

Joe would never forget the first time he saw her. It had been by firelight and her hair had looked startlingly blonde in contrast to the crowds of oriental heads he had been surrounded by for so many months.

It had been love at first sight for both of them and they had travelled back to England together to inform Fliss' horrified family that they were going to get married. Joe had invited his parents over for the wedding at Fliss' insistence, but their visit had not been a success. Neither his mother nor his father had been able to forgive Joe for the years he had been out of touch. The fact that he was now marrying and planning to live three thousand miles away from them did nothing to heal the wounds. His mother insisted on making pointed remarks about how they couldn't afford to come over to England whenever they wanted to visit their grandchildren. The obvious wealth of Fliss' family served only to fan the flames of her bitterness.

Everyone told them they were far too young but the marriage had still seemed to be a success.

'What made you do it, Fliss?' Joe asked.

'Do what?'

'Leave me?'

'I was just bored. Paolo came along and he made my heart race again, like it had when I first met you. I was missing that feeling. Weren't you?'

He didn't reply.

'It had all become so easy and comfortable,' she continued. 'We were heading for middle age and I didn't feel ready for that. Hugo was such hard work to bring up. You were always lost in your own thoughts. I felt that the pair of you were dragging me down all the time. I needed to escape.'

'But you took him away from me. How could you have done that?'

She fell silent and he knew better than to press the point. He knew there would never be a satisfactory answer to that question.

'I'm planning to go to the Philippines in the next few days on business,' he said.

'You lucky bugger. Perhaps you'll find a new wife out there.'

He ignored the comment. 'I'll take my mobile so you can contact me if anything happens to Hugo.'

'Oh God, I hope nothing else is going to happen.'

'Well, just in case.'

'When you get back,' she said, 'I think we should go and look at a few schools. Just so we know what the options are if that place doesn't work out.'

'I think you're right. I'm sorry if I've been prickly. Always feel that you can talk to me about Hugo.'

'Okay.'

That evening Joe went round to see Doris, taking a pizza for them to share. She was cleaning the windows when he came in, rubbing much harder than he thought must be wise given her recent operation. He had been to a cash machine on the way over and had drawn out several hundred pounds. He put it in an envelope and gave it to her.

'This is for you, to buy food and whatever you need for a while. I'm going to fly out to Manila to see what I can find out.'

'You going to Manila to research my story?' she grinned, pleased at the thought.

'Yeah. Where do you think I should go? Could I visit your family?'

'Sure. They live in a little village north of Manila, long way north, almost in Baguio. I draw you a map and write their names. They pleased to see you. Give them this.' She passed back the envelope of money without opening it. 'They need money.'

'You'll need some. How will you eat?'

She shrugged.

'Here.' He opened the envelope and counted out two hundred pounds. 'You have that. I'll give the rest to your family.'

'Okay.' She left the money lying on the table. 'Another man to speak to. His name Jeremy Pevensey. He looked after me when I arrive in Manila. Gave my family money while I was trained, helped me to get my boob job. Very kind man. He friend of Maisie. They work together very close. Tell him Doris says hi.'

'How do I find him?'

'I give you mobile number. He drinks in Manila Hotel very often, entertaining important clients. He's English Lord. Very rich. Very important man in Manila.'

CHAPTER TWELVE

The Manila Hotel provided a cool, dry sanctuary from the heat and rain of the tropical evening outside. Joe sat on a stool at the bar and looked around the room. Doris had given him a description of Jeremy Pevensey and he hoped he would be able to spot him. He wanted to observe the man from a distance.

'He's big man,' Doris had said, puffing her cheeks full of air and holding her arms out in front of her to indicate the size of the man's belly. 'Always laughing. Very jolly fellow. He has big voice, always louder than all around him. And he wears white suits which show how he sweats.'

The bar was full of people and it took Joe a while to accustom his eyes to the atmospheric gloom. His time clock was telling him it was late morning and he felt wide awake. The early-evening drinkers came and went, and then others started to arrive having had their dinner, settling in for late-night sessions. None of them seemed to fit the description he had been given.

Eventually, when the bar was almost empty, he gave up and retired to bed, to stare sleeplessly at the ceiling. The following morning his body felt disorientated. He breakfasted slowly before making his way out into the town. He spent the day wandering around the massage parlours, most of which were closed during the morning anyway, and asking questions of anyone he could find. He could tell from the looks in their eyes that everyone had heard of Jeremy Pevensey, but they all shrugged or suddenly lost their ability to speak English when he asked how he could find the man. He tried phoning the number Doris had given him but it was always on message service. He didn't want to leave a message. If the man wanted to avoid meeting him he didn't want to warn him he was there.

By the evening, his legs were aching and his clothes were sticking to him with sweat. He returned to the hotel to swim and spend another evening in the bar, waiting.

The barman was all smiles. 'Yes, Lord Pevensey often drinks here. He's a very good customer.' But he had no idea if his Lordship was expected. Joe picked at the snacks on the bar top and gazed around him at the same crowd he had seen the night before. He was beginning to wonder if he had made a mistake and wasted his money on this trip.

Almost at the point of giving up for the second night, he noticed a stir of movement at the door, and three men came in together. One was obviously the dominant character. He was wearing a white suit and shoes, dabbing his face with a handkerchief as he looked around the room for a spare table. The two men hovering at his side were altogether smaller, slightly rodent-like in the way their eyes darted around. Someone waved to them from one of the tables and they made their way through to join a group which was already well established.

'My dears,' the big man boomed. 'You have started without us. We must catch up immediately.' He signalled to a waiter. 'Bring us gin and tonics.'

He sank into a low sofa and the two smaller men had to scurry around borrowing chairs from other tables in order to become part of the group with him.

The waiter was there almost immediately, and Joe watched in awe as the big man downed his drink in one and signalled for another. All the other men in the group appeared to be deferring to him, laughing at his jokes, goading him on to talk more. This, Joe thought, must be his man.

Turning his back on the group he pulled out his phone and dialled the number Doris had given him. It started to ring. From the corner of his eye he saw the big man pull a phone from his pocket, whilst still finishing off whatever story he had been telling.

'Yes?' he said.

'Jeremy Pevensey?' Joe enquired.

'Speaking.'

'My name in John Weston. I'm in Manila for a few days and a mutual friend suggested I should make contact with you.'

'Who's that then?'

'Maisie Martin.' Joe waited to see what sort of response this would elicit.

'Maisie!' The big man emitted an explosion of laughter. 'How is she? The old devil.'

'She's fine. Could we get together?'

'Sure, sure. Do you want to come to the house in the morning? Come for coffee and pastries, about eleven.'

Joe wrote down the address which Pevensey dictated to him and hung up. Sliding his phone back into his pocket he swivelled back round on his chair. Pevensey was putting away his phone and was already back in charge of the conversation, telling a new story which he obviously found deeply amusing, his whole body shaking with suppressed merriment. It didn't look as if he was trying to avoid meeting anyone.

Joe slipped out of the bar and went up to his room to sleep.

Pevensey's villa in the suburbs of the city had the same colonial air as his clothes. There were wide sloping lawns, immaculately manicured, and an imposing facade of pillars and verandas. A servant, presumably the butler, in a formal white coat and black trousers let Joe into a large front hall with highly polished, dark wood floors and ceiling fans keeping the hot air moving.

'Lord Pevensey is on the terrace,' the man said. 'If you would like to follow me.'

143

They came through onto a patio at the back. A swimming pool glittered in the sunlight, the water obviously only just settling from its owner's exertions. Pevensey was pulling on a full-length towelling robe and pushing his wet hair back from his forehead, using his fingers as combs.

'Weston?' he asked, extending his hand. 'Good of you to pop over. Bring us coffee and pastries, Fred,' he instructed the servant. 'Come and sit down.'

Joe found himself being steered to a heavy wicker chair beside a table where two women sat. They looked like mother and daughter. The young one didn't look much more than fourteen.

'This is Betty,' Pevensey boomed, 'and her daughter, Doris.'

'Doris?' Joe shook their hands deliberately formally. They both averted their eyes and were obviously ill at ease in the men's company. 'That's an unusual name for this part of the world.'

'I call them all Doris,' Pevensey chuckled. 'Anyone who works for me is either Fred or Doris. I don't have enough of a brain left to remember a million different names.'

'You're working here?' Joe asked the girl, trying to put her more at ease.

'She's just starting today,' Pevensey said. 'Aren't you, my dear? Her mother here has brought her into town and she's going to start training at one of my establishments. I think she's going to be a great success. Aren't you, my dear? You're going to earn lots of money to send back to your lovely old mother here?'

The girl blushed and lowered her head even further. Her mother remonstrated with her, obviously telling her to speak when she was spoken to.

'Don't worry, my dear,' Pevensey said. 'She's just a bit over-awed. It's all very new for her. Once she's mixing in with all the other girls she'll get her confidence up. She'll be chirping away like a little canary in no time, won't you Doris, eh?'

The girl raised her head just long enough to nod and smile and then lowered it again, staring at her hands, which lay inertly on her lap.

The servant reappeared, carrying a tray filled with pastries and coffee, and laid it down on the table in front of them.

'Fred,' Pevensey said. 'Would you take these two lovely ladies and get them something to eat. Betty here then needs some money and her fare home and young Doris will need to be taken down to the boarding house, where she can meet the other girls she'll be training with.'

'Yes, your Lordship.' Fred gave a little bow and signalled to the two women to follow him round the side of the house, leaving Joe and his host alone together.

Pevensey poured them each a coffee and let out a deep sigh of satisfaction. 'It's a wonderful world when you can help a few people out, don't you think, Weston?'

'The two ladies, you mean?' Joe asked.

'Yes indeed. You have no idea the poverty some of these poor people have to live in. They rely on their children to earn enough money just to put food on the table. The money Fred will give her will be enough to feed the rest of her family for six months. And the girl will be able to learn a profession which will mean she'll be able to earn a living for years to come. Probably even lead to her finding a decent husband.

'It's no good just pouring aid money into these places. If you give them food they'll eat it and be hungry again a few hours later. You have to give them the means to earn money for themselves. That way you break the poverty chain. What do you think?'

'What will she be trained to do?' Joe asked.

'Masseuse. She won't be much good to start with, but the other girls will soon have her up to scratch. They're wonderful with their hands these people. So, tell me how Maisie is.'

'She's fine. Business seems to be booming for her.'

'Marvellous. Marvellous.' Pevensey popped a pastry into his mouth. 'She does great things for these girls. Arranges for them to get out of this country, where there are so few opportunities for them, and takes them off to the lands of the free. Great work. Funds it all from her own pocket, you know.'

'Funds what?'

'Their airfares, whatever paperwork they need. Then they pay her back out of their wages once they've found themselves jobs.'

Joe could imagine exactly how that would work, with Maisie refusing to hand any of the girls' money over to them, forever telling them they still owed her, baffling them with talk of interest still outstanding, keeping them permanently enslaved.

'How does she get them work permits?' he asked.

'God knows,' Pevensey laughed. 'The woman's a miracle worker. I dare say she goes in for all sorts of behind-the-scenes jiggery-pokery. But who cares if she's helping the poor girls to a better life?'

Pevensey leant forward as if to confide something deeply confidential. 'She even pays for them to have the odd snip here and there with the plastic surgeons, to help them feel better about themselves.'

'How long have you known her?' Joe asked.

'Oh, a good few years. She wasn't much older than that young girl you just met when she first came to me. She was a Doris too, but she wanted to be an individual. She had obvious management potential. She was running a couple of the businesses by the time she was twenty and she told me she shouldn't have to have the same-name as all the ordinary working girls. Always very status conscious was Maisie. She asked me to suggest another name, so I came up with Maisie and she took to it like a duck to water.'

Another pastry disappeared between his permanently masticating jaws.

'Very ambitious young lady,' he went on. 'I introduced her to a chap called Mike Martin who I'd been doing a bit of business with, and she set her sights on him. Poor old bugger didn't stand a chance. Been trained in the arts of seduction, you see. When a girl like that sets her cap at a chap he might as well kiss goodbye to any hope he might have of a peaceful bachelordom.'

'Martin was unmarried?'

'Not sure he was, now that you ask. But it wouldn't take Maisie long to see off a rival. She's a character is Maisie.'

'I've never met her husband,' Joe said. 'What's he like?'

'Mike?' Pevensey filled his mouth again as if to give himself time to think while he chewed. Eventually, he said. 'Between you and me, I think he's a bit of a dangerous character. He was always completely straight with me, always meticulous about paying his bills on time. One of nature's gentlemen. We did a bit of business together, created some companies, bought and sold a few shares. He made me a lot of money, I have to give him that. But over the years I've heard a few stories.'

'What sort of stories?' Joe persisted.

'I don't know that I would want to repeat them.' Pevensey was obviously finding it hard to resist the temptation to gossip. 'Well, I did hear he once executed this chap at a board meeting of one of his companies in the Middle East. Some executive who spoke out of turn. They say he stood up, cool as a cucumber, walked round the back of the chap and slit his throat, in full view of everyone. Blood all over the boardroom table. There are a few tales like that around, but I sometimes think he encourages them himself just to rattle his opponents. I mean, would you cross swords with a man who had a reputation for doing that sort of thing?'

'No, I guess not. Did you know he was a major fundraiser for the government these days?'

Pevensey let out another joyful bellow. 'I didn't know that, but it doesn't surprise me. He'd fit in well with that lot. All sorts of politicians have been out here on an "educational" at one time or another. They all find their way to me somehow. And they all expect to get services on the house. Makes you weep, doesn't it? And my father couldn't understand why I wouldn't want to take up my seat in the House of Lords! So,' Pevensey changed the subject, 'how long are you in town?'

'A few days.'

'You must sample one of our establishments while you're here. Best in Manila. Everyone says so. Probably the best in the whole of the Far East. Which hotel are you at?'

'The Manila.'

'Tell you what we'll do. Can't manage tonight, but tomorrow evening I'll send a car to collect you at, say, seven? The driver will take you to the Golden Heaven. It's my favourite. Some of the girls there…' He seemed to go off into a dream for a few seconds. 'Well, you'll see for yourself. Then the car will bring you back to the hotel and we can have dinner together. All on the house. Anything for a chum of Maisie's.'

'That's very kind of you,' Joe said.

'Not at all. Will you be staying for lunch?'

'It's very tempting,' Joe said, 'but I do have an appointment out of town this afternoon. In fact, I really should be going.'

He left Pevensey happily tucking into another pastry and caught a taxi back to the hotel. He had ordered a rental car for two o'clock and he needed to work out exactly where he was going.

The scenery passed in a haze of steam as he drove through the jungle on winding roads which occasionally surprised him by turning into spanking new highways, only to revert to potholed side roads again without warning. The rhythmic sound of the windscreen wipers toned into the roar of the air conditioning and the noise of the water on the surface of the road. It made Joe feel lost even though he could still find his position on the map. As he drove further from Manila the villages became more basic, the scenery more dramatic and overbearing. It was like travelling back in time through a prehistoric landscape of giant leaves and tangled, ancient roots.

The signposts told him he was heading towards one of the towns on the map Doris had drawn for him, but it never seemed to materialise. The petrol gauge flickered dangerously close to empty and the jungle-covered mountains seemed to stretch in every direction as far as the eye could see. Joe began to panic. What the hell would he do if he ran out of fuel? The number of passing cars had dwindled to the occasional lorry filled with workers sitting in the open, apparently oblivious to the rain which poured down on them. They did not look like the sort of people who would be sympathetic to a stranded tourist. Joe thought of all the stories he had heard about kidnapping and murder in the jungles of the Far East. Who would ever know if he simply vanished out there?

The emergency light started to blink and he lifted his foot off the accelerator to conserve the last few litres, coasting as gently as he could, cursing every incline that forced him to use more valuable fuel. Just when he was about to give up, a side road appeared through the mists. It looked as if it might lead to a village. He turned onto it and the car bumped down a track and finally cut out, coming to a halt beside a plantation.

Joe sat for a few minutes as the windows steamed up around him. He was going to have to do something. He couldn't just sit there, hoping someone would come to his rescue. He climbed out and was instantly drenched. Opening the boot he found a petrol can and set off down the track.

He must have walked for three or four miles before he came across a clutch of wooden buildings standing out of the mud on stilts. A group of women watched him from the veranda. None of them spoke. He could see an elderly tractor parked at the back of the buildings. Maybe they had some fuel.

'Petrol?' he asked hopefully, holding up the can to illustrate his plight.

One of the women rose lazily from her chair and went into the house, shouting for someone. A few minutes later an elderly man came out, blinking, obviously freshly woken from his afternoon sleep. He beckoned Joe over.

'I've run out of petrol,' Joe said. 'Do you have some I can buy?'

The man took the can from him and shook it, as if to check Joe was telling the truth.

'A hundred dollars,' he said.

'A hundred dollars?' Joe realised he was not in a strong bargaining position. 'For that much?'

'A hundred dollars,' the man nodded.

'Twenty.' Joe proffered a soggy note. The man shook his head and handed back the can.

Joe pulled out two more notes. 'Fifty,' he suggested.

The man stared at the money for a few moments and then took it with a dissatisfied grunt, as if he resented doing this stranger such a favour. He led Joe round to the back of the house and found a large rusty can of fuel. Joe prayed it would be of a high enough octane to make the car run. When the can was full he showed Doris' map to the man and asked the way to the town he had seen on the signposts.

'Back to highway,' the man grinned, happy now the transaction was satisfactorily completed. 'One kilometre on, turn to left. You're there.'

Joe thanked him. If the man was telling the truth he had been closer to the town than he had to this place. He cursed himself for choosing the wrong option. He should have stayed on the highway.

He trudged back to the car. The rain had abated and his clothes began steaming in the sun. The tractor fuel made the car cough alarmingly as he pulled back onto the road, but at least he was moving. As soon as he got to the town he would fill up with decent petrol and try to dilute the bad stuff.

Just as the man predicted, a signpost took him to the town on the map within ten minutes and the first thing he saw was a service station. As the garage owner filled up the tank, the sun went in again and the rain became heavier than before. Joe showed him the map and asked for directions to the village nearest to Doris' mother's home. The man gave him directions with a broad, gold-toothed smile. Joe drove on for another half hour until he found a settlement, seemingly without a name. The main street was a made-up road, although mined with potholes which had filled with water and gave no clue as to how deep they were until the car had plunged through them. The side streets were dirt tracks. A few locals walked about their normal business in the rain, covering their heads with broken umbrellas or sheets of cardboard. The children didn't bother to shelter at all. Small boys played football in the mud as if the sun was out.

Following the lines which Doris had drawn, he made his way down a track, past a church. The wheels of the car lurched and bumped through puddles sending sheets of mud up over the windows, which made it impossible to see where the road forked or turned. The clouds had grown so heavy it was starting to feel like night, even though it was still only late afternoon. His relief at finding the fuel was draining away and Joe sensed a new twinge of panic. He did not fancy the idea of having to spend the night in the car, lost in the jungle, or with his wheels stuck in the mud.

He spotted a local shop, with an assortment of plastic basins, brushes and fruit on display at the front, sheltered under a sagging canopy. He pulled up and climbed out of the car, his feet sinking into the soft ground and his shirt immediately soaked as he ran across to the store.

The map was drenched through but he could still just make out the lines Doris had drawn. He pointed them out to the old man who was sitting on a stool inside the shop, listening to the radio. The old man laboriously took out a pair of glasses and placed them on the end of his nose.

'Ahhh,' he moaned, as if being asked to cut off his own limbs. 'Ahhh.'

'Do you know this village?' Joe asked.

The old man looked up at him and down at the map again. The rain crashed onto the canopy outside and Joe could feel sweat breaking through inside the shirt which was already sticking to him. The shopkeeper pulled himself up off his stool and walked on crooked legs to the front. He waved the map in the air and pointed to the road ahead.

He indicated that Joe should turn right and then left and pointed at the map once more. Joe picked up a packet of biscuits and gave him far too much money for them, waving aside any suggestions that he should receive change.

The old man bowed his thanks, repeatedly, and went over the directions one more time. Joe splashed his way back to the car, which had now misted up so much he could see nothing through the windows at all. He opened the packet of biscuits and pushed one into his mouth while he waited for the windows to clear and then moved cautiously off.

The old man's instructions gave him confidence that he was heading in the right direction, but he was still very unsure exactly where the tracks were actually leading him. Then he spotted a church and knew that Doris had drawn one on her map. He stopped the car and realigned himself. If this was the right church then he was very close to Doris' mother's house. The map was now almost unreadable, the ink having spread into multi-shaded stains either side of each road. Joe let the car crawl forward.

As he came round behind the church he saw a row of shacks and, at the end of the row, a bungalow that wouldn't have looked out of place in Cape Cod, or in an old-fashioned English fishing village, complete with clapperboard walls and window boxes.

Joe stopped the car and checked the map one more time. This had to be the house. He ran across, with his head down, and huddled in the narrow porch, pressing on the bell. He heard musical chimes coming from inside the house and, a few moments later, the door opened.

'Excuse me,' he said, 'Tikki?'

The woman standing in front of him didn't look much older than Doris. She was wearing what looked like a cocktail dress and rather more make-up than he would have expected in the middle of the jungle. She clutched a can of Diet Coke in her hand. Her feet were bare and she was very small. She looked at him with no particular expression on her face.

'I'm a friend of Tikki's daughter, Doris,' he went on, speaking extremely slowly as he had no idea how much English this woman would understand – if any. 'I've come from England and Doris asked me to come and visit Tikki. Is this the right house?'

'Sure,' the woman shrugged but made no attempt to invite him in.

'Are you Tikki?'

'Yeah. You American?'

'Yes.' Joe held out his hand. 'My name is Joe.'

'Oh yeah. I know plenty of American Joes.' She laughed and it sounded as if she was genuinely amused by the memory. She didn't bother to shake his hand. 'Not so many Americans here now.'

'No,' Joe said. 'I guess not. May I come in for a moment? I'm kinda wet.'

'Sure.' She stood back to let him past.

There was a wide-screen television on in the corner of the room, showing what looked like a Mexican soap opera. The house was pristinely clean compared to the mudbath outside the front door, and filled with possessions. There was a large stereo system and a bar stacked with bottles. There were shelves of dolls in national costumes from around the world. A giant air-conditioning system hummed monotonously in the corner of the room.

'Don't wet the carpet,' Tikki snapped. 'Stand there. I get a towel.'

He stood, dripping on the lino, until she returned with a towel covered in pictures of Mickey Mouse. He gave his hair a rub and dabbed inadequately at his clothes. She stood watching with an amused expression.

'You a big guy, Joe,' she said, flirtatiously. 'You a good friend to Doris? You know what I mean?'

'Just good friends.' Joe found himself blushing and tried to laugh it off. 'Doris is a very nice, hard-working girl.'

'Oh, sure.' Tikki gave another attractive laugh. 'I taught her to work hard. Lazy girls end up with nothing in life. I always work hard.' She gestured around the room as if to prove her point. 'Take off wet clothes. I find you robe and dry them for you.'

She disappeared again. As he started to undo his shirt, he remembered the envelope of money which he had changed into American dollars at the hotel, and which was still in his bag.

'Doris asked me to give you this,' he said, handing it over when she came back with a dressing-gown displaying the Manila Hilton's logo on the breast pocket.

She opened the envelope and flicked through the notes inside. Satisfied, she opened a drawer in an ornate, Italian-style chest, and dropped it in without a word.

'You want a Coke?' she asked as he changed.

'Please.'

'Okay. Give me clothes and I'll dry them. Take Coke from the bar.'

She disappeared through another door, and he wandered across to the bar to find a drink. It looked as well stocked as any hotel bar.

'So, Doris says "hi", yeah?' she said as she came back in.

'Yeah. Actually, I have another reason for coming to see you.' He sat on one of the leather sofas, crossing his bare legs and trying to maintain some semblance of dignity.

'Oh yeah?' She laughed again and he blushed.

'I'm a writer and I'm sort of writing a book about Doris.'

'Doris is famous? What she done to become famous?' Tikki was suddenly shrill. 'Has she been stupid girl and made trouble?'

'No, no, nothing like that. I just think that it's an interesting story, a girl who starts life in the Philippines and ends up in London. I thought it would make a good book. So I wanted to ask you a bit about her early years. Background colour. That kind of thing.'

'Will Doris be paid for this book?'

'Yes. That was some of the money, there.' He nodded towards the chest of drawers.

'How much will she get?'

'It depends how successful the book is. The more information I can get about her the more money she's likely to earn.'

Tikki appeared to be thinking this one through. 'Okay,' she said, eventually. 'Ask me questions.'

'So, when Doris was born, did you live in this house?'

Tikki's laugh tinkled through the room again. 'No way. You see the houses next door when you drove up?'

He remembered the line of shacks he had passed. 'Yes.'

'We lived in house on the end.'

'How many of you?'

'I live with my mother and father. They still there. With my sister and her husband and with my husband.'

'So, how many children were there when Doris was little?'

'Doris had two sisters and two brothers. And my sister, she had three more. There were many people in that house. No bathroom, no running water. Difficult, difficult times.'

'Who made the money?'

155

'My father. He worked in the village, cleaning up in the shop. My husband and my brother-in-law, they travel to the cities to do construction work. They were always away. Whenever they come back, *boom* one of us got pregnant again.' She laughed uproariously at the idea.

'So, who earned the money for this?' He gestured around the sparkling little room.

'I did.' She banged her chest proudly. 'Tikki went to work and made the money to buy everything. My husband and my brother-in-law built it.'

'Where is your husband now?'

'He is away, working in Saudi Arabia.'

'How did you earn the money?'

'I went to see Lord Jeremy Pevensey. He helped me so much. He paid for me to have an operation so *poof* no more babies.' She patted her stomach affectionately. 'Then I worked as masseuse at the Golden Heaven. I was very good masseuse. Made very happy customers and received many tips.' She smiled proudly.

'Who looked after your children while you were in Manila?'

'My mother. She is a very good woman. Very hard-working. She wanted her daughters and her granddaughters to be a big success and she looks after the children so we can have big-time careers.'

'How did Doris get into the business?'

'Jeremy very nice man. He always talked to me like I was his friend when I gave him massage and I told him about my children. He said I should bring the girls to meet him and he would make sure they had big-time careers like Tikki.' She laughed happily. 'I was so proud of them.'

'How old were they when you took them to meet him?' Joe asked, remembering the photograph of the laughing girls which Doris had had in her room.

Tikki wrinkled her brow, trying to work it out. 'I think they were fifteen, fourteen and thirteen. They were very pretty girls.

And very polite. And very hard-working. Their grandmother, she brought them up so well, so strict, in the old-fashioned days. You know what I mean? Here, look,' she said as she went into the bedroom and re-emerged with a photograph in an ornate frame. It was a picture of a group of girls in what looked like dancing outfits. They were all waving and laughing at the camera. It was the same group of girls as the photograph he had seen in Doris' Brighton bedroom, but must have been taken a year or two later. They were all wearing make-up and posing in a childish mockery of provocativeness.

'These are all our girls,' Tikki explained. 'That is the Doris that you know in England.' Joe looked closely and could see that it was, although she had matured and grown thinner since the photograph was taken. 'The others are her sisters and her cousins. Lord Jeremy called us all Doris because he couldn't remember all our names.' Tikki laughed and Joe forced himself to smile.

CHAPTER THIRTEEN

The Mercedes limousine arrived at the hotel for Joe at exactly the time Pevensey had predicted. The driver, who introduced himself as Fred, was a respectful but jolly man in short sleeves and sandals. As he held up an umbrella and ushered Joe into the back seat of the car, he pointed out the bar and suggested Joe should help himself to a drink on the way.

'Is it far?' Joe asked.

'Sometimes there are traffic jams,' Fred said cheerfully, before closing the door and leaving Joe cocooned in quiet luxury, able to watch the street life passing by the darkened windows, knowing he was invisible to the people he was spying on.

The building that housed Golden Heaven was not as smart as the people working there. A doorman in a uniform which would not have looked out of place outside a five-star London hotel came to open the door and usher Joe out. He led him across the pavement under another umbrella and through a rather ordinary-looking glass shop door covered in credit card stickers and hurriedly written notices about opening and closing times.

It was like walking into a public aquarium, except the illuminated tanks on either side of the heavily carpeted, unlit reception area were filled with girls rather than fish. The doorman introduced Joe to a young woman dressed in a uniform that suggested she would be more suited to selling airline tickets or hiring out cars than organising a massage parlour. The doorman explained that Joe was a friend of Lord Pevensey's. The lady bowed her head with due respect and led him gently around the displays.

'Please take your time deciding. If you would like a drink while you are making up your mind, please let me know and I will be pleased to serve you. All our girls are fully trained masseuses and will be happy to satisfy all your requirements. Please take your time choosing.'

She backed away, smiling and bowing discreetly. Joe joined the other furtive-looking men as they ogled the women behind the glass, trying to make what seemed impossible choices. The younger, and presumably more popular, girls were working hard to be chosen, pouting, waving and flirting with their unseen admirers on the dark side of the glass. One or two of the older ones were sitting down, busying themselves with their reading or sewing, or just gossiping with one another as they waited for some regular customer to ask for them. They all had numbers pinned to them.

Joe picked a girl who seemed to be brimming with self-confidence. He wanted someone who was likely to talk and be indiscreet. This must have been a stage that all the Dorises had been through and he needed to find out as much about it as possible.

He beckoned over the lady in the uniform. 'Number seventeen,' he said.

The lady smiled sweetly, as if to say that he had made a wise choice, and spoke into a microphone. There must have been a loudspeaker on the other side of the glass because the girl he had selected gave a little jump of excitement at being chosen and hurried out of a door at the back of the aquarium. Joe's guide took him to another door and showed him through. The girl of his choice was waiting for him with her eyes demurely downcast, a sweet smile and dimpled cheeks. Her hair reached down below her waist.

She led him up a flight of stairs, collecting a pile of clean towels from a laundry woman who sat behind a hatch at the end of the corridor.

'Welcome to Golden Heaven,' the girl said, reciting her much-rehearsed speech as they approached the door of the room they had been allocated. 'My name is Doris and I hope that you will enjoy yourself here today.'

She ushered him into the room, which was laid out very like the one Rod had taken him to in London, complete with a bathtub and a bed. She started to run the bath and helped him to undress, her fingers unselfconsciously brushing against his skin as she peeled the clothes away. He kept asking questions, which she answered like a pre-recorded tape.

'How long have you been working here?' he asked as her fingers grazed against his hips.

'Only a few months.' She slid his trousers down, kneeling gracefully to lift them over his feet.

'Where did you come from before?'

She named a village as she folded his clothes neatly onto a stool, but he didn't catch it.

'So, who brought you here?' he asked, trying to ignore the fact that he was now standing naked and aroused in the middle of the room as the water continued to tumble into the bathtub.

'I was looking for work and a friend introduced me to Golden Heaven.' She tested the temperature of the water.

'Do you enjoy it?'

'Oh yes. It is very interesting work. I meet many interesting people. Lots of handsome men like you.' She giggled and pulled her T-shirt off over her head. She noticed him looking at her small, perfect breasts. 'You like my tits?' she asked, caressing them teasingly. 'They are only little. Tomorrow I have an operation to give me beautiful, big, new breasts. If you come back next week I will look different. Would you like that?'

'Why do you want to make them bigger?' Joe asked. 'They look beautiful now, to me.'

160

She laughed, as if he was just being kind with his words, as if she knew that all men secretly liked big breasts.

'I have been offered to go to London for a trip. I want to go very much, but European men like big breasts. Isn't that right?' She indicated he should get into the bath.

'Some of them,' he said, guardedly, as he lowered himself into the hot water. She took her skirt off. She was wearing nothing underneath. 'What are you going to be doing in London?'

'I am going to see the Queen and all the sights,' she said, her eyes sparkling.

'I meant for work.'

'There are many good jobs in England for a hard-working girl like me. I will earn much more money and be able to help my family by sending some back.'

'Are your family in difficulties?'

'Oh, sure. It is very hard to live in the Philippines without education. But in London, with my new big tits...'

'Where are you going to have this operation?'

'At the Santa Christa Hospital. A very nice hospital. And it is all being paid for by the Golden Heaven. They are good employers.'

'Where is this hospital?'

'Close. Just down the street.'

'Can I come and visit you after the operation?' he asked. 'I could bring you some flowers.'

'That would be so sweet,' she said, climbing into the bath on top of him, her hair cascading down around him as she bent her head in concentration.

As Joe came out into the street, Fred the chauffeur sprang out of the waiting car and opened the back door for him. The rain had abated, leaving the pavements glistening with water. Passing cars sent up sheets of spray which reflected the bright lights of the buildings.

'His Lordship said to take you back to the Manila Hotel for dinner,' Fred said.

Pevensey was in the bar, just as he had been the first night that Joe had seen him, surrounded by a new group of sycophantic men, all laughing at his jokes and encouraging him to tell more stories.

'Ah, John, my dear friend!' He didn't stand, but he held up his arms in a theatrical gesture of welcome. 'Come and join us, come and join us. How was Golden Heaven?'

'It was great, thank you.' Joe was embarrassed to have everyone in the group know where he had just come from, but they all nodded their agreement on what a great place Golden Heaven was.

'I have big plans for a revamp,' Pevensey said. 'I want to do the Golden Heaven up from top to bottom. Make it look as good as this place.' He gestured around the five-star hotel.

They all nodded their agreement at the wisdom of this idea.

'How many places like that do you have?' Joe asked, innocently.

'Half a dozen. Eventually they will all be little palaces.'

'So, how many people do you have working for you?' Joe enquired.

'Difficult to say. Bit of a floating population. Then there are the ones who get invited to travel by people like your friend, Maisie. I suppose we have a couple of hundred on our books at any one time.'

After two large drinks, Joe was steered through to the dining room with Pevensey's arm around his shoulder. The big man seemed to be resting most of his weight on Joe, as if he was having trouble holding himself up.

'It's good of you to join us,' he said, quietly. 'Sometimes colonial company can be very trying. It's refreshing to see someone from the outside world every now and then.'

'It was kind of you to invite me,' Joe replied.

As they reached the table, Pevensey indicated that Joe should sit next to him. The meal had already been ordered and discreet waiters were placing the food in front of the diners as soon as they were settled.

'How did you come to be living in Manila?' Joe asked.

'Long story, old boy,' Pevensey grinned sheepishly. 'When I finished at university, the family wanted me to go into law. They wanted someone to administrate the family trusts and all the rest. All deadly boring stuff. I told them I needed a break before I got down to business. I took myself off on the hippy trail for a few months, overland to India, all that stuff.

'When I got out here I thought I'd arrived in heaven. After a childhood in a draughty great pile in Norfolk, and then on to Eton and Oxford, the tropics were like a dream come true. The women were beautiful and willing and the cost of living was nothing. I had a private income which would have been perfectly adequate in England, but meant I could live like a prince out here.'

'Didn't your family try to make you go back?'

'Of course they did. Tried to cut off my money, but the trustees wouldn't let 'em. They tried to tempt me back with the prospect of marriage to some tasty little heiress. But why would I want to marry some woman who would give me a hard time, when I could have all the women I wanted out here and they would never give me an ear-bashing about anything? I'm telling you, it's paradise out here. Don't you think so?'

'It certainly has a lot to commend it,' Joe agreed as the aromas of the food drifted up from the table and he sipped at the champagne which had been poured into his glass.

'Of course it does.' Pevensey's eyelids were becoming heavy and it looked as if he might be about to doze off. He rallied himself and raised his voice to the whole table. 'And I'm the luckiest man in the world, to be able to afford to entertain my friends like this whenever I want.'

There was a murmur of agreement from around the table and they all raised their glasses in a toast to their host.

Joe found the Santa Christa Hospital eventually, although the flowers he had bought in the hotel florist's were starting to look a little droopy by the time he eventually walked in. It was a building which couldn't have been more than ten years old, but which already had an air of degeneration and neglect.

The reception area was stark and empty, the curling lino tiles smelling of disinfectant. A man in a sweat-stained shirt sat in a chair in one corner. On a table next to him stood an electric fan, a kettle and a few dirty mugs.

'I'm here to visit Doris, from the Golden Heaven,' Joe said in what he hoped was a no-nonsense voice.

'Golden Heaven girls?' The man grinned, showing a gappy row of teeth a similar colour to the walls outside. 'Third floor.'

Joe thought about using the lift, but decided against it and started up the stairs. By the time he reached the third floor he was bathed in sweat.

Voices echoed all over the building from the curtainless, carpetless rooms and bare corridors. Someone somewhere must have dropped a kidney dish for a clattering sound was reverberating endlessly. There were several doors to choose from, each with a small window of reinforced glass. Joe peered through the first and saw a couple of beds which seemed to be occupied by men, although it was hard to see through the jungle of tubes and pipes attached to them. The next one had a child sitting up in a bed with a huge bandage around his head. He was surrounded by his extended family, all fussing over him at once.

In the third room he saw four beds, and on the nearest one he could make out a mass of dark hair spread on the pillow. He cautiously opened the door and poked his head round. The hair rose from the pillow and a pretty face looked at him with a sleepy smile. He was about to speak when three other identical

164

heads lifted themselves up in the other beds. They were all young, round-faced and pretty. He had to rack his memory to think what Doris had looked like. They all smiled sweetly.

'Doris?' he asked, tentatively.

'Yes,' they all answered.

'Hi, Mr John,' the one in the furthest bed said and he breathed a sigh of relief.

'Hello, Doris,' he said, walking over to her bedside. 'How are you feeling?'

'Feeling tip-top,' Doris laughed, pulling down the sheets to show the enormous bandaged bust which had blossomed inside her hospital gown. 'Do you think the English men will like these, Mr John?'

'I'm sure they will, Doris,' he said, laying the flowers down on the end of her bed, since there were no tables or surfaces in the room. 'Are you all in here for the same thing?'

'Sure,' Doris said. 'Show Mr John your new breasts!'

The other girls all giggled weakly and pulled down their sheets to show him their proud new possessions, straining at their dressings.

'We all going to London together next month,' Doris crowed happily.

'Listen,' Joe said, getting out a note pad and a pen. 'I live in London. I'll give you my telephone number and address. If you get into any trouble over there and need a friend, just call me. In fact, call me anyway. I'd like to see you again.'

Doris giggled sleepily. She had dark rings under her eyes and he guessed she was meant to be resting after her operation. He ripped out the piece of paper and folded it into her hand.

'And your friends as well. If any of you need anything, just call or write to me.'

'What the fuck are you doing in here?' a familiar voice roared into the room from the doorway.

Joe jumped and turned to see the surgeon from the Wimpole Clinic standing with his hands on his hips. This time it was even less obvious that he was medically qualified. He was wearing a short sleeved Hawaiian shirt covered in vivid pink flamingos against a red sunset, and white trousers so thin they were almost see-through. The same medallion nestled in his chest hair, but his tan had improved since Joe saw him last.

'I know you from somewhere,' the doctor said, narrowing his eyes as he tried to picture where Joe's face might fit in his memory.

'I don't think so,' Joe protested.

'You were visiting the other fucking girl in London. What is it with you? You kinky for girls in hospital beds or something?'

'I think you're mistaking me for someone else. I'm a friend of Jeremy Pevensey. I came to see how Doris here, was.'

'Everyone's a friend of fucking Jeremy Pevensey,' the doctor said. 'Anyone with a glass in their hand is a friend of his. You're up to something.' He pushed his face close to Joe's and Joe could smell alcohol on his breath. 'Who do you fucking work for?'

'I told you, I'm just a friend.'

'Get the fuck out of here and leave my patients alone,' the doctor said, turning on his heel and striding out of the room.

'I mean it,' Joe said to Doris as he went towards the door. 'Contact me when you get to London.'

She gave a weak little wave and he left. He went back down the stairs and out through the reception area. The man in the chair had disappeared. Everything was silent. He sauntered out into the street and turned to go back to the hotel. The two men hit him with the full weight of their bodies. Neither of them was as tall as Joe, but their combined strength knocked him off balance and sent him spinning down some greasy steps to a service area beneath the hospital.

There was a clattering of falling bins all around him and his head hit something sharp as the wind was knocked from his chest, leaving him struggling for breath. He was unable to work out what was happening in the sudden darkness of the underground area. A fist drove itself into his face and something, he guessed it was a boot, came up between his legs into his groin, making him scream with surprise and pain.

He heard the click of a knife being opened and felt a razor-sharp edge pressing against his cheekbone.

'Stay away from our girls,' a voice hissed in his ear. The knife made a quick downward sweep and he felt a warm bubbling of blood on his cheek as he passed out.

There was no way of knowing how long he had been lying there before the persistent ringing of his phone brought him back to consciousness. He was amazed it was still in one piece after the battering he had had. He felt weak and dizzy and disorientated. He eventually managed to pull the insistent phone out of his pocket and switch it on.

'Joe,' Fliss' voice came down the line as clearly as if she were calling from the next street. 'It's Hugo. He's gone again.'

Joe shook his head, trying to clear it enough to make sense of this piece of news which was being sprung on him from the other side of the world.

'How long has he been missing?' he asked, groggily.

'Did I wake you up?' Fliss asked.

'It's okay. How long has he been gone?'

'About eight hours.'

'Okay. I'll get the first available flight back,' he said. 'Let me know of any developments.'

He snapped the phone off and sank back against the wall, waiting for the dizziness to clear. After a few minutes he thought he could manage to stand. He pulled himself to his feet and paused for the wave of nausea to pass, before making his way back up the steps and into the street. Passers-by pulled back when they saw his face. A few people spoke to him, perhaps asking if he needed help, but he had to concentrate all his energies on putting one foot in front of the other and remembering the way back to the hotel. Every part of him was filled with a searing pain from his head to his crotch. The crowds on the pavement parted in his path.

He saw a taxi parked by the curb and made his way across. The driver looked frightened by the sight of him but Joe didn't give him any chance to argue. He opened the back door and collapsed onto the seat. The driver said nothing when Joe asked for the Manila Hotel, driving in silence.

The driver took the money Joe offered him as the hotel doorman opened the door, without making any comment. The doorman helped Joe up the steps to reception.

'I think I need a nurse,' he told the shocked-looking receptionists. 'Just to clean me up a bit. I was attacked in the street.'

'Would you like us to call the police?' one of them enquired.

'There's no need. I doubt they would be able to find the men. It was very dark and I didn't get to see their faces. Could you please ring the airline?' He pushed his crumpled air ticket, which had been in his pocket with his passport, across the counter. 'Ask them to book me onto the next flight back to London.'

'Certainly, Mr Tye,' she said, grateful to be given something she was trained to deal with. 'We will send the doctor to your room, and let you know when the flight is confirmed.'

'Thank you.'

Joe made his way up in the lift, aware of the people all around him who were torn between wanting to stare and wanting to avert their eyes. When he finally stumbled through the door of his room and looked in the mirror he was shocked by just how bad he was. The cut on his cheek seemed to have unleashed a cascade of blood down his neck and chest, soaking into his shirt. From the amount of blood, it looked as though he had had half his face cut away.

He went through into the bathroom and ran the tap, splashing water gingerly onto his face. As the dried blood washed off he was able to see the extent of the cut, which had stopped bleeding but was still vivid and raw.

The white porcelain of the basin was stained with blood. He stripped his clothes off and washed himself down, pulling on a hotel robe. He went to find himself a brandy from the mini-bar, leaving dirty footprints across the white tiled floor. He drained the miniature bottle in one gulp and collapsed onto the bed. He dozed for a few moments and was woken by a light tapping on the door.

'Who is it?' he called out.

'Doctor,' came the reply.

Joe opened the door and an earnest young man came in, carrying a black bag. He examined the cut with no expression on his face.

'You really need to have stitches in this,' he said.

'Can you do that for me here?' Joe asked. 'I don't want to have to go into a hospital.'

'Sure. Come and lie on the bed.'

An hour later, with his face stitched and dressed, having been given a shot of something for the shock and a tetanus booster, Joe drifted into a deep sleep, haunted by imaginings of what might be happening to his son all those thousands of miles away, while he could do nothing but wait for a seat on a plane.

CHAPTER FOURTEEN

Jeremy Pevensey always prided himself on being able to get on with everyone. It was one of the reasons he liked living in the Far East, people were always remarkably pleasant to him. They were usually so grateful for the help he gave them in bettering their lots in life.

But Christopher Rose was a man Jeremy found almost impossible to charm. The man appeared to have to dominate every relationship and every conversation. His arrogance and rudeness seemed to know no bounds and left Jeremy unable to think what to say when in his company.

He understood that the man was a great surgeon, because Mike and Maisie had told him so. And he could see that Rose brought happiness to many hundreds of people by making them more like their own fantasies of themselves. But he didn't see why that meant the man should be so charmless to everyone he met along the way.

It was, therefore, with a sinking feeling in the pit of his stomach, that Jeremy saw Fred bringing the surgeon through into the drawing-room, where he was lying with his shirt open and his belly bared to the cooling breeze of the fans, planning his evening's activities.

'I could fix that for you,' Rose gestured towards Pevensey's stomach. 'A spot of liposuction and all that would vanish.' He made an unpleasant sucking noise, before continuing, 'you'd be able to see your dick again for the first time in years.'

Jeremy gave a wan smile. 'Kind offer, Christopher. I'll consider it and let you know.'

'Bloody bad for your heart,' Rose continued, sitting himself down on a wicker sofa and lighting a cigar. 'Carrying all that weight. Lucky you've lived as long as you have.'

'Ah, well.' Jeremy pointed to the cigar. 'We all have our little indulgences.'

'Ha!' Rose let out a bark of laughter. 'Touché. What do you know about a bloke called John Weston?'

'The American?'

'Yes.'

'Not much. He said he was a friend of Maisie's. I've been showing him a bit of hospitality while he's in town. You know how one does.'

'I know how you do,' Rose sneered. 'Did you check up on him at all? Did you talk to Maisie about him?'

'No,' Jeremy felt uncomfortable being cross-examined in his own house. 'Why would I? He obviously knows her. He seems a perfectly decent sort. Why? Are you worried about him?'

'He was nosing around the girls at the clinic. Taking flowers in to one of them. He left his name and address in London with her.' Rose waved the piece of paper Joe had written on under Jeremy's nose.

Pevensey smiled. 'That's rather sweet. He was at Golden Heaven last night. He must have struck up a relationship with one of them and went to visit her.'

'Wake up and smell the fucking roses, Jerry,' Rose shouted. 'That is not normal behaviour for a man like that. He's not exactly your average brothel-goer who thinks all tarts have golden hearts.'

'Well, I don't know,' Pevensey blustered.

'Well I do fucking know,' Rose stabbed the air with his cigar to emphasise his point. 'He was nosing around another of the girls in London. I met him there a couple of weeks ago. Don't you think that is a bit of a coincidence? Twice in a matter of days? Two different girls? Two different bunches of bleeding flowers? He falls in love a bit fucking easy, doesn't he?'

'What possible other motive could he have?'

'Jesus Christ. No wonder you had to come out here and live amongst the savages. You have no bleedin' idea, do you?'

'If you are going to talk to me like that I would ask you to leave my house.' Jeremy did his shirt up in an attempt to increase his authority in his own home.

'Oh shut it,' Rose snarled. 'He could be a journalist. He could be a policeman or someone from immigration. He could be looking into their working papers, or maybe someone after Maisie and her husband, for all we know. He could be anyone and you've just let him waltz in and see whatever he wants to see. You are a big, fat, bleedin' kid, Jerry.'

'You think that?' It was beginning to dawn on Jeremy that he didn't actually know anything about this American who called himself John Weston. But then he always thought it rather ill-mannered to cross-examine people who came to visit him. If they wanted to tell him about themselves then that was fine. If they preferred to keep their details quiet, he was quite willing to respect that. Perhaps he should have been a little more cautious.

'Well, anyway, I got the security boys at the clinic to give him a bit of a warning,' Rose went on. 'If he's just a casual nosy parker, or some do-gooder, he'll go scuttling back home pretty smartish. If he's something more official we'll soon know about it.'

'Maybe I should give Maisie a call,' Jeremy said. 'To see if she does know the man.'

'Maybe you should,' Rose agreed. 'Shut the stable door now the horses are all over the fucking shop!'

Jeremy got through to Maisie almost immediately on her mobile business line. After a brief exchange of pleasantries, which obviously bemused Maisie and infuriated Rose, Jeremy got to the point.

'I've had a visit from a man called John Weston. He claims to be a friend of yours.'

There was silence at the other end of the line as Maisie took in this piece of information.

'He's an American,' Jeremy said. 'Late thirties, quite tall, very personable.'

'I met a man of that name a few weeks ago.' Maisie seemed to be weighing her words carefully, as if trying to work out a puzzle as she went along. 'Claimed to be a potential client, wanting to rent a housekeeper. He is no friend. I did not hear from him again after introducing him to a girl.'

'Oh,' Jeremy looked crestfallen.

'Give me the fucking phone,' Rose said, springing to his feet and snatching the receiver from him. 'Hi, Maisie. It's Chris Rose here. This American bastard has been nosing around the clinics. I've seen him in London and out here, pretending to be visiting the girls. It's fucking funny behaviour.'

'I don't know how to find him,' Maisie said. 'He left me no address and no number. He told me his house in Belgravia was being redecorated.'

'I can help you there,' Rose smoothed out the crumpled piece of paper. 'He gave his address and phone number to the girls in the clinic. Told them to contact him if they had any problems in London. He said to ask for "Joe".'

'Give me address and number.'

Rose dictated them down the phone.

'It's not Belgravia address.' Maisie sounded affronted. 'It's Earls Court.'

'He's had a little accident in the street over here,' Rose told her. 'Met with some unsavoury characters who didn't like the look of his face. My guess is that he'll be slinking back to London pretty sharpish.'

'We will be waiting for him.'

When Max had arrived back at the house in Ditchling Avenue, after the incident in the café with Joe, and discovered that Doris had fled, his fury had been uncontrollable. As the other members of the household sat quietly in the kitchen, waiting for the storm to pass, he had rampaged from room to room, tearing and smashing everything that came to hand. Mattresses, crockery, clothes; the trail of devastation followed him from floor to floor until eventually he came to Doris' mean little room in the roof. For at least five minutes he ricocheted around inside, until there was nothing left and the window through which she had made her escape had been smashed from the frame, leaving the hole open to the night sky above.

His temper had been building ever since he had started to regain his senses in the casualty department of the hospital. The café owner, very wisely, had told the ambulance men, and the accompanying policemen who had answered his 999 call, that he had been out the back when the incident occurred and had no idea what had happened.

'I heard a noise,' he had told them. 'And when I came out I found him on the floor in that state. I don't know anything else. There was no sign of another person.'

Max had been just conscious during this and took his cue from the man, swearing that he could remember nothing about the attack at all, that his memory had been wiped clean right back to several hours before.

He had lain, and then sat, simmering, while they cleaned up the wound on the top of his head and dressed it, before driving him off to hospital. Anyone who came near him could tell from the cold, hard stare in his eyes, that Max was not someone who would welcome questions. The policemen knew exactly who Max was and realised he would not be changing his story. They assumed he had fallen out with a dissatisfied junkie customer or had had a run-in with an ex-boyfriend. Either way, they couldn't have cared less. It was just one more thing to go on Max's file, waiting for the day when they eventually had something concrete on him and were ready to pull him in.

When he had finished wrecking the house, Max stood in the front hall, panting, his hunger for revenge still not sated. His eyes flickered in his ugly head like some prehistoric reptile searching for new prey. Everything was silent around him as a plan hatched in the primeval swamp of his brain. He ran out of the house, not bothering to close the door after him, to his elderly, elegant Porsche and took off across town in an angry roar of acceleration.

His destination was a suburban mansion in Dyke Road, with views out across the town to the tranquil sea beyond. All was peaceful inside the house. The master, whose income supported the grand edifice, had not yet returned from his work in the City. His wife was watching the children in a concert at their school a few miles away.

The Filipino maid was working in the laundry room, folding clothes, which had just come out of the washing machine, into neat piles. She planned to iron them later while watching the little black-and-white television which her employers had given her in the scullery.

There was a back door from the scullery to the terraced garden behind, where the swimming pool lay peacefully under its cover and the barbecue stood waiting for the weekend. It was this door that Max kicked in. It was not locked but he didn't have any patience left in him for subtleties like door handles.

He grabbed the maid by the throat, just as he had Joe a few hours earlier, lifting her clean off her feet and smashing her head back against the wall. He then pushed his face so close to hers that his lips brushed against her ear as he spoke.

'My Doris has run away from home, Doris,' he said. 'And I'm broken-bloody-hearted. I want her back and I'm relying on you to help me. Otherwise I'm going to kill you. Do you understand?'

She didn't respond, too terrified to move.

'Do you understand?' He shook her and she emitted a squeak of confirmation.

'The moment you hear from her you will ask her where she is. You will tell her you want to run away too and you want to join her. Ask her for her address. And you will then give me that address. Do you understand?' He shook her again and her eyes rolled in her head like marbles, her teeth clicking together.

'If you hear from her and do not tell me, I will know. I will know because you are not the only one. One of the others will tell me if you hold out on me, and I will find you wherever you are and kill you. Any girl that doesn't do as I tell her, dies. Very slowly and painfully. Do you understand?'

She nodded and then slumped onto the floor as he let go of her. She sat there, silently sobbing into her hands as Max slammed his way out of the house. There were several more Dorises for him to call on before the night was over.

Joe was waiting in the departure lounge of Manila Airport when he received a call from London. His face was hurting and he noticed that people were giving him a wide berth.

'Joe, is that you?' a woman's voice asked down the phone.

'Yes.' He tried to move his jaw as little as he could when talking, to minimise the stabs of pain.

'It's Annie. I'm calling from the flat. Hugo's here.'

'On his own?'

'He just turned up, looking for you. I found him asleep in your room when I went in to look for a T-shirt. What shall I do?'

'Ring his mother.' Joe dictated Fliss' number. 'And tell them both I'm about to board a plane and should be back in London in around fifteen hours.'

'He wants to talk to you.'

'Put him on.'

'Hi, Dad.' Hugo's voice sounded blissfully untroubled.

'What are you doing there, Hugo? Your mother's worried. You have to stop doing this. You're supposed to be at school.'

'I wanted to see you.'

'I told you I was going to be away for a few days.'

'I forgot.'

'Annie is going to ring Mummy. You must talk to her and tell her you are fine. Okay? I'll be back soon.'

'Okay. Love you Dad.'

'I love you too, son.'

He hung up and slumped back into his seat. Relieved and despairing at the same time. And just slightly proud of a boy who could be so unconcerned about the dangers of the world outside his homes and school. Other passengers waiting for Joe's flight were starting to fill the seats around him and he noticed a group of three local girls huddling nervously together. They kept checking their tickets and boarding passes, their eyes darting around them as if unsure whether they were in the right place. Every so often they would dissolve into giggles.

Joe noticed that they all had large, well-rounded breasts which they seemed particularly keen to show off in tight T-shirts. It was as though they were new acquisitions which they were exceptionally proud of, if a little uncertain how to wear. If he hadn't been in so much pain from his face, he would have talked to them. He was willing to bet money that they all answered to the name 'Doris'.

At the same time as Joe was waiting for his plane, Cordelia had popped into the Gloucester Place flat to see Doris. She blinked with surprise as she walked in. The place was so startlingly clean. The windows had been polished to such a level there didn't appear to be any glass in them. The sunshine streamed through, bouncing and reflecting on the dozens of different polished surfaces. Doris was on the phone in the kitchen, absent-mindedly wiping a work surface as she talked. She hadn't heard Cordelia coming in.

'You just go,' she was saying. 'You don't put up with any more of her shit. She's ignorant woman. Thinks you her slave. You come here. I give you address. Then we maybe get jobs and earn money and go back home together. Yes?'

Cordelia waited patiently as Doris dictated the Gloucester Place address to someone at the other end and hung up.

'They won't be turning up in the next twenty-four hours, will they?' she asked, making Doris jump and give a little shriek of surprise. 'It's just that I need to use the flat tonight for some American visitors I've got to pick up from Heathrow. I was going to ask you to come over to Earls Court for the night.'

'That's okay,' Doris said, recovering herself. 'My friend is working for a bad woman in Brighton. Makes her work night and day. But she not yet ready to leave. She is frightened. She just want somewhere to go if things get too bad. We go to Earls Court now?'

'I need to get in some shopping. You want to come with me? You've done a brill job cleaning this place up.'

'I like to work. My grandmother always told me that hard work was direct route to heaven.'

'Yeah, my Nan comes out with stuff like that too,' Cordelia said. 'Come on, let's go shopping. The limo's waiting downstairs.'

Two hours later they arrived back at the flat, laden down with bags from Selfridges food hall. They stocked the fridge with champagne, Coke, beer, smoked salmon and a dozen different ready-made dishes, and completely filled the bread bin and piled high the fruit bowl.

'Your visitors very hungry people,' Doris commented as she emptied the last of the bags.

'They are people who like to have what they want when they want it,' Cordelia agreed. 'And we like to keep them happy.'

When they had finished putting everything away, Doris packed her overnight bag and they went back down to the street to find the limousine. The driver was circling the block while he waited for them to come out.

Had they drawn away two minutes later, Doris might well have recognised the Porsche that turned into the street and nosed slowly along the curb as if looking for an address. She would certainly have recognised one of the three men who climbed out of the car, once they had found what they were looking for and had parked around the corner.

Joe's face throbbed agonisingly throughout the flight, keeping him in a permanent state of half-sleep as he swallowed pain-killers every few hours in the dark roar of the plane's economy section.

He didn't see the girls in their tight T-shirts again until they were all queuing to get through passport control at Heathrow. The official in the booth carefully inspected every non-European passport that went by, and seemed to want to know more about the girls and their reasons for coming into the country. Joe was too far back in the queue to be able to hear exactly what was being said, but he saw another official being summoned to question the girls. The queue waited with a nervous, suppressed impatience to be through the ordeal. No one wanted to make a protest about the delay, for fear of drawing attention to themselves and becoming the next objects of scrutiny.

After what seemed like an age, the officials seemed to decide the girls deserved the benefit of the doubt and let them through. The queue continued to edge forward. When Joe reached the front he saw the hard stare of the woman in the booth resting on his face.

'What happened to you?' she asked, trying to compare the picture in the passport with the reality a few feet away from her.

'I had a car accident,' Joe lied. 'I cut my face on the windscreen.'

179

'No seat-belt?' she enquired and, for a moment, Joe wondered if that would be enough of a criminal act to have him barred from re-entering the country.

'Faulty seat-belt,' he replied. He could feel himself blushing at the lie, but felt confident a little extra colour would not be noticeable amongst the dressings and bruises.

She nodded him through and he made his way to the baggage reclaim area. The three girls were already there, waiting for their luggage to emerge. When it came it consisted of the same pitiful little sports bags he had seen in the bedrooms in Brighton and Eaton Square. They could easily have taken them on board as hand-luggage had they been a little more worldly-wise.

His own bag came out immediately after theirs and he found himself pushing his trolley through the customs channel just behind them as they went ahead, tottering on their cheap platform shoes. A few, apparently bored, customs officials watched them all pass, perched on the edges of their desks. The girls looked like obvious targets for searching to Joe, but maybe that was the point, they simply looked too obvious. None of the officials moved to stop them. In fact, none of them actually registered any facial expressions at all.

Joe came out through the swing doors onto the public concourse behind the girls. There were lines of waiting friends, relatives and taxi drivers leaning over the rails, watching the faces in search of the ones they had come to meet.

A chill of horror rippled through him as his eyes came into direct contact with Max's. For what seemed like an eternity Max's watery gaze did not flicker, and Joe thought he was about to jump over the rails and attack him. The eyes disengaged and Max ducked down, coming under the rails and moving towards Joe in the crowd of arriving passengers. Joe looked for an avenue of escape but there was none. Max walked directly at him and Joe prepared himself to punch first. Then Max spoke.

'Good evening ladies,' he said to the three girls. 'My name is Max and I am your driver for this evening.' The girls giggled and allowed him to steer them towards the exit. Joe could not help thinking that they were like little rabbits gratefully accepting the hospitality of the biggest and baddest wolf in the forest.

As he looked around him, Joe realised that a number of other people were looking at him, glancing quickly away as he caught their eyes. It was the state of his face that was attracting attention. But it was also acting as a disguise. Max's gaze had simply been attracted by a man with a bandaged face.

As Max loaded the delighted girls into his Porsche in the short-term car park, and Joe found a taxi to take him to Fliss' house, Cordelia's limousine slid to the main doors of Terminal Four. Heads turned as the driver got out and walked smartly round to open the back door and allow Cordelia to step out. She was wearing a blonde wig and a light summer dress which showed off her figure in every way. Any passers-by who troubled to make a judgement as to who she might be, would probably have decided she was a member of a girl band, or a young soap opera star off to New York and the big time.

'Thanks, mate,' she said to the driver. 'I could get used to this lifestyle.'

'Me too,' he grinned. 'Beats mini-cabbing.'

She gave him a wink before throwing her head back and striding into the terminal with the confidence of a supermodel.

She walked across the concourse to the arrivals hall, exactly where Max had been standing just a short time before. She had checked from the car that the flight she was meeting was on time. She had also memorised the pictures which had been faxed to her of the men she was to meet and accommodate. She bought herself a bottle of water and waited patiently with the crowd, watching the arrival doors.

Two flights came through without her targets on board. Then she saw them. They were both in their forties and looked like old-fashioned salesmen in their dark single-breasted suits and conservative ties. They had neat haircuts and handsome, open faces. Cordelia made herself known to them and they both allowed their eyes to roam approvingly up and down her body. She smiled sweetly, biting her bottom lip with her perfect white teeth.

'If you would like to follow me,' she said, with a flutter of her eyelashes and a dip of her head. 'There's a car waiting. Did you have a good flight?'

The two men made stumblingly flirtatious conversation as they attempted to keep up with her brisk pace. Cordelia was anxious to get out of the airport as quickly as possible. She preferred to be on home territory. There were too many cameras and security staff in airports.

The men sat either side of her in the back of the car and one of them allowed his hand to rest on her bare thigh. The other man followed suit on her other thigh. Both of them ran their fingers upwards, gently easing her legs apart and pushing up her skirt.

'I think we should get to know each other a bit better first, don't you, guys?' Cordelia said, firmly placing both their hands on their own bulging laps and crossing her legs. 'I should try to get a few minutes sleep if I were you. What with the jet lag and all.'

The men exchanged knowing glances and stayed silent, staring out at the dreary passing scenery of West London, darting the odd glances at Cordelia's pert profile when they thought she wasn't looking. Cordelia didn't miss a single look.

The driver dropped them outside the block of flats in Gloucester Place and unloaded their luggage from the boot. The men picked the cases up themselves and followed Cordelia up the steps and into the block. The driver climbed back in and drove away to find a parking space, whilst Cordelia exchanged greetings with Bernie, the doorman. They then made their way up in the lift.

There was no sign of any forced entry on the front door of the flat. It was only once Cordelia had inserted her key and pushed the door open in a grand gesture, that the sight and smell hit them. The flat, which had looked like a show home from a glossy magazine when she and Doris had left it, now resembled a particularly foul squat. Everything that could be torn up and destroyed was lying in the centre of the room, like a bonfire awaiting a match. Blinds, furniture, pictures, curtains, rugs, kitchen equipment, bottles from the bar, everything was slashed and smashed and tossed onto the heap. Even the parquet flooring had been ripped up and added to the chaos. Wires hung from the demolished ceiling and everywhere on the walls and windows there seemed to be shit smeared and spread in wild, foul-smelling, nonsensical graffiti.

'Jesus Christ,' one of the men said, covering his mouth and nose with his hand.

'What the fuck happened here?' the other asked, backing away, his eyes darting in all directions, as if expecting an ambush.

Cordelia already had her phone out. 'Car' she said, and the number gave a few rings. 'It's me,' she said as soon as the driver picked up. 'We have to get out of here quickly. Bring the car back to the entrance. Fast as you can.' She pushed the men back outside the door. 'We'll find you somewhere else,' she told them.

As they went down in the lift with all their luggage, she put the phone to her mouth again. 'Len,' she said.

'Dad,' she said when Len replied. 'It's me. We can't use the flat. Someone's been there. You'll have to set us up with a hotel room or an alternative address. We'll be in the car.'

The car hadn't managed to get back to them by the time they emerged onto the street and the three of them stood together, Cordelia silent and thoughtful, the two men suddenly nervous and showing their jet lag. Cordelia felt vulnerable in her flimsy dress, exposed on the empty pavement as the traffic streamed by in the cooling night air.

CHAPTER FIFTEEN

Hugo, in his pyjamas and dressing-gown, was sitting in the kitchen with Geoffrey, his grandfather, when Joe arrived at Fliss' house. They had obviously just eaten and Rosa, the Spanish housekeeper, was busy tidying around them.

'Good God!' his ex-father-in-law exclaimed as he saw Joe's face. 'What the hell happened to you?'

'Minor road accident in Manila,' Joe lied fluently, catching Hugo in mid-air as the boy launched himself across the room, wrapping his legs around his father's waist and his arms around his neck. Joe staggered back under the force of the welcome. 'Boy, you are putting on weight,' he laughed.

'Want a drink, old man?' Geoffrey asked.

'Thank you, yes. That would be very welcome.'

Geoffrey poured them each a scotch and Joe sat down at the table.

'Manila, eh?' Geoffrey said. 'Knew a chap whose son went out there and never came back. Pevensey. Member of the Landowners' Association. Place up in Norfolk somewhere. Boy went completely native apparently. Runs a string of brothels.'

'I met him,' Joe said. 'He seems to think he's landed in paradise.'

'Dare say he does,' Geoffrey said, sitting down beside him. 'There's not many of us who haven't dreamed of doing something similar at some stage or another, eh?'

'What's a brothel?' Hugo enquired.

'Hugo and I have been having a chat.' Geoffrey went on, ignoring the question. 'I was telling him I think he'll end up being a great explorer one day. Or possibly a habitual escapee from some prison camp somewhere. That school doesn't seem to be able to hold onto him for ten seconds.'

'Don't encourage him, Granddad,' Joe said, with what he hoped was the expected solemnity of a responsible father. 'He causes his mother a lot of grief with these escapades. And he has got to stop it.'

'Oh, I've told him that,' Geoffrey agreed. 'He understands all that. Don't you, lad?'

'Yes, Granddad.' Hugo had clambered onto his father's knee and was studying the dressing on his face carefully. 'Is Manila really cool?'

'It was exciting,' Joe said. 'Where's your mother? I thought she would be here.'

'She's gone to a party with Paolo,' Hugo said. 'Prince Charles is going to be there.'

'She said they won't be late,' Geoffrey said. 'She left me on sentry duty. To make sure he doesn't dig his way out again.'

'What's happened to Nanny Harris?' Joe asked.

'Nanny Harris has gone into semi-retirement now Hugo's boarding. About time too. The woman's older than I am. I believe as we speak she's staying with friends on the Isle of Wight.'

Hugo appeared not to be listening, suddenly absorbed in his own thoughts.

'How did you get all the way to London, Hugo?' Joe asked.

'I was having a Sunday out with Ben and his family. They live in Chiswick. So I caught a bus to Earls Court. I forgot you were going away.'

'That's terrible,' Joe said. 'Ben's family must have been worried out of their minds.'

'Sorry,' Hugo said and grinned. 'Where is Manila anyway?'

'In the Far East. But don't keep changing the subject. You've got to understand that it isn't safe for a little boy to be running around London on his own. You must never go anywhere without telling us or your teachers where you are. Do you understand?'

'Yes. The Far East is near Japan, isn't it?'

'You're changing the subject again. Do you understand how important it is you don't keep doing this?'

'Yes, Dad.' There was an edge of impatience in the boy's voice. 'You don't have to keep going on. I understand. Will you be taking me back to school?'

'Is it that bad?'

'No. It's boring, mainly.'

'Hugo was telling me he doesn't really have many friends,' Geoffrey said. 'I was explaining that sometimes it takes a bit of time to build up friendships. But those are the ones that last.'

'The others don't like me,' Hugo said, all his attention going into building a pyramid with the various plates and cups and glasses that were still standing around on the table.

'Why do you think that?' Joe asked, feeling a stab of pain in his heart.

'They tell me. They're always saying how weird I am. I get fed up with it.'

'Well, your mother and I will start to look around for another school. A day school,' Joe said. 'But you do have to go back for the rest of this term at least.'

'No offence,' Hugo said. 'But do we have to go in the Fiat?'

'No,' Joe laughed. 'We'll try to arrange for something less embarrassing. Come on, let's get you to bed.'

His tiredness from the trip, coupled with the throbbing pain in his cheek, all added to the weight of sadness that pressed on Joe's heart as he put Hugo to bed in the room which he and Fliss had spent so much time organising for their baby son when they were waiting for him to be born. There was a stack of old soft toys, each of them carrying a different memory, and

187

pictures on the wall which the boy had probably outgrown. Pride of place now went to the computer, and the television which doubled as a PlayStation.

Joe found one of Hugo's favourite books and settled himself on a beanbag beside the bed. He read aloud until Hugo's breathing had sunk into the steady rhythm of sleep.

By the time he was coming back downstairs Fliss and Paolo, both in evening dress, were letting themselves in through the front door.

'What happened to you?' Fliss wasn't able to stop herself from laughing at the sight of Joe's face. She seemed to have had a bit too much to drink.

'A little accident in Manila. It's nothing.'

'Have you seen Hugo?' she asked.

'Yes.'

'Have you given him a talking to?'

'I've tried, but I don't think it'll have much effect,' Joe said, coming the rest of the way downstairs. 'It's like water off a duck's back. He seems to be totally without fear.'

'Well, you've got to get a grip on him,' Fliss said. 'You're supposed to be his father.'

Joe opened his mouth to respond, but changed his mind. Paolo gave an embarrassed cough and moved as if to escape through to the kitchen.

'Darling, wait,' Fliss commanded him. 'I need your support. Neither of you seem to be taking this seriously. Why does everything always end up being my responsibility?'

'I'll take him back to the school tomorrow and talk to the headmaster myself,' Joe said, feeling his temper rising and forcing himself to control it. The worst thing for Hugo now would be for him and Fliss to go to war. 'I'll need to rent a car. I don't think it will help his credibility to turn up in my old Fiat.'

'You can take the Range Rover,' Paolo volunteered, eager to show he was being supportive. 'We're not using it tomorrow.'

Joe was about to decline and then thought better of it. It was time to be gracious. He was going to need Paolo as an ally. 'Thank you,' he said, curtly, before turning back to Fliss. 'Then you and I will start looking at local schools where he can be a day boy.'

'I'm not sure we should allow him to get away with it that easily…' Fliss started.

'Let's talk about this when I'm less jet-lagged and you're more sober,' Joe said, irritably.

Fliss took a deep intake of breath and glared at him. 'Piss off, Joe!' she said, and stormed off upstairs.

Paolo exchanged a sympathetic raised eyebrow with Joe and showed him to the door, pulling out a bunch of keys from his pocket. 'The Range Rover is parked in the mews at the back,' he said. 'Take it home and then come back and get Hugo in the morning.'

'Cheers.' Joe took the keys and nodded his appreciation. He had a feeling Paolo genuinely wanted to help him with Hugo, and he resented feeling grateful.

'Bloody hell, Joe!' Cordelia exclaimed as he came into the kitchen in Earls Court. 'What happened to your face?'

Doris was cleaning the cooker while Cordelia and Annie sat drinking wine at the table.

'I bumped into your friendly plastic surgeon in Manila,' Joe said to Doris.

'Mr Rose?' Doris looked shocked. 'Mr Rose was in Manila again? That man works so hard. He helps so many people.'

'Chris Rose did your operation?' Cordelia asked her.

'You know this man?' Joe asked Cordelia, slumping down into a chair and allowing Annie to pour him a glass of wine.

'Everyone knows Chris Rose,' she replied. 'He did Mum's face. Several times. He's supposed to be the best in London. Dad's used him to patch himself up once or twice and I know a few blokes he's given completely new identities to.' She pointed at Joe's face. 'He did that to you?'

'Well, not personally. But I'm pretty sure he instructed the gentlemen who did.'

'He's working with Maisie Martin?' Cordelia seemed to be trying to work out something. 'Seems a bit strange.'

'Why?' Joe asked.

'Well, no offence, Doris; but have you seen the mess her chest's in? Not exactly precision surgery. Why would Maisie want to fork out for one of the most expensive surgeons in the world just to do a botched-up job like that? She could have got a first year medical student to do it for a bag of jelly beans.'

'You want I cook you something, American Joe?' Doris piped up cheerfully.

'No, I'm fine thanks,' he said. 'Are you staying here at the moment?'

'Cordelia need apartment for important clients. So I have come here to look after you all.' Doris gave a little giggle of pleasure at the prospect.

'Lucky she came here, as it turned out,' Cordelia said. 'We can't have been out of there for more than a couple of hours before someone let themselves in and destroyed the place. It's a right mess.'

'Where are your "important clients" then?' Joe asked, unable to keep a hint of sarcasm out of his voice. 'Are they camping out in my room?'

'They're at the Savoy,' Cordelia replied. 'They had an empty suite. Thank God.'

'So, who trashed the apartment?'

'Gawd knows,' Cordelia said. 'But Dad's pretty sure it's someone linked to Mike and Maisie Martin, and he's very pissed off about it. He thinks they want to put him out of business.'

'Which business is this?' Joe asked, but Cordelia ignored the question.

'I'm not so sure, myself,' she went on. 'I've got a feeling that if it was Maisie's people, they may have been looking for Doris rather than trying to reach out to Dad. I think they were giving her a warning. I don't think they know the flat has anything to do with Dad.'

Joe looked across at the Filipino who appeared completely unconcerned at the possibility she might have been the target of the attack. It was as though she had complete faith in her new-found friends and their ability to protect her.

'I saw Tikki while I was in the Philippines, Doris,' Joe told her.

'Ah, yes,' Doris smiled broadly. 'My village is beautiful, no? One day I would like to go back and build myself a house, right next to my mother's. And start family of my own.'

'What the hell are you doing here, then?' Annie enquired.

'You need money to build a nice house and buy furniture,' Doris said, her face filled with seriousness.

'If Chris Rose is involved in whatever scam the Martins are pulling, here,' Cordelia was thinking aloud, 'he would be the one we need to get to, if we want to find out what's going on. He would be the weak link in the chain. He has a big mouth and a lot of weaknesses.'

'What sort of weaknesses?' Joe asked.

'Drink, coke, cannabis, pretty girls.' Cordelia shrugged as if to say the list could go on for ever.

'Could you get to him?' Joe asked.

'I couldn't, no,' she said. 'He's known me all my life. He would never open up to me. You need someone new, someone he'd want to impress.'

They both turned simultaneously to look at Annie, who had been listening to the conversation with as much of her mind as the wine bottle had left her with.

'What?' she wanted to know.

'He'd show you a good time,' Cordelia said. 'He throws money around like there's no tomorrow. You could go to him as a potential customer and let his aged hormones do the rest.'

'I don't need a facelift,' Annie protested. 'Do I?'

'You don't have to commit yourself,' Cordelia said. 'Make an appointment and tell him you're worried about your future career. Tell him you want to be sure you're doing the right things to make your face last. You're an actress. You can do it.'

'He's hardly going to tell me all about importing illegal Filipinos at an appointment,' Annie protested.

'Make him fancy you,' Cordelia said. 'Shouldn't be hard. You're quite attractive really. Specially to an old geezer like him.'

'Thanks!'

'Get him to ask you out and take it from there. It shouldn't be beyond your skills to get him talking. I'm sure Dad would be happy to pay for any information you get out of him.'

'Hang on.' Joe rubbed his eyes to try to force the tiredness away for a few more moments. 'This could be dangerous. These people are killing girls who threaten to expose them.'

'*Killing*?' Annie rocked back in her chair. 'They're *killing* people?'

'We don't know that for sure,' Joe admitted. 'But a body has been found which would seem to be one of Doris' friends.'

Doris stopped her work and sat down at the table with them, sinking into the chair as if finally defeated by exhaustion, both from her endless work and from being reminded of her missing friend.

'They aren't people to kid around with,' Joe said. 'I just thought I ought to warn you of that before you go off on some mission of discovery.' Cordelia squeezed Doris' hand comfortingly. 'I really have to go now,' Joe said and stumbled away to his room, collapsing onto his bed fully clothed as sleep took over.

'What do you think then?' Cordelia asked Annie once Joe had gone. 'Would you give it a go?'

'Sure.' Annie drained the wine bottle into her glass. 'Sounds like Mr Rose could be exciting company.'

'Attagirl!' Cordelia said and Doris gave Annie an excited round of applause.

Joe was woken by his phone ringing. At first, as he fumbled around trying to find it, he thought it must be Fliss calling to discover why he hadn't yet arrived to pick up Hugo. It wasn't. It was Adele.

'Listen,' she said, her voice urgent and discouraging of any small talk. Not that Joe could have mustered any anyway. 'Marion Ray's in town and she wants to see you again. Can you make lunch at the Dorchester?'

'What's the time?'

'Nine o'clock.'

'Shit. No. I wouldn't be able to make that. I have to get Hugo back to school.'

'Can't his mother do that?'

'No.' Joe didn't intend to get into a conversation with Adele about his relationship with his ex-wife. 'I could make it for tea-time. Ask if I can see her for cucumber sandwiches at about four. She'll like that.'

'Christ, Joe,' Adele sounded angry. 'I thought you were keen for this job. She's not the sort of person you mess around.'

'I'm not messing her around, Adele,' Joe remained firm. 'I just can't make lunch. Let me know if she can see me later.'

He hung up and went in search of some breakfast.

Two hours later he and Hugo were heading down the motorway to Sussex.

'I was serious with what I was saying last night, you know,' Joe said.

'What was that?' Hugo asked, most of his attention focused on making Paolo's CD player work.

'About running away from school all the time. You can't keep doing it. Your mother and I understand you don't like it there and we will look at other schools. But it'll take a little time. If you keep going off on your own you're likely to end up getting into real trouble.'

'Yeah, yeah. I know, Dad. Don't keep on.'

'But if I don't keep on you just do it again.'

'I understand!' Hugo spoke firmly and Joe decided to let silence fall for a few minutes, to give the boy time to think over his words, and for him to make sure he didn't lose his temper.

'Dad,' Hugo said a few minutes later.

'Yeah?'

'How come we never get to see your Mum and Dad?'

'You have seen them.' Joe protested, taken by surprise. 'They came over for your christening.'

'Oh, right! Like I remember that.'

'We went over there when you were five.'

Hugo gave him a look which suggested he wasn't going to be fobbed off quite so easily.

'It's a long way to America from here,' Joe ended lamely.

'Did you run away from home?'

Joe couldn't stop himself from laughing. 'I suppose in a way I did. But I was eighteen, not eight, when I left home. There's a big difference.' He remembered the stifling boredom of his parents' well-meaning company which had eventually driven him to leave the country altogether. He could all too easily imagine the effect which Hugo's dull-witted peer group might be having on him.

'I think children are more mature these days,' Hugo said.

'I dare say you are,' Joe agreed, trying not to smile. 'But not that much. It also happens to be legal to go wandering around on your own when you're eighteen. It is not legal for you to keep walking out of school when you're eight.'

'I didn't walk out of school this time. I walked out of Ben's house.'

'You know what I mean. Doesn't anyone ask you what you're up to? Bus conductors, ticket collectors, those sorts of people?'

'Not often. When they do I just tell them you're meeting me off the train or the bus or whatever. That always makes them happy.'

The phone rang and Hugo was glad of the diversion. He answered it and passed it over.

'It's for you,' he said.

'Joe? It's Adele. She can see you at three, but only briefly. It would have been better if you had been able to get there for lunch.'

'I'll be there at three,' Joe promised. 'Thanks for setting that up.'

'You're welcome,' Adele said and hung up. Joe could tell she hadn't yet forgiven him for putting Hugo before his work.

When they reached the school, Joe made sure he parked Paolo's car directly outside the front door, so any passing boys would be able to see Hugo descending from it. He then steered the small boy in to see the headmaster. He noticed Hugo seemed utterly unconcerned by the prospect of being told off, whereas he was feeling decidedly jittery himself.

As he listened to the headmaster pontificating about Hugo's duties towards his school, his friends and his family, Joe became increasingly convinced they had to find another school. The man sounded like he was speaking from a pulpit placed firmly in the nineteen-fifties. Once or twice Joe was tempted to intervene on his son's behalf, but, since Hugo appeared not to be listening anyway, he decided to save his energies.

'Run along now, Hugo, and find out which class you are supposed to be in.' The headmaster eventually dismissed him, obviously having decided he had imparted enough wisdom to the lad for one day.

Hugo, waking from whatever daydream he had been in, jumped up, kissed his father goodbye and disappeared. Joe felt sick with unhappiness as he watched the dark panelled door closing after his son.

'Mr Tye,' the headmaster said. 'You have a remarkable young man there. You can trust us to make the most of him.'

'To start with you had better concentrate on keeping him under armed guard,' Joe replied, the unexpected compliment having taken him by surprise.

'Oh, I don't think we'll be having any more trouble. It always takes them a while to settle down. I think he's learnt his lesson.'

Joe didn't share the headmaster's confidence.

On the way back to London he stopped at a service station to buy himself a sandwich and a black coffee. The jet lag was starting to creep up on him again. He drove straight to the Dorchester, parking Paolo's car amongst the limousines on the forecourt, relieved that he hadn't arrived in his Fiat Panda. He slipped a ten-pound note into the doorman's hand with the keys and told him he would be with Miss Ray if they needed him.

The sitting-room of Marion Ray's suite was filled with people on telephones. A publicist was shouting at a journalist and an assistant was arguing about a dress that should have been delivered. Two men in suits sat with their briefcases on their laps and their phones to their ears as they carried on a conversation with one another at the same time as the people on their phone lines. Another woman was changing the flowers and Marion Ray's secretary promised to let the star know Joe was there.

'So there you are, you genius writer,' Marion Ray's voice cut through the babble of the room like a knife as she emerged from the bedroom with a hairdresser and make-up artist trailing behind her. 'These people are driving me mad. They want to take my picture and I keep telling them, "I'm an old woman. It's the grey hairs and wrinkles that make me interesting", but they want me to be twenty again!' She elbowed the others aside and sat beside Joe, her hand on his knee, her eyes only inches away from his, her voice like a runaway train.

'My dear, you look terrible! What happened to your face?'

'A little accident,' Joe tried to wave it aside. 'It was nothing.'

She seemed happy to change the subject. 'I read the book you did for Garbo. It was stunning! Wonderful! I wept. How did you ever get her to tell you all that? All the childhood stuff. So lyrical. So beautiful. You must be a magician as well as a genius writer.'

'Thank you. I...'

'Will you be able to make me sound as wise and interesting? Can you do it for me? Can you make them weep for me?'

'Of course,' he laughed, allowing the tidal wave of flattery and enthusiasm to wash him away. 'But only if you can find the time to talk to me.'

'Time, pah!' She flapped her hands at him as if trying to cool his face. 'If I had more time I would be a rich woman!'

'Take a week off and we'll go to a mountain cabin somewhere,' Joe coaxed. 'It'll be like an extended therapy session for you.'

'My God, doesn't that sound like heaven. Let's do it. Get your people to contact my people and arrange dates.'

'Couldn't we just do it between us?'

'I need my diary. I don't have it.' She called to her secretary. 'I don't have my diary!'

'I can get your diary,' the girl said, smiling calmly.

'I don't have the time. We have to do these damn pictures. Talk to her.' She waved Joe and the secretary towards one another like a matchmaker. 'Let's make it work. You're a genius. I want to spill my heart out to you. We have to do this thing.' She leant forward, and kissed him on the unbandaged cheek and then was gone, back into the bedroom in a flurry of activity, shouting orders at the photographer waiting for her inside.

'She's starting work on a new film,' the girl said apologetically. 'There's no chance she could allocate more than a few hours to you until that's over.'

'I'll take whatever time she can spare,' Joe said.

'I'll ring your agent when I've found some slots,' the girl promised, before hurrying off into the bedroom in answer to a call from her employer.

Joe went back downstairs, his mind reeling from the chaos of the scene he had just left. Focussing once more on the matter in hand, he went in search of Paolo's Range Rover, to return it to its rightful owner.

CHAPTER SIXTEEN

Mr Christopher Rose, surgeon to the stars, looked very different in his Harley Street consulting room from the figure which Joe had described to Annie a few days before. His pin-striped suit had creases as sharp as scalpels and the blood-red handkerchief in his top pocket matched his tie and socks to perfection. His grey hair swept back and his skin tanned, he gripped Annie's hand in a firm greeting. She felt herself being carried away by the sheer force of the man's personality before he had even opened his mouth.

'Good afternoon, my dear,' he boomed. 'Come in and tell me what's on your mind.'

He guided her to a deep armchair, filled with exotically patterned cushions, returning to sit in his own wing-backed chair behind a mighty oak table, upon which a single yellow legal pad and silver fountain pen lay waiting.

He took her details. She gave her parents' address and the number of the mobile that Cordelia had lent her.

'So,' he put down his pen and steepled his immaculately manicured fingers in front of him, resting his chin on the top. 'What do you think I can do for you?'

'I don't know really,' she giggled rather foolishly. 'I'm a model and actress and I want to make sure that my career lasts as long as possible. I don't want to leave it too late to start taking little nips and tucks which might help to keep me looking young. I also,' she realised she was moving away from the script which she and Cordelia and Joe had worked on together, but she couldn't help herself, 'have a little mole which I am slightly afraid may be growing.'

He listened patiently, took a few more notes, and then invited her to step behind an antique screen, lie down on the couch and allow him to examine her.

As Annie lay back, Rose washed his hands ostentatiously in a nearby basin, dried them on a snow-white towel, and then sat on a stool beside her. She felt vulnerable and trembled as his fingers confidently and lightly touched the skin on her face, testing, lifting, moving. He examined around her eyes and under her chin. She was sure he would be able to feel she was shaking.

'And where is this mole?' he asked.

'On my shoulder.'

'Would you mind unbuttoning your blouse and showing me?' he said.

She unbuttoned with clumsy fingers and he gently lifted the material away to reveal her bra. The strap covered the mole and he moved it aside, examining the skin beneath with minute attention. She felt the slightest whisper of his breath on her bare skin.

'Very good, my dear,' he said, sitting back. 'Would you like to put yourself together and then come back out? Would you care for tea?'

'Thank you, yes.'

Almost as soon as she had sat back down in the chair an elderly secretary brought in a tray with a china teapot and matching cups and saucers. She poured them each a cup of tea through a silver strainer and presented Annie with hers, offering her a plate laden with delicate biscuits. All the while Chris Rose continued to write on his note pad. As soon as the other woman had gone, and the heavy consulting room door had clicked shut behind her, he laid down his pen and took a sip from his tea.

'To be honest, my dear, I think it's too soon for you to worry yourself about cosmetic surgery, although I think you are very wise to be thinking about it so far in advance. I am also fairly confident your mole is quite harmless. In fact, rather fetching. But it's always wise to keep an eye on these things, just in case.

'If you're absolutely determined to have some sort of cosmetic treatment I would like to recommend you to a colleague of mine. An excellent man whose work is, I believe, superior to mine in many ways.'

'Oh,' Annie was startled. She hadn't expected this.

'This is only if you absolutely insist on going ahead.'

'I see. Why would you not take me on as your own patient?' she asked.

'It's a question of ethics, Annie. May I call you Annie? It's a question of ethics. I think you're one of the most beautiful creatures I have ever clapped eyes on. I am very much hoping you'll agree to have dinner with me some time this week. Were I to take you on as a patient, it would be quite impossible for me to make any such suggestion. Does that make sense?'

'Yes,' she squeaked, suddenly finding it hard to get air into her lungs. She had imagined, when she had set out from Earls Court on her mission, she would be the one in control of this seduction. They had carefully planned how she would work her way into his affections with a number of visits and consultations – it was a meticulously constructed campaign. Now he had taken over control and she could do nothing to get it back. Everything Joe and Cordelia had told her about his reputation increased her nerves and intensified the excitement of his presence. She took a sip of her tea and almost swallowed it the wrong way.

'Would you, for instance,' he continued, 'be free for dinner tonight?'

'Tonight? Um, yes. I think so.'

'How splendid! Would you like me to pick you up from,' he glanced down at his notepad, 'your home?'

201

'No,' she said quickly. 'I live with my parents. I'd rather meet you somewhere.'

'Why don't you come to the house?' he said. 'I'll give you the address. Shall we say half past seven?'

'Okay.'

She came back out into Harley Street, reeling from shock and wondering whether she'd made a terrible mistake in allowing him to move so fast. She felt a familiar sensation of breathlessness at the prospect of the adventure that lay ahead.

Joe and Rod cautiously pushed open the door to the Gloucester Place apartment. There was a buzz of flies in the foul air and they both pulled their T-shirts up to cover their faces as they went in. Joe strode straight to the French windows and threw them open to allow some fresh air in. He stepped outside onto the balcony and took some deep breaths. Rod joined him.

'Bloody hell,' Rod said. 'They meant business, whoever they were.'

'It looks like it. Thank God Cordelia and Doris weren't here when they arrived,' Joe said.

'If they had been I think we'd be fishing bits of them out of skips by now,' Rod agreed.

Joe said nothing for a moment. The thought of anyone hurting Cordelia made him feel surprisingly angry. He hadn't realised quite how fond of her he was becoming.

'You think it could be the same people who cut up the other girl?' he asked.

'Could be,' Rod said. 'But then again, it could just be a rival firm, looking to hurt Len's business.'

'Do they really still behave like that?' Joe asked. 'It sounds like something from Soho in the sixties.'

'If anything it's got more cut-throat since the stakes got higher. In those days they were squabbling over a few tatty little illegal spielers and a few hundred low-rent hookers. Nowadays, with drugs and all the rest, it's big money. There's a lot of people who would be delighted to take over a slice of Len's business.'

'He told me he was winding his business interests down, preparing for retirement.'

'And you believed him?' Rod raised an eyebrow and Joe didn't reply for a moment, staring back into the wrecked flat.

'He's not into drugs, is he? He always told me that was a business he refused to be part of. Too dirty...' Joe's voice trailed away as he saw Rod's expression of disbelief.

'They all say that,' Rod said. 'Nobody gets a good press for being a drugs baron. A bit of good old-fashioned GBH, a bit of bank-robbing, or cat-burglary, a few gambling interests. The great British public likes all that. It's what you might call 'user-friendly' crime, cops and robbers stuff. But drug dealers and dope fiends, that's a different matter. That conjures up images of innocent kids overdosing in back alleys and old ladies being mugged coming out of the post office by addicts desperate for their next fix. Never mind that about a quarter of the law-abiding population use drugs every weekend, and then go back to school or work on a Monday morning without another thought.

'The public relations war has been well lost in the drugs business. So anyone who wants to set themselves up as a loveable rogue, as old Len most certainly does, is not going to want to advertise the fact that most of the criminal money in the world today comes from the pockets of kids in nightclubs. Of course Len's into drugs.'

Joe stared at him. 'Do you know this for a fact?' he asked eventually.

'Yeah, of course. Everyone in the force knows Len's dabbling.'

'So why don't they close him down?'

'He's a useful man. He comes up with good information from time to time. And we always know where to find him.'

'You mean, he's an informant?'

'I wouldn't put it that bluntly, but that's the sort of idea. The authorities know that if they ever want to get the real evil bastards…'

'Like Mike Martin?'

'Precisely. If they are ever going to get them, then they'll need the help of relatively decent blokes like Len.'

'But Len's a drug dealer?' Joe was having trouble coming to terms with the information Rod was imparting.

'You've been reading too many tabloids,' Rod sighed. 'You ever used drugs?'

'From time to time.'

'You shop at Sainsbury's for your groceries?'

'Sometimes.'

'And buy your booze there?'

'Occasionally.'

'Think the managers at Sainsbury's should be locked up for supplying you with what you want?' Rod raised his eyebrows questioningly. 'The only difference between drink and drugs is that we've decided to hand management of the drugs industry over to the criminals. If we hadn't done that it would be neatly placed somewhere between brewing and pharmaceuticals in the great global business jigsaw, earning billions for the tax men instead of providing a living to any fly boy willing to risk a jail sentence.'

Joe fell silent after Rod's outburst.

'What's Cordelia's role in all this?' he asked after a few moments' thought.

'Very minor. She's only a kid. Len wouldn't want her being put away at such a tender age. He has big plans for his girl. I would imagine she meets couriers off the planes, brings them into town and makes sure they're comfortable and have everything they need, until such time as whatever they are carrying can be moved on, and they are free to go back to wherever they've come from.'

'I saw her with some guys at the Lanesborough,' Joe said.
'You mean they were carrying drugs?'

'I would guess so.'

'Thank God for that,' Joe said. 'I thought she was on the
game.' He blushed when he realised that Rod was watching him
with an amused expression.

'And that worried you, did it?' Rod asked with a grin.

'Fuck off.' Joe grinned back.

'Well,' Rod said. 'We can't work here until it's been cleaned
up a bit. So, shall we see if we can find a quiet corner in a pub?'

When Annie arrived at Chris Rose's house in Grosvenor
Square, just a few doors away from the American embassy, he
answered the door himself. It looked as if he had only just got
in from work. He had taken off his jacket and tie, but was still
wearing his suit trousers. His shirt was as immaculately pressed
as if he had just put it on. There was the faintest hint of
expensive cologne in the air.

'Come in, my dear.' He held the door wide with a theatrical
sweep, leading her upstairs to a grand reception room, with
windows looking out over the square. Cleo Laine's voice was
crooning softly in the background.

'I've just got in and I was about to take a quick shower.
Would it be too terrible of me to sit you down here with a glass
of champagne and a little caviar? I'll be right back.'

While her host was out of the room, Annie wandered
around, examining the original works of art on the walls, the
sculptures and the furniture. There were shelves full of heavy,
illustrated art books, side by side with works of erotica. A
portrait of Chris as a young man, by Patrick Procter, hung next
to a nude woman by Lucien Freud.

She kept dipping into the caviar and sipping at the large
flute of champagne which he had left her. By the time he
returned, in a silk shirt and Armani trousers, she could already
feel herself slipping luxuriously beneath the surface of her

common sense. Everything was simply so smooth and oiled by money. It was the life she had always imagined herself leading when, as a frustrated schoolgirl, she used to dream about leaving home. She shook herself mentally, recalling what this man involved himself with in order to live like this.

She allowed him to steer her to a sofa and refill her glass. He cut her an elegant little line of cocaine on an antique hand-mirror and held it up for her to help herself. A warm glow of well-being settled onto her like a wonderful homecoming.

'I thought, if it's all right with you,' he said, after sniffing up another line himself, 'we would have a little supper at home. If you don't like the idea, we could pop down the road to the Mirabelle or the Connaught. But I just thought it would be so relaxing to stay here and get acquainted.'

Annie sat back and listened as he talked about art and love and travel. She sipped more champagne and puffed on a joint which he rolled for her, after taking the ingredients from a small, inlaid box on the mantelpiece.

When it was time to eat he led her through to a dining-room where a cold supper had been laid out by invisible hands, the candles lit, the ice bucket filled. They talked on through the meal and then he led her back to the sitting-room, describing a meal he had recently enjoyed in Manila. Through the haze of good feelings, she could dimly remember her briefing from Joe and Cordelia.

'So,' she said, as they settled onto the sofa and he put his arm around her shoulders. 'How come you were in Manila? Was it work or holiday?' She could feel the intensity of his desire for her, it was like a heat emanating from every part of him. She felt in imminent danger.

'All the girls out there,' he said, undoing the buttons on her blouse, 'want to have perfect breasts. Like these. I give them just that.'

'Implants?'

'That's right.' He slid his hand inside and lifted her breast free of the material, leaning over to kiss it.

'I've wondered about those. Do you think I should have something done to mine?' she asked as he gently slid her down on the cushions.

'You wouldn't want what they have,' he laughed. His eyes were glazed from the mixture of champagne, smoke and chemicals. The young skin of the girl in his hands was making his mouth water. 'They're just being used as a walking postal service.'

'What do you mean?' She laid her head back, allowing him to continue but focussing her attention on what he was saying.

'I mean,' he said, 'I pack them in Manila and unpack them again in London, or New York or Paris. They're just mules.'

'Pack them with what?' Her ears pricked up at what he was saying. She knew this could be the information that Joe and Cordelia had sent her for.

'With some of the pretty powder we've enjoyed this evening,' he said.

'I know what I'd like to do,' she whispered, slipping out from under him and standing up, relieved to bring to an end his attentions on the sofa. After all, she now had what she'd come for.

'What is that my dear?'

'I feel like dancing,' she said, buttoning up her blouse and running her fingers through her hair.

'Dancing?'

'Absolutely!' She made a few sample moves around the room. 'Let's go to Tramp, I've never been there.'

'It's late now,' he protested, thrown by her sudden change of pace. 'Why don't we stay here tonight and go dancing another night?'

'Oh, come on,' she laughed, teasingly, anxious not to anger him, trying to appear like an innocent, tipsy girl. 'Don't be an old bore.'

'Whatever you want,' he smiled bravely and pulled himself off the sofa.

An hour later they were dancing in Tramp. Annie was feeling good. She could see that she was exhausting him. At two o'clock she asked to leave. Once they were outside on the pavement, she told him she was getting a cab to take her home.

'Why don't you come back to Grosvenor Square?' Rose asked, obviously unsettled by the way he was losing control of the situation. Watching her body moving on the dance floor had increased his appetite for her.

'I should be getting back,' she said. 'My parents don't like me staying out all night.'

'I'd like to see you again,' Rose said. She smiled but didn't reply. A taxi drew up beside them. 'But I've got to go to New York for a couple of days. May I ring you when I get back?'

'Sure,' she said, pecking him on the cheek and climbing into the cab. 'When are you due back?'

'Here.' He hurriedly scribbled some information on the back of a calling card and passed it through the cab window to her.

'Okay,' she grinned. 'See you then. Thanks for a great evening.'

Everyone sat silently round the kitchen table in Earls Court the following morning, listening to Annie's story. Even Doris had stopped work and was sitting with them, although she was still wearing the yellow rubber gloves that Angus had bought her in recognition of his gratitude for all the cleaning she had been doing.

'You should think about asking her to stay here full-time,' he had enthused to Joe the day before, after discovering the stains on the lavatory were not actually immovable as he had believed, although it had taken Doris the best part of two hours of scrubbing to prove it. 'She's improving the environment for all of us. She's a great girl. She never stops. She's been sorting through my wardrobe for me, mending holes in pockets, taking things to the launderette that have been nestling in dark corners for years.'

Angus too was in the kitchen, a mug of tea half raised to his lips as Annie explained exactly why 'Maisie's Amazing Maids' had all been having their 'beautiful new breasts' stolen.

All eyes turned to Doris' flat chest and she too looked down at it with her mouth hanging open.

'I was carrying drugs in my tits?' she asked, incredulously. 'All that time?'

'Apparently he's a busy man, Mr Rose,' Annie said. 'Especially with all the flying back and forth to Manila and New York and Europe. He can't always do the operations as soon as the girls get to their destinations. So they have to keep carrying the stuff around until he has a spare afternoon in his diary.'

'Bloody brilliant!' Cordelia exclaimed.

The tension was broken and they all laughed.

'I'm amazed they packed you with cocaine and not heroin,' Cordelia said as the laughter subsided. 'Mostly that's what's been coming in from that part of the world. Coke normally comes in straight from South America.'

They all looked at her, shocked by her apparent knowledge of the subject. She blushed. 'Just what I've heard.'

'It does seem a long way round,' Joe agreed. 'But I guess with mules this effective,' he gestured to Doris, 'it's worth going to a bit of extra trouble.'

'So, when are you planning to see him again?' Angus asked. 'This Prince Charming.'

'Piss off, Angus,' Annie said. 'He wants to see me again, when he gets back from New York in a couple of days.'

'Do you know exactly when he's due back?' Cordelia asked.

'As a matter of fact, I do.' Annie produced the card Rose had given her. 'He told me the flight number and everything. I think he's hoping I'll be at the airport waiting to meet him. The man is seriously in heat.'

'Good work, sister,' Cordelia said, scooping up the card as Joe's phone rang. He moved away from the noise of the others to answer it.

'Joe?'

'Yes.'

'It's Adele. *Sunday International* want to buy serialisation rights to the Doris book. Could you and Doris get down to meet the editor and their people today?'

'Will you be there?'

'Of course.'

'The story has got a lot more interesting.' He told her what he had just heard and for the first time since he met her, Adele was lost for words. 'They may also be interested in the fact that Maisie, who runs this operation, is married to Mike Martin.'

'Mike Martin? The government's money-man?'

'That's the man. He has a very shady past indeed. In fact, he may be worth a book all of his own one day.'

'Okay.' Adele was obviously thinking on her feet, spotting a potential big killing on the horizon. 'Bring Doris to the office and we'll all go down to the meeting together. We can talk in the cab. This could be a very good deal.'

'We'll be there in an hour.'

He hung up and went back into the kitchen. 'Okay, Doris. We're on our way to the big time. We're going to meet a newspaper editor who wants to buy the rights to the book. If we get this right you may be able to build your house next to your mother sooner than you think. You may even be able to put in a swimming pool.'

'Which paper?' Angus asked.

'*Sunday International*,' Joe said.

'Good God,' Angus slopped his tea over himself, and Doris dabbed at him with a drying-up cloth. 'You'll need to tart her up a bit. They'll want glamour.'

'We can do that,' Annie jumped up. 'Can't we, Cordy?'

210

'Yeah!' Cordelia was up too. They each grabbed an arm and whisked the startled-looking Doris away to Annie's room.

Half an hour later Doris emerged, as if from a magazine make-over. Joe was startled-by how pretty she was with a little make-up and the right clothes to show off her fragile little body.

'You look wonderful,' he said.

'Thank you, American Joe,' she gave him a radiant smile, obviously proud of the way she looked.

They took a taxi to Regent Street. All through the journey Joe explained, very carefully, what it was the newspaper would be looking for, and warned her to say nothing unless he or Adele said it was all right.

'If you tell them anything before they have signed contracts, they'll print your story and you'll get no money at all,' he said. 'Let Adele take care of the business first and then we can start to answer their questions. Okay?'

'You the boss, American Joe,' she laughed and gave his hand an affectionate little squeeze.

On the trip from the agency to the newspaper offices, Joe filled Adele in on the details of the story so far.

'Okay,' Adele said as the taxi finally drew up. 'Let's go. Just remember we're selling the rights to a major book here, not some scummy newspaper exposé. That way we will more than double the sort of money they're willing to pay. Doris, you keep silent until we've got their signatures.'

'Yes, Ma'am,' Doris said, but Adele was already out of the cab and striding away. Joe and Doris ran to catch her up.

They were taken to a room where a group of executives in shirtsleeves were waiting for them. The editor introduced himself and they all sat down with coffee, orange juice and Danish pastries.

'So,' the editor said, 'what have you got for us, Doris?'

'At this stage,' Adele interrupted, 'I'll do the talking. Doris is writing a book about her experiences as a white slave, ghost-written by Joe Tye here, a name I'm sure you're all familiar with.'

The editor inclined his head slightly to concur that he had indeed heard of Joe.

'I believe we have bought one or two of your previous books, Joe,' he said.

Adele cut in again, determined not to allow the editor to trick either of her clients with charm. 'Then you'll know how reliable and professional he is. If this story wasn't hot, Joe wouldn't be on board.'

Joe tried hard not to smile as Adele moved her hype into top gear.

'All you need to know at this stage is that this girl was white-slaved into Britain, along with dozens of others, from the Philippines. She was brought here by an agency which is owned by a woman called Maisie. Maisie's partner in life is Mike Martin.'

She paused for effect. All the men around the conference table had sat up a little straighter. She now knew she had their full attention. She said nothing, waiting for their response.

'We are very interested in any story that might lead towards Mr Martin,' the editor admitted. 'We have a pile of files on him. We know where he's come from and we are just waiting for something big to pin on him. We already knew, by the way, that he's married to a woman called Maisie. It happened on a beach in Phuket. We bought photographs of the ceremony, but haven't had an opportunity to use them yet.'

'This is the biggest thing imaginable,' Adele said. 'The white slave trading is only the tip. It involves the mutilation of young girls' bodies and big-time drugs trafficking. It will blow your minds. And we can prove it all.'

'Fire away,' the editor said.

'No. I must have a confidentiality agreement from you first, just in case you're not able to meet our asking price and I have to go somewhere else.'

'We could agree a price now,' the editor suggested.

'You'll offer us more once you've heard the rest,' Adele said. 'I can guarantee that. Just sign this confidentiality agreement and then I'll tell you everything.' She slid two sheets of paper across the table to him.

The editor picked up one sheet and passed the other to an in-house lawyer sitting beside him. They read them through, agonisingly slowly, and then exchanged looks. The lawyer mouthed something. The editor then nodded, and signed both copies before pushing them back across the table. Adele took one copy and gave the other to the lawyer.

'These girls are being used as human parcels,' she said. 'To carry drugs around the world. In Manila they are told they can have breast enhancement operations for free, to make them more attractive to European and American men. To increase their chances of landing rich husbands.

'A top British surgeon then flies out and does the operations. The girls are thrilled. What they don't realise is that their breasts have been enlarged with bags of the highest-grade cocaine. When they arrive in England, America or mainland Europe, they're found jobs as cheap domestic labour. Then they're told they've developed lumps in their breasts and will have to have operations to remove them. The same surgeon opens them up, takes out the bags and sews them back up as quickly and crudely as possible.'

All the newspaper executives automatically glanced across at Doris' chest. She kept her eyes on the floor.

'And Martin's wife is behind all this?' the editor asked Joe.

'She runs the traffic in girls. Whether she knows about the drugs is another matter,' Joe said. 'But I would imagine she does.'

'There's more,' Adele said.

'Go on,' the editor told her.

'Some of the girls have started to complain about the way they're being treated by the people who employ them as servants – people in some of the finest families and homes in the land, incidentally. As a result they've started to disappear. It's pretty certain they're being killed. A torso has been found in a skip up north, a torso which had previously had its breasts crudely removed.'

'Jesus,' the editor said, and there was a collective sigh of astonishment and delight around the table. This was the sort of story that kept them all in the newspaper business – a story that would shock and titillate their readers, while at the same time ruffling the feathers of the establishment.

'When will the manuscript be ready to see?' the editor asked.

'In a month,' Adele said, 'if we can agree terms today. The research has already been done. Joe has been to Manila and met Doris' family and the people who introduced her to the massage parlour business. He's met with Maisie, posing as a potential customer, and he's interviewed Doris for days on end.'

Joe suppressed another smile. Adele was good at making a little sound like a lot.

'How much are you asking for?' the editor wanted to know.

'Half a million. Half now and half on delivery.'

There was another collective sigh. Even Joe's eyes flickered towards his agent for a second. Doris showed no emotion, keeping her gaze on the tips of her fingers, which lay peacefully in her lap.

'I was thinking more along the hundred thousand line,' the editor said, after a long pause.

'No,' Adele stood up.

'But I could double it,' he said, 'as long as there were a few guarantees.'

'Like what?'

'I would want Joe to make contact with Mike Martin and ask him a few questions, using our phones here with a tape running. And I would also want Joe to show us the work in progress. Say, once a week.'

'I wouldn't be willing to go below four hundred thousand,' Adele said, still standing.

The editor fell silent for a moment. 'No,' he said. 'We couldn't stretch to that.'

'Okay,' Adele bent to pick up her briefcase.

'We could say a quarter of a million. Then we'll sign the papers today, and give you the down-payment.'

'Make it three hundred thousand on the same terms,' Adele said.

The editor stared at her and everyone waited. 'It's a lot of money, Adele,' he said, eventually.

'It's worth it, and you know it,' Adele retorted.

'Very well,' the editor nodded and there was a hiss of escaping air as everyone stopped holding their breath. 'We'll pay three hundred thousand.'

CHAPTER SEVENTEEN

The kitchen in Earls Court had become a council of war. After dropping Adele back in Regent Street, Joe and Doris had returned home to try to take in everything that had happened. Joe had rung Rod and asked him to come over. Cordelia and Annie were both sitting at the table, painting their nails, and Angus had joined them, not wanting to be left out of any excitement that might be happening on his premises.

'The point is,' Joe said, 'if the *Sunday International* is going to start stirring things up, the Martins are going to want to get rid of the evidence as quickly as possible. That means any girls who are in the country, and might incriminate them, are in even greater danger than they were before.'

'They can't just go around killing people wholesale,' Annie protested. 'This is England in the new millennium, not Chicago in the nineteen-twenties.'

The others all looked at her.

'Am I being incredibly naïve?' she asked.

'What have they got to lose?' Rod asked. 'No one would miss a few Filipinos who are working in the country illegally. No offence, Doris.'

'No, sure. No problem,' Doris replied in rather a small voice.

'Doris has the telephone numbers of quite a few of them,' Joe said, turning to Doris. 'If you told them how much danger they were in, would they believe you and come to a secure house?'

'Some of them would,' Doris said. 'But some of them are too frightened of Max and of Maisie.'

'There are also some new girls who came in on the same flight as me,' Joe said. 'I guess they'll still be in Brighton, waiting for their operations or for employers to be found. We really need to get them all to somewhere safe.'

'Where would we take them?' Cordelia asked.

'They can't come here!' Angus chipped in quickly. 'I'd be in so much trouble with my lease if other residents saw hundreds of illegal immigrants trooping up in the lift.'

'Oh shut up, Angus,' Annie said. 'There isn't anyone in this block who hasn't worked out that you're sub-letting to half the world.' She turned back to the others. 'Don't you think we should involve the police?'

'No!' Angus jumped back in. 'We don't want them sniffing around here.'

'He's right,' Rod agreed. 'The police wouldn't know where to start. They'd trample all over everything and the Martins would get away scot-free. This needs to be sorted privately.'

Cordelia appeared to be relieved at this decision, although she said nothing.

'So, where should we take the girls?' Annie persisted.

'The best place would be back to the flat in Gloucester Place,' Rod suggested.

'But they know about that,' Cordelia said.

'That's why it's good,' Rod said. 'They wouldn't expect us to go back there after they trashed it.'

'Unless we decide to let them know where we are,' Cordelia said, a plan hatching in her head.

'Lure them in, you mean?' Rod asked, his eyes lighting up at the prospect of some action.

'The apartment's a big mess still,' Cordelia warned. 'Dad's arranging for decorators and contract cleaners.'

'We can clean it.' Doris brightened up at the prospect of some serious housework to take her mind off the complicated web which had been spun around her.

'Yeah,' Joe said. 'Tell your Dad not to worry, that you'll organise the clean-up.'

'Doris can call all the girls she knows,' Rod said. 'And she can tell them to call any others they know. But these new girls in Brighton will have to be fetched. Who's going to do that?'

'There are some ugly characters down there,' Joe said. 'One in particular. I'd better go because I know the layout of the house.'

'It'll need more than one of us, then,' Rod said. 'I'll drive you down there and lend a hand.'

'I'll come,' Angus piped up. 'I've always been very fond of Brighton.'

'It won't be a day at the seaside, mate,' Rod said.

'No, no, quite. Serious business,' Angus blustered. 'Quite understand. Still, very happy to do whatever I can.'

'What if one of the girls Doris is calling spills the beans to her minders?' Annie asked. 'What if someone's in the room with them when they take the call.'

'Then we'll be ready for them,' Cordelia said. Everyone turned to her and it was obvious, from the look on her face, she meant what she said.

'Maybe we should stay with you,' Rod said.

'Too right, mate,' Cordelia grinned. 'Don't think you're going anywhere till you've helped with the clearing up.'

'Are you taking drugs?' Maisie's voice was shrill with suppressed anger. She hated having to deal with scum like Max. She hated the fact that, although she felt herself to be superior to them in every way, she still had to rely on the sheer brute force of their muscle to get things done.

Max grunted something non-committal back down the line. Maisie continued talking.

'Listen to me,' she said, speaking slowly. 'There is a man getting too close. He calls himself John Weston, or he calls himself Joe Tye. He has been to the clinics in Manila and London. He may have been to others, I don't know. He knows about the Montgomerys. He may know much more. It is time to clean up.'

'Yeah,' Max smiled happily at the prospect. 'He's been down here too. I owe him a beating.'

'Dispose of all the girls you can find as quickly as possible,' Maisie continued, ignoring the interruption. 'We don't want any evidence left behind.'

'Some of them are still carrying,' Max protested blearily. 'We need Rose to unpack them. Where the fuck is Rose?'

'Rose is on his way back from New York tonight. We can't wait for him. You'll have to operate on them yourself when you dispose of them.'

'What about this Joe guy?' Max was obviously fighting to keep a grip on reality. Whatever chemicals he had filled himself with were gradually seeping into his brain, making logical thought harder to grasp.

'Leave him to me,' Maisie said. 'I have an address. And you pull yourself together bloody quick or shit will hit everywhere. Understand?'

Max let out another guttural sound which suggested to Maisie it would be an hour or two before he started making sense again. She hung up angrily.

'How come you're such a little creep then?' the fat boy asked, and his two sidekicks sniggered.

'Get lost,' Hugo replied, concentrating on trying to make his football bootlaces join in some semblance of a bow. He was anxious to escape from the changing room as fast as possible. He was always getting into trouble for being the last to get anywhere, and the rest of the team had disappeared some time ago. The fat boy and his friends were now the only other people in the changing room and they were in no hurry. They were off games.

The more Hugo struggled with the laces, the more stubborn they became. He would have liked to have gone out with them trailing in the mud, but he had been in trouble for that several times as well. He couldn't understand how everyone else found it so easy to get changed in the allotted time. It seemed an impossibility to him.

'I think Creepy Tye-Dye needs a little help with his boots,' the fat boy sneered.

'No, I don't,' Hugo responded, adamantly.

'Don't argue with me, Tye-Dye!' The fat boy showered him with indignant spittle. 'Hold his arms while I "help" the little baby who can't do up his own laces.'

The other boys grabbed Hugo's arms and gripped him painfully. Hugo kicked as hard and as fast as he could, as if pedalling an imaginary bicycle. He caught the fat boy in the stomach and between his legs, knocking the wind out of him and making him squawk.

'You gay little bastard!' the red-faced bully screamed, frantically snatching at the flailing legs and ripping both badly laced boots off his feet.

'Let's go!' he shouted to his companions and the three of them ran out of the room, bearing their trophies with them.

Hugo sat for a moment in the silent changing room, catching his breath and staring at his bootless feet. His socks had unravelled down around his ankles. He wondered if he should borrow someone else's boots, just in order to get himself out onto the pitch and to avoid further trouble with the teachers. He decided that would be stealing.

After a few moments, when his heart had stopped thumping, he stood up and wearily changed back into his school uniform. He rummaged through his pockets to check how much money he had left from what his mother had given him before he left London. It seemed like enough. Opening his locker he pulled out a kitbag and checked that it contained his maps and train timetables. Satisfied, he snapped the locker door shut and slung the bag over his shoulder.

He made his way out of the changing room and crossed the playground outside quickly, diving into the woods which surrounded the grounds. Once out of sight of the school he hummed cheerfully to himself.

As Joe, Rod and Angus sped down the motorway towards Brighton in Rod's car, Hugo was sitting on a train going in the opposite direction. He had bought himself an Internet magazine and was deeply absorbed in his reading as the countryside sped by outside the window.

The three men in the car were equally absorbed in their own silent thoughts. They were relieved to have got out of the flat in Gloucester Place, where they had been all morning, helping to clear up. They had done as much of the heavy work as they could, and had then started to get on the women's nerves.

'For God's sake, you three,' Cordelia had exploded eventually. 'If you can't do anything useful then go and find the girls in Brighton.'

'I think we should be here with you,' Joe said, doubtfully. 'What if the heavies turn up again?'

'We can look after ourselves,' Cordelia assured him. 'Can't we ladies?'

The others had agreed with loud bravado, although they looked a little more half-hearted than Cordelia. Two new Filipino girls had already arrived, after urgent calls from Doris, and more were expected to turn up through the morning and afternoon.

When the BMW reached the outskirts of Brighton, Joe started to give instructions for Ditchling Avenue. Rod parked the car a few doors away from number forty-two and they sat for a minute, watching the street. An elderly woman came past, walking her dog. A group of young people appeared at the far end of the street and strolled towards number forty-two. They looked around furtively and then sauntered up the steps. One of them rang the bell and knocked, while the others darted looks up and down the street.

'Seems like they aren't open for business,' Rod said.

'Maybe they've already cleared out,' Joe suggested.

'Or maybe Max is already tracking down the Dorises,' Angus added.

They watched as the youths continued trying to attract someone's attention in the house. Eventually they shrugged at one another and wandered off. The street was now completely empty of people.

'Let's take a look,' Rod suggested.

He and Joe climbed out of the car and Angus struggled to clamber through from the back seat, tripping over the front seat-belt as he went and sprawling onto the pavement.

'That's inconspicuous,' Rod commented as Angus stood up, dusted himself off and joined them for the short walk to the front door. Rod led them past the steps to the gate at the side of the house. He opened it. It was unlocked, and they simply sauntered through. The alleyway at the side of house was green with moss. Water ran down the walls from leaking gutters and overflow pipes. There was a high fence between them and the alley for the next house. As they reached the corner of the building they paused.

The small garden behind was a jungle of weeds and junk. A bicycle, which someone seemed to have been trying to dismantle, lay next to a discarded bathroom suite. There were boxes of old newspapers which had become sodden and turned to solid grey lumps. Rod had his back to the wall of the house – just like in all the police television programmes, Angus thought. Rod edged round the corner to peer in at the window. The kitchen was empty. The patio doors leading out onto the garden were cheap replacements. Rod produced a screwdriver from his inside pocket, inserted it into the crack of the door and levered it sharply. Whatever lock he had found gave way without resistance and he slid the ill-fitting door open. They silently made their way in.

The table on which Joe had seen various of the inhabitants sitting during his last visit, was covered with discarded wrappers from fast-food outlets. There were saucers piled high with ash and cigarette ends, next to clusters of unwashed mugs. A stale odour hung over everything.

Joe took the lead and made his way cautiously up the grubby stairs to the first floor. The house appeared to be empty. As they tiptoed across the hall, the silent air was shattered by an explosion of ringing and banging on the front door. It seemed there were more customers in search of Max. The three men froze where they were and waited. They could hear voices outside. There was more ringing and banging and then the voices faded.

Joe moved on, peering cautiously into the first room which was full of mattresses. It was a few seconds before he saw Max, since the man was sitting so still amongst the tangle of blankets, sleeping bags and rubbish. He was naked but his assortment of tattoos had made him merge into the background.

His eyes were open and he was rocking back and forth very slowly, playing with a huge erection. Joe froze, waiting for Max to say something or make the first move. The ugly eyes were fixed on him, but didn't seem to be able to see anything.

Rod and Angus were standing beside him now, all three of them staring at the scene.

'This is the man?' Rod asked.

'That's him,' Joe confirmed.

'Jesus. Looks like he's having an interesting time.'

'Maximilian?' Angus stepped in front of them. 'Is that you?'

'Maximilian?' Rod repeated. 'You know this guy?'

'I used to,' Angus said. 'Intimately. In fact, if you turn him over and look at his buttock, I believe you'll find my name there, on a four-leaf clover.'

'I think I'm happy to take your word for that,' Rod said.

'I used to come to Brighton a lot when I was younger,' Angus said, as if that explained everything.

'Kinda rough trade isn't he?' Joe suggested.

Angus didn't reply.

'He's not going to be bothering anyone for a few hours,' Rod said. 'Let's check the rest of the house.'

They made their way systematically through the house, searching each room as they went. There was no one else there.

'This was Doris' room,' Joe said as they reached the top. 'The one she escaped from.'

'Let's have a look, then,' Rod said, pulling back the bolt on the red door.

There was hardly any light inside the room, the broken skylight having been blocked up with a piece of wood which had already grown sodden from rain. There was a rat-like scuffle of movement and the three men drew back quickly. No one jumped out at them and the room fell silent once more. Rod cautiously pushed the door further open and the light from the passage fell onto a huddled group of bruised and frightened faces.

Joe guessed they were the same three girls he had seen coming through Heathrow a few days before. But they were no longer the jaunty, giggling little adventuresses. Now they looked more like refugees crushed into the back of some boat or lorry.

'It's okay,' he said, stepping forward. 'We've come to get you out.'

One of the girls started to cry. Without their strutting bravado they looked more like children than women. As they emerged into the light it was easy to see that they were still carrying Chris Rose's packages inside them, their kilo-sized breasts hanging uncomfortably from their skinny little frames. The T-shirts they had worn so proudly at Manila Airport were stained, and their skirts torn.

The extent of their bruises became more obvious in the light. One of them must have been punched in the mouth because her lips were swollen in a grotesque parody of a pout. Another had a vicious slash of dried blood down the side of her face, as if she had been cut by a knife or razor. They looked at the men with wide, frightened eyes, as if expecting to be hit again.

'Come on,' Rod said. 'Let's get out of here before Angus' chum comes down from whatever planet he's visiting, or some of his troops arrive.'

With the girls in tow, he led the way back down the stairs, pausing at each corner to check there wasn't anyone waiting to ambush them. When they reached the hall they made a dash for the front door and the girls started to scream. Max was stumbling out of the room where he had been crouched earlier. His eyes seemed to be spinning in his head.

Rod tore open the front door and the girls ran out. A group of white youths, all sporting matted dreadlocks, were making their way up the steps. Max lurched towards the door, his erection swinging in front of him. The youths looked shocked and then started to laugh as Rod, Joe and Angus followed the girls down the steps.

'This way,' Joe shouted and they headed to the car. Angus climbed into the back seat and the three girls crawled in on top of him. Joe managed to get into the front passenger seat, with the door still hanging open as Rod hit the accelerator and they sped off down the street. The boys had let themselves into the house and closed the door behind them.

Once the men had left for Brighton, Cordelia, Annie and the growing band of Filipinos had set about the flat in Gloucester Place like an army of invading charladies. They had stopped off at the supermarket on the way over and armed themselves with every possible brand of cleaning liquid, mops, brushes, buckets, scourers and a dozen pairs of rubber gloves.

As the others set to work in the foul-smelling rooms, Doris had got out the fluorescent green, fur-covered book in which she kept all her telephone numbers, and continued calling the girls she hadn't already reached. She was feeling increasingly agitated about all the girls who she knew Max could hunt down if he wanted to. She knew that none of them would have found such a supportive group of friends as she had. They would all be out there on their own.

Throughout the afternoon more and more girls appeared at the door to the flat as the dirt and chaos yielded to their ferocious attack. At three o'clock Rod, Joe and Angus arrived back from Brighton with their girls.

Joe's phone rang just as Cordelia was explaining to Rod and Angus what she wanted them to do next.

It was Adele on the line. '*Sunday International* want you to go down to their offices and make the call to Martin this afternoon,' she said.

'Okay,' he replied. 'Tell them I'll be there in half an hour.'

When Hugo arrived at Victoria Station he pulled out his *A to Z* and opened it on the page he had marked. Squinting up at the street names, he located where he was on the map. Hitching his bag back onto his shoulder, he set off to follow the route he had worked out for himself on the train. He had a look of extreme determination on his small face.

The walk to Earls Court took him the best part of an hour. He was feeling both hungry and thirsty by the time he reached the block of flats in Bramham Gardens, but he didn't have any money left to buy anything. He began to imagine how his father would greet him. He knew Joe would be cross to start with. But then he would soften up and ask Hugo if he had eaten anything. Hugo began to picture himself with a Big Mac, large fries and an even larger Coke, munching happily as his father told him once again how unwise it was to be wandering around London on his own.

The street door to the block was standing ajar, the spring not strong enough to push itself the final inch to lock, so he didn't have to buzz himself up on the intercom. He pushed his way in and let the door close under its own steam again as he went to the lift. Once again it didn't quite have the strength to click shut.

When the lift deposited him on the top floor he pressed the front door bell to the flat.

The accountant who occupied the other room had come home early from work. Unusually for him, he had taken the afternoon off. Finding himself the only person in the flat for once, he decided to take a long, leisurely bath. He had a date that night and he wanted to look his best. He had just lowered himself into the bath and picked up his book when he heard the bell. As he wasn't expecting anyone, he decided to ignore it. Everyone else in the flat always seemed to have such active social lives. He was fed up with taking messages and answering the door for them when he had just got home from a hard day's work. As far as he could see they all just lounged around the flat all day anyway. He continued to read his book.

Hugo pressed the bell again and then sat down on the floor to wait. He was disappointed. He wasn't just hungry and thirsty, he was also tired and feeling just a little in need of a hug from his father.

He heard the lift clicking into life and descending to pick someone up. There was a clanking of doors from one of the lower floors and then the mechanism started to haul the lift back up towards the top floor once more. Hugo's hopes lifted. Perhaps this was his father coming home. Or, if not, he hoped it would be Cordelia or Annie or Angus. He thought about standing up to greet whoever it was, but his legs were too tired.

The lift gates were pushed open and two slender legs in neat high heels clicked out in front of him. He looked up beyond the short skirt and expensive silk blouse and found himself gazing directly into Maisie's expressionless eyes.

'Hello,' she said after a moment's pause.

'Hello,' he replied. 'I don't think anyone's in. Have you come to see my Dad?'

She held out her hand and smiled. 'My name's Maisie.'

'How do you do.' Hugo solemnly shook the hand which wasn't much bigger than his own. 'I'm Hugo Tye.'

'Yes,' Maisie lied without a blink. 'I know.'

'How do you know?' Hugo asked, interestedly.

'Your father sent me to come and find you.'

'How did he know I would be here?' Hugo was amazed. Maisie hesitated for a second. 'Did the school ring him already?'

'I guess,' she said. 'He asked me to look after you until he's free.'

'Oh, good,' Hugo said. 'I'm quite hungry actually.'

'What do you want to eat?' Maisie asked, her usual snappy manner beginning to return.

'McDonalds?' Hugo enquired hopefully.

'Sure. Let's go.'

Hugo was pleased to see she seemed to be in as much of a hurry as he was to get to some food. Outside the block she walked briskly to a yellow Mercedes SLK with a personalised number plate, MM 2.

'My husband has MM 1,' Maisie explained as she saw Hugo's eyes resting on the plate.

'Cool car,' Hugo said with genuine admiration.

'Sure,' Maisie shrugged and flicked open the locks to let him in. She was anxious to put some distance between them and Earls Court, while she thought how to make use of this unexpected windfall.

CHAPTER EIGHTEEN

'Mr Martin?' Joe was startled to get through to the man himself so easily. The editor, who was sitting beside him with headphones on, had said this number was direct, but Joe had still imagined he would have to go through a secretary or some other screening process.

'Who's speaking?' Martin's voice was patrician without being educated. He sounded like a man who was used to being listened to.

'My name's John Weston. I'm a writer and I'm doing a piece on the international movement of labour in the modern world.'

'Are you sure you have the right number, Mr Weston?' Martin growled.

'Well,' Joe continued, determined not to be intimidated, 'I've been looking into the popularity of Filipino maids worldwide, trying to explain the phenomenon.'

'I don't think you have the right number, Mr Weston.'

'I understood you and your wife run an agency for maids from the Far East.' Joe spoke quickly, before Martin could hang up.

'Who told you that?'

The fact that Martin hadn't yet cut him off was encouraging. The tape recorders were running and the editor was listening intently, deliberately not looking at Joe, as if anxious not to distract him.

'I saw an advertisement in *The Lady* magazine for "Maisie's Amazing Maids". Your wife is Maisie, isn't she?'

'My wife and I run our businesses quite separately.' It sounded as if Martin was relaxing, deciding he was dealing with a lightweight. 'Who did you say you were working for?'

'I'm freelance.'

'I don't think you have a story here, Mr Weston. My wife runs a small employment agency for domestic help. It's not part of any great international labour movement.'

'Are you aware that a number of the girls your wife brings over do not have work permits?'

Martin's tone hardened again. 'I think you have been misinformed. I think you should be talking to my wife. Or perhaps to her lawyers.'

'And that they are all needing breast operations when they arrive here, which leave them badly scarred. Are you aware of any of this, Mr Martin?'

There was a long pause. For a moment Joe thought Martin might have hung up. 'I know nothing of the day-to-day running of my wife's businesses,' he said eventually. 'I suggest you channel your enquiries through her lawyers.'

'Could you give me their number?' Joe asked, innocently.

'No, I could not,' Martin's tone was becoming more aggressive.

'Were you aware that your wife was using these girls to smuggle drugs into the country?'

There was another silence and then Martin came back on the line with a new, gentler voice.

'Mr Weston, it seems you are determined to get a story from nothing here. How about we make an appointment for you to come in and chat to my wife and me over a cup of coffee? I'm sure we could put your mind at rest.'

'I would like to meet you,' Joe said, an involuntary shiver running through him. 'But I think I'd prefer a public place. How about the bar of the Lanesborough Hotel?'

'We'll be there tomorrow evening at six,' Martin said. 'I'm sure we'll be able to answer all your questions and satisfy you that there's no story here.'

Martin hung up and Joe sank back into his seat. The editor pulled his headphones off, and the technician who had been operating the tape machine rewound it.

'We'll wire you up,' the editor said. 'Although he's bound to expect that. We'll have photographers posted around the hotel. We'll need to have proof that he turned up to the meeting. I doubt you'll be able to get him to give anything away, but at least we'll be able to link his name to the story. It's a start.'

The moment he had hung up on Joe, Mike Martin pressed the button for his wife's mobile number.

'I've had a journalist on my private line,' he said as soon as she answered. 'Says his name is John Weston.'

'John Weston is a journalist?' Maisie asked.

'You know him?'

'I met him. He pretend to be a client. Also he ask questions at clinics in Manila and London. His real name Joe Tye.'

'What clinics?' Martin snapped.

'Girls need plastic surgery. We help them.'

'He thinks you're running a drugs importation business.'

Maisie didn't reply.

'Whatever you are doing, you stupid bitch,' Martin snarled, 'you had better cover your tracks fast.'

'Already working on it.' There was an uncharacteristic quiver in Maisie's voice, as if she was genuinely frightened of her husband.

Martin hung up and sat thinking for a few moments. Apparently having reached a conclusion, he shook his head sorrowfully and lifted up the phone again. He pressed a button and the line was answered before it had even rung.

'Yes, sir.'

231

'I've got a cleaning up job that needs doing urgently,' Martin said quietly.

By late afternoon the flat in Gloucester Place was buzzing like a beehive. There were girls everywhere. The windows were thrown open and a strong smell of disinfectant had banished the stink of human waste. Anything that could not be repaired was being sacked up and taken out to be disposed of. The girls chirped happily to one another as they worked, and there were televisions or radios on in every room.

'Our Doris', as Cordelia and Annie had christened her, was still on the phone. Every Doris she had contacted had given her two or three numbers for others who they had travelled with or stayed with at some stage in their journey from Manila. She was following them all up. The web just seemed to be spinning out into infinity.

The flat was already heaving with young Filipino girls who had been working in London and had been able to get there immediately. There were still more to be brought in to safety, girls who either lived out of the centre or who hadn't yet been reached. They were all talking at once as they worked, exchanging horror stories about the families they had been working for. Most of them had lost their breasts.

'You must come,' Our Doris was saying to the girl who still stubbornly refused to leave the house on the hill overlooking Brighton. 'They know where you are. They come find you. It not safe to stay in house. Come here. We protect you.'

'I'm frightened, Doris,' the girl admitted. 'Max say he kill me if I run away from family here.'

'Max gonna kill you anyway. We protect you from Max.'

The girl fell silent, torn between her fear of going outside the house and the thought of Max coming back to find her again. She was still sore from his last visit. Her breasts were also hurting. They seemed to have grown hard over the previous three weeks and one of them had moved, rising frighteningly up towards her shoulder. She had no one to tell about her worries. The thought of going to be with other Filipino girls was tempting, even if it did mean she would have to leave the sanctuary of her scullery.

'Okay,' she said, eventually. 'I come. Same address you gave before?'

'Sure,' Our Doris gave a little clap of excitement, almost dislodging the phone which she had wedged between her shoulder and ear. 'See you soon. Call if you get lost in London.' She hung up and dialled the next number on her list.

The girl in Brighton went to her bedroom, which nestled behind the washing machines in the utility room. She swiftly packed all her possessions into the small sports bag she had arrived with in England just a few weeks before. She checked the pile of small change she had been accruing since coming to work at the house, one day finding a pound coin down the back of a sofa, another day finding a fifty-pence piece on the floor of one of the children's bedrooms. She had squirrelled away just enough to buy a ticket to London. Our Doris had told her how much it would be.

Quickly brushing her hair and pulling it into a ponytail, she hurried back out into the kitchen, desperate now to get out of the house and away from the street before any of the family came home and stopped her.

Max was waiting by the Aga. He was wearing gloves, a long black overcoat and a very nasty smile.

'Where the fuck do you think you're going, Doris?' he asked, turning her name into a savage sneer. 'Going to visit your friends?'

The girl couldn't answer. She had frozen to the spot, her jaw rigid with fear, her mind a blank.

'Where do you think you're going?' Max asked again, his voice rising in anger at her silence, like a school bully determined to prove his authority. He slithered towards her, adjusting his gloves as if preparing for a surgical operation. She let out a whimper of fear but was unable to make her legs move.

He grabbed her around the throat and threw her back across the Aga. She could feel the heat from the lids of the hotplates. Within seconds it became painful. But it was Max's grip on her windpipe that hurt the most, and he seemed very reluctant to let go.

'Tell me the address you were going to!' he insisted, tightening his grip. Her arms hung loosely at her sides. She couldn't muster the courage to fight back. 'Fucking tell me!' he screamed into her face.

'Same place as before,' she managed to gasp.

'You sure?' Max held his face close to hers. 'They've gone back there?'

The girl nodded and Max could tell she was too frightened to lie. Completely terrified by the situation, the girl passed out and slumped lifelessly against the hot Aga. Max released his grip and dropped her on the floor. He would come back for her later and finish the job if necessary, but first he had to get back to the flat in Gloucester Place and put a stop to things once and for all.

Now that Max had started, there was no stopping him. As he drove towards London he breathed deeply through his nose to keep himself calm and to ensure the adrenaline didn't take over until he wanted it to. He parked the car in a side street off Gloucester Place and walked deliberately slowly towards the block.

He didn't expect to be given any trouble by the porter. Max had learned long ago that men tended not to want to get into arguments with him. He liked to see the fear in other people's eyes when they saw him approaching. Even when he was walking along the seafront in Brighton he could see people crossing to the other side of the pavement in order not to encroach on his space. It had taken many years to make himself look this frightening, but it had been worth it.

He let himself into the building and walked past the reception desk without giving the porter a second look. As the lift doors closed behind him, Bernie lifted his internal phone and pressed a button.

'Miss Jones,' he said. 'That friend you asked me to look out for. He's on his way up in the lift.'

'Cheers, Bernie,' Cordelia said. 'I'll buy you a drink later.'

She hung up and clapped her hands to attract the attention of all the girls.

'Quickly,' she shouted, 'he's on his way.'

Like well-drilled soldiers they scuttled to their various posts. All the radios went off, leaving just one television in the sitting room. Our Doris sat on the sofa as if watching it. Everyone else vanished.

A few moments later there was the sound of a blade at the door. Our Doris gave it a nervous glance, before returning her eyes to the screen. The blade passed down the crack in the door and there was a clicking sound as the lock gave in to an expert's wrist action.

The door burst open. Our Doris let out an involuntary shriek and jumped to her feet as Max came hissing across the room. He grabbed her by the arm, almost lifting her off the floor, and pressed the blade against her throat.

'Cleaned the place up nicely, then,' he whispered into her ear, looking around at the half-repaired flat. 'Pity I'm going to have to get your blood all over the walls.'

'Help me,' she pleaded.

'There's no one here to help you, Doris,' Max said. But in the time it took him to get the words out he found himself lifted off his feet and carried across the room on a surge of angry arms. Someone was clinging tightly to his wrist, pulling the knife away from Our Doris' throat. The girl's long, hard nails were breaking his skin and blood was beginning to seep out from between them. Max didn't even have time to cry out as he was dragged down to the floor.

Piranha-like fingers were tearing at him from every angle as he thrashed around, trying to save himself. They yanked on the rings in his ears, nose, lips, eyebrows and nipples, holding him down in a dozen different places. He could feel the clothes being ripped from him, his skin being torn. Illustrations from tattoo parlours around the world, elaborate patterns, names and dates, were being muddied with his blood as the vengeful girls stripped him naked.

His knife was pulled from his hand and he was too busy trying to protect himself from the blows to be able to look for it. The next thing he knew it was pressed against his left eyelid and someone else, with strong, bony little fingers was gripping his exposed scrotum as if crushing walnuts.

His mouth opened to scream but no sound escaped as more fingers forced a damp piece of dishcloth between the sharpened teeth. It had been used to clean the walls and the cleaning fluids dripped into his throat, the fumes rising up into his nasal passages, making his eyes sting and his stomach retch.

'We're really pissed off with you, mate,' Cordelia said, cheerfully, putting a little pressure on the knife and allowing the point to prick the skin of his eye socket. A small rivulet of blood ran down and he blinked to try to get rid of it. 'We've spent all day cleaning up your bleedin' mess. We don't want any more of it. Do you understand?'

Max, too frightened to nod his head in case he drove the knife point in any further, gave a little squeak of acknowledgement.

'What we want you to do,' she continued, 'is write a little letter to the authorities. Just telling them all about the Dorises here and who you work with. We know all about you, Max, so we'll know if you're leaving out any good bits. We know you've been killing 'em off. We know about Chris Rose and his little operations. We know who your employers are.

236

'We don't intend to shop you. You don't have to worry about that, as long as you do whatever we tell you. We just want some insurance, to make sure you and your bosses don't think you can ever interfere in one of our operations again. Copies of your confession will be lodged with a number of different lawyers and they'll be under instructions to release them to the police if we tell them to, or if anything happens to me or my Dad or anyone else close to us. Which includes all the Dorises. Do you get it?'

Max gave another little squeak. Our Doris pushed her way to the front of the crowd with a large pad of lined paper and a pen. Other girls released his right arm, but Cordelia kept the knife pressed into his eye and made no attempt to remove the cloth from his mouth. The naked, blood-smeared Max sat up gingerly, and lifted his knees so that he could press against them as he wrote. His hand was shaking. The girl attached to his scrotum neither tightened nor loosened her grip.

'Okay,' Cordelia said. 'Let's start this story from the beginning.'

'The job's done,' the voice on the phone said.

'Good.' Mike Martin stood up from the table he was sitting at with several government ministers, a handful of civil servants and two offshore banking specialists. He walked to the window with the phone to his ear. 'Are you clear of the place?'

'There's a complication,' the voice told him.

'What is it?' Martin kept his voice steady. He wanted everyone else in the room to assume it was a routine business call. They were talking amongst themselves, taking no notice of him, used to him being interrupted by calls.

'There was a boy at the flat with her.'

'Explain.'

'He's some kid. Says his father is a writer called Joe Tye who's a friend of your wife's.'

Martin chose his words carefully. 'Was he there when you were working?'

'No.' The voice sounded hurt that Martin could imagine he would do such a thing. 'He was in the other room.'

'Okay. Keep him safe and out of sight. I'll contact you.'

He snapped the phone shut and went back to the group. They were deep in their own conversation, and obviously hadn't been taking any notice of his. He sat down and resumed his place in the discussion. An hour or so later he glanced casually at his watch.

'Gentlemen,' he said. 'You'll have to excuse me. I've agreed to meet my wife for a spot of shopping before we go out to dinner. I'm going to have to leave you to it. I don't think you need me any more, do you?'

There was a murmur of agreement and Martin left the building at a leisurely pace, talking to several people on the way out.

Rod had taken Angus back to his flat in Camden Town after dropping Joe at *Sunday International*. Actually, it was more of a bedsit than a flat. Angus was sitting on the edge of Rod's un-made bed in his vest, underpants and socks.

'You know John Travolta in *Pulp Fiction*,' Angus said, as Rod rummaged through his wardrobe.

'Yeah,' Rod said.

'Well, that's a good look. Very sinister. Very threatening.'

'Okay,' Rod pushed the hangers along the rail and pulled out a black suit. 'Try that. You'll need a white shirt. Do you have one?'

'Well…'

Rod sighed. 'Do you have any clothes of your own?'

'Of course,' Angus replied indignantly. 'But I've always gone more for the Noel Coward style. Never seen myself as a "hard man".'

'Okay,' Rod said, pulling open a drawer. 'Let me look.'

Half an hour later Angus was standing in front of the mirror looking as if he were on his way to a funeral. Rod had managed to find a black tie and a pair of black lace-up shoes. A generous scoop of hair gel had pulled Angus' hair back, giving his face a sinister, skull-like appearance which his thick, floppy fringe usually disguised. Rod was staring at him and shaking his head doubtfully.

'It's the eyes that give you away.' Rod said.

'What do you mean?' Angus prepared himself to be offended. He had always prided himself on his 'bedroom eyes'. When he was a young actor, casting directors used to compare him to Terence Stamp, and he was sure that over the years they had lost none of their darkly lashed allure.

'They're too soft,' Rod said. 'Anyone looking into them will see that you couldn't hurt a kitten.' He looked around the room. 'Here,' he said, 'try these.'

He handed Angus a pair of small, round, Ray-Ban shades. Angus slipped them on and smiled menacingly at himself in the mirror. Rod was right. He looked deeply frightening.

'Don't bloody lose them, mate,' Rod warned. 'They cost me a fortune. Here, you'd better wear this.'

'What?' Angus lowered the glasses so he could see better. 'Oh no,' he said at the sight of the shoulder holster and gun. 'I don't think we have to go that far, do we?'

'Just put it on and stop complaining or we'll give the part to someone else.'

Angus gave him a dirty look, but slid the jacket off so Rod could strap the holster over the shirt.

'You don't have to actually get it out,' Rod said. 'In fact, you'd better not in case it goes off by mistake. Just unbutton your jacket so he can see it. Okay?'

Angus pulled the jacket back on, replaced the shades and posed in front of the mirror again. He had to admit, if only to himself, that it felt good. He could feel himself getting into the part.

A fax machine in the corner of the room gave a couple of rings and then clicked into life, grinding out sheets of handwritten paper. Rod read each sheet as it came out, passing them on to Angus when he had finished.

'Fucking hell,' Angus said as he read.

Joe was still at the *Sunday International* offices when Fliss called him. It was growing late in the evening and the school had finally noticed that Hugo had gone again. There was an edge of panic in Fliss' voice.

'They don't know when he actually disappeared. No one has seen him since before their games period this morning.'

'Why didn't they inform us earlier?' Joe asked.

'Another child said they thought he'd gone to matron to get off games. Everyone assumed she'd put him to bed.'

'No one checked?'

'Apparently not. And I've been out all day, so if he came here there was no one in.'

'What about your father?'

'He's been at some Landowners' Association meeting, and Rosa went visiting her relatives. There was nobody here for him!' She was beginning to sound hysterical.

'He's probably okay, Fliss. He seems to be able to look after himself pretty well.'

'I know,' she said. 'But he's very little and a lot can go wrong, Joe.'

'Okay. Have they informed the police?'

'The local force, yes. They're out looking for him in Brighton. They told me to check he hasn't turned up with you.'

'I'm not at the flat. I'll try ringing them.'

'I tried. There's no reply.'

'I'll go straight there. Hold on.' He stood up and addressed the meeting. 'I'm sorry, urgent family business. I'll call you.' He walked out of the office, talking to Fliss on the phone as he went. 'His friend Ben, whose people live in Chiswick. Can you ring the school and get their number? Then ring them and check he isn't there.'

'Okay.'

They both hung up and Joe started to hunt for a cab. He wanted to get back to the flat as quickly as possible. If Hugo was waiting there, Joe didn't want to risk him becoming bored and wandering off again. This time, he told himself, they would not be going back to that school. No taxis appeared and he ran to the next street. He could see a few, but their 'for hire' lights were all out. He ran on, irrationally thinking that at least he was getting closer to home while he waited.

After twenty agonising minutes he came upon a taxi which was just disgorging its passengers. He raced towards it, shouting, terrified it would set off without him, or someone else would slip in and steal it. When he did finally sink into the seat, he had trouble finding enough breath to tell the driver where he wanted to go.

They crawled through the evening traffic. As the cab pulled up outside the block in Bramham Gardens, Joe saw the accountant getting out of a taxi with a girl. They met at the front door.

'Hello.' The accountant grinned cheerfully. It seemed to Joe that the man was a little drunk. The girl had made a big effort for the date and had forced her rather large legs into a mini-skirt and dangerously high heels. She too appeared to be drunk, but Joe thought it might just be the outfit unbalancing her.

'Hi,' he replied as they made their way to the lift together. 'Have you been out all evening?'

'Yes,' the accountant replied proudly. 'We've been for dinner in the West End.'

'Now he's luring me back to his place for coffee,' the girl giggled, and the accountant looked simultaneously sheepish and triumphant.

'You didn't see a small boy hanging around the flat before you left, did you?' Joe asked as the lift carried them upwards.

'There was no one in the flat when I left,' the accountant said. 'Someone did ring the bell while I was in the bath. But by the time I'd got out they'd gone.'

Joe fell silent, willing the creaking old lift to speed up. If that had been Hugo, perhaps he had just gone to get himself something to eat and would be back later. But then why hadn't he rung Joe's mobile to find out what time he would be back? Perhaps he was scared of getting into trouble.

The flat was dark and silent, and Joe felt a cold shiver of despair running through him. His child was lost and he felt as if his whole world had spun out of control. He had no idea what to do next. The accountant ushered his date into his room, and went down to the kitchen to make the coffee he had promised. Joe dialled Fliss' number. It was engaged. It seemed an age before he did finally get through to her.

'I'm at the flat. He's not here,' he said, the moment she answered.

'Ben's parents haven't seen him either,' she told him. 'I've given them both our numbers so they can call if he does turn up there.'

'I'm going to check the fast-food joints around the area,' Joe said. 'Then I'll come back here and check he hasn't turned up. I'll call you again.'

'Should one of us go down to the school in case he turns up there?' Fliss asked.

'What good would that do?'

'I just need to be doing something. We might be able to make the police take it more seriously.'

'Let me think about it.'

'I can't just sit here, doing nothing, Joe,' she protested, but he had already hung up. He was having enough trouble coping with his own emotions, he couldn't cope with hers as well, not yet, not till he had sorted out his thoughts and decided on a plan of action.

He grabbed a picture of Hugo off his bedside table and ran out of the flat. He took the stairs. He couldn't bear the thought of being stuck in the lift again as it laboriously ground its way from floor to floor.

Once outside, he ran in a circuit around the area. Within a quarter of an hour the muscles in his legs were screaming with pain and he could hardly get enough breath into his lungs to ask at each sandwich bar and fast-food joint he went to whether they had seen the little boy in the picture. Some of them barely gave the photo a second glance before shaking their heads. Others stared at the picture for what seemed like several minutes before deciding that they didn't think he had been into their place that evening.

When Chris Rose emerged from customs at Heathrow, having just stepped off the flight from New York, he was surprised to find a driver waiting for him, holding up a piece of card with his name on.

'I'm Christopher Rose,' he told the big, uniformed man. 'Is this car for me?'

'Yes, sir,' the chauffeur replied, with a broad, disarming grin.

'I didn't order one.'

'Courtesy of Miss Maisie,' the driver said, taking over the wheeling of the trolley and heading out to the limousine, which was parked on the tarmac in its designated area.

The driver opened the back door and Rose got in, sinking his tired frame into the brown leather seats. The driver stowed the luggage in the boot and climbed into the driver's seat. He started the engine and indicated to pull out into the traffic. Just as the car moved forward and Rose poured himself a scotch from the decanter in front of him, the door on the other side opened and Angus stepped in, sitting himself down next to Rose.

Rose heard the locks on the doors click automatically, and the screen behind the driver's head purred up to provide privacy as the car accelerated away.

'Who the fuck are you?' Rose asked.

Angus looked just as sinister as he had intended – an undertaker with attitude. He had tried out a number of accents on Rod and they had both decided that a Scottish burr, with just a hint of Glaswegian, was the most threatening.

'My name is not important, Mr Rose,' he growled, looking straight ahead as he spoke. 'You only have to listen to what I have to say.'

'I don't have to do fucking anything,' Rose protested, and Angus was pleased to note there was a quiver of fear in his aggression.

'You might as well,' Angus said. 'We have to pass the time somehow.' He allowed a long pause and Rose didn't interrupt. 'It has come to the attention of my employers that you have been involved in a little import/export business.'

'What the fuck are you talking about?'

'Just shut the fuck up and listen!' Angus barked, still without turning his head. 'We're willing to turn a blind eye to everything that has happened so far, and not even ask for any commission, provided you do as we ask.'

Rose said nothing. He waited for Angus to continue. Angus made the pause last as long as he dared before going on.

'Some of the girls who have been under your scalpel are still carrying...packages. We want you to do the operations to remove them.' Another pause. 'We then want you to provide the highest-quality reconstructive surgery to all the girls you've botched up so far. We want them to be as perfect as they were when they first met you. We don't require them to look like page three pin-ups, but we don't want them to look like they've just crawled out from under a multiple pile-up on the motorway either. We know you can do it, Rose. You have the finest of reputations.'

Rose made a rumbling noise which could have been a denial or an acceptance of his own genius with the knife.

'The operations are to be carried out at the Wimpole Clinic,' Angus continued. 'And you are to cancel all other patients until every single girl has been repaired to our satisfaction.'

'And who is going to pay for all this work?' Rose asked, his courage beginning to return as he realised that whoever this man was, he wasn't connected to the police or customs and excise. 'I don't come cheap, you know.'

'This will be your charitable contribution to a group of people less privileged than yourself,' Angus said.

'Fuck off!' Rose yelled.

'Perhaps,' Angus said, keeping his tone low in dramatic contrast to Rose's shouting, 'you had better read this before you make any final decisions.'

He passed over a few folded pieces of paper. Rose switched on the reading light beside him and unfolded them. Angus was grateful for the extra light. The gloom of the car's interior had been almost impossible to penetrate through Rod's Ray-Bans. The papers were faxed copies of what looked like a school essay, handwritten on lined paper. As he started to read, Rose felt a wave of nausea ripple through him. His forehead throbbed and his stomach churned. Max had written down the entire story, including Rose's part in it, in minute detail.

'This is a complete fucking fabrication,' Rose blustered as he got to the end, taking a swallow of whisky and slopping most of it down the front of his Armani jacket. 'You realise that, don't you?'

'Of course,' Angus bowed his head in acknowledgement. 'If you say so. But if we were to give this to the police, and then introduce them to the girls, some of whom still have kilo bags of coke in their tits, and the rest of whom are left with some pretty appalling stitchwork over their ribcages, they would be bound to ask a few questions.

'If, for example, they were to ask those same girls whether they knew who had done this to them, and every single one of them pointed their dainty little fingers at you...' Angus let his words hang in the air. 'Do you see how they might be forced to think that this statement had more than a little truth to it?'

'Who the fuck are you, you bastard?' Rose asked.

'Doesn't matter,' Angus said. 'Please give me your passport. We'd like to ensure you don't leave the country until this job is completed. Once all the girls are restored to good health, we'll return it to you.'

'Piss off!' Rose said.

For a second Angus wondered what he should do. Then a genuine anger at the man's arrogant face got the better of him. With a roar, he leapt across the car and grabbed the startled surgeon by the hair, slamming his head back against the window.

'Give me the fucking passport!' he shouted and, to his surprise, realised he had a gun in his hand and was pushing it up the distinguished surgeon's nostril.

Rose handed the passport over as meekly as a chastised schoolboy. Angus slipped it into his pocket and reholstered the gun. This was what they had always told him at drama school. If you wanted to give a convincing performance of an emotion like anger, you had to feel it.

He leant forward and poured himself a drink with slow, easy movements. Rose sank down into his seat, his head spinning with a mixture of pain and confusion.

Angus hadn't enjoyed himself so much in years, not since his last season in pantomime. As soon as he had dropped Rose at his house, he would take himself off for a night's clubbing. No point having the free use of a limo if you didn't do a bit of cruising.

CHAPTER NINETEEN

It was a nightmare from which they had no way of waking. As the hours ticked by and the streets began to empty for the night, it became more undeniable to both Joe and Fliss that Hugo had vanished. Joe had half hoped that, as people disappeared from the crowded pavements into their homes, his son would be left standing there, suddenly visible.

As they telephoned each other, back and forth, they racked their brains to think of places he could have gone to. They tried to visualise all the things that might have gone wrong, searching their minds for clues as to where he might have ended up, constructing scenarios, many of which were almost too terrible to bear.

Fliss started phoning the casualty wards of hospitals in Brighton, London and all places in between. No one had had an unidentified child brought in to them. She had been ringing the school every hour. When she detected a hint of impatience in the headmaster's voice on the fifth or sixth call, her self-control gave way and she screamed abuse down the line at him, threatening to sue the school for every penny they had. Paolo gently took the phone away from her, apologising on her behalf before hanging up.

The police were as soothing as they could be, their highly-trained, impersonal voices assuring both parents that it was early days and the chances were still high that he had simply fallen asleep somewhere and would turn up in the morning.

Just the thought of their tiny son curled up asleep in some unknown corner was too much to contemplate.

While Fliss spent her time making frantic phone calls, Joe kept tramping round the streets. He had instructed the accountant to ring him on his mobile immediately if Hugo turned up at the flat. No one else had come home and the accountant was now blissfully asleep in the arms of his plump date.

The London police came to Fliss' house at about one in the morning. They assured her they were doing everything possible, and asked questions about Hugo. Fliss called Joe and he walked up to the house from Earls Court, peering into every darkened corner as he went.

When he was finally sitting in Fliss' kitchen with a cup of tea and a policeman and a policewoman asking solicitous questions, he found himself unable to stop crying. The police obviously expected Fliss to try to comfort him, but that would have been impossible. They had not touched, not even shaken hands, since the day she had announced she wanted to leave him. Fliss had to avert her eyes from his tears and busy herself sorting through photographs of Hugo, trying to find a good likeness. Fliss' father squeezed Joe's shoulder as he left the room with Paolo. Both of them felt they were intruding on the broken couple's private grief.

When the police left, Joe went back out onto the streets. He was a man in a trance, too tired and unhappy to make any rational decisions. At half past five it felt as if a new day had started without Hugo being in it, and Joe didn't think he could stand the pain. Sitting heavily on a waste bin outside a bookshop he dialled Rod's number. He was surprised how quickly his friend answered.

'Did I wake you?' Joe asked.

'No,' Rod laughed. 'I just got back from a run.'

Joe didn't say anything, not knowing where to start and unable to trust his voice not to crack.

'You okay?' Rod asked.

'Hugo ran away from school again yesterday morning. He hasn't turned up anywhere.' Joe spoke as succinctly as he could, afraid that if he used too many words he would not have the strength to prevent himself from crying again.

'Twenty-four hours is too soon to think the worst,' Rod said.

'Easy to say.'

'Sure. Where are you?'

'Earls Court Road.'

'Go home and lie down for an hour. I'll come over as soon as I can.'

'Thanks.'

Joe was grateful. He felt in need of someone who would be able to tell him what to do next. Fliss had Paolo and her father. Joe felt lonely. The flat was silent. He couldn't tell if the others had got back and were asleep in bed, or whether they were still at Gloucester Place. For a few seconds, as he opened his bedroom door, he thought he might find Hugo tucked up in his bed, but there was no one, just a palpable emptiness. He lay down and closed his eyes, not expecting to be able to sleep.

The next thing he heard was the accountant's alarm clock going off in the next room. He was startled to find himself lying on the bed fully dressed. Then the horror of the situation came back to him. He forced himself to get up, and went into the kitchen to make a cup of tea. He had just put the kettle on when the doorbell rang and he heard the accountant letting Rod in. Joe poked his head out of the kitchen door to let his friend know where he was. He was surprised to see Rod carrying a pile of newspapers.

'Hello, mate,' Rod said, putting his arm round Joe's shoulders and giving them a squeeze. 'How're you feeling?'

'Numb,' Joe said. 'What's with all the papers?'

'You're not going to believe this.' Rod slapped them down on the table. All the front pages carried pictures of Mike and Maisie Martin.

249

'What's happened?'

The headlines didn't make sense to Joe. He was too tired to be able to focus his mind on the text.

'Apparently, Maisie strung herself up late yesterday afternoon. Just in time to make today's early editions.'

'Strung herself up?'

'Hung herself. Committed *hari kari* or whatever they call it, at their flat in Marble Arch. The sadly bereaved husband found her when he went round to pick her up for a little late-night shopping and dinner.'

'What?' exclaimed Joe. 'You mean she committed suicide?'

'So they say. Apparently, she knew she was about to be exposed as a drug runner and slave-trader and all the rest, so she topped herself rather than face the music. At least that's what her loving husband says.'

'Mike Martin says that?' Joe knew he was being slow, but he was having trouble getting the story into focus in his brain. Had he really caused all these headlines with one call to Martin? The kettle started to steam but he ignored it.

'He says a lot of things,' Rod continued. 'Like how shocked he is to discover that his wife was running all these illegal businesses without his knowledge.' Rod made a wry face. 'About how heartbroken he is to lose the woman he loved. About how ashamed he is that such things were happening under his nose without him knowing anything about it, blah dee blah dee blah.'

'My God.' Joe picked up one of the papers and stared at the pictures. There was one of an older woman he didn't recognise. 'Who's she?'

'She's the first Mrs Martin. The one who got dumped when Maisie turned up. You can imagine what a field-day she's having. She's already agreed some six-figure deal with your friend at *Sunday International.*'

250

'She hung herself?' Joe stared incredulously at the picture of Maisie. She looked so beautiful, so composed. It seemed impossible to think she would do such a thing.

'Of course she didn't bleedin' hang herself,' Rod said, pouring water from the boiling kettle into a couple of mugs.

'What do you mean?'

'Martin must have done it. Or had someone do it for him. Someone must have tipped him off that people were beginning to notice what was going on and he needed to find a scapegoat, preferably one who couldn't put her side of the story.'

'It was me,' Joe sank into a chair, still staring at the paper.

'What was you?'

'I tipped him off.'

'What do you mean?'

'I rang from the newspaper yesterday, to get his comments on the story. I used another name, but it was me.'

'Bloody hell.' Rod sat down beside him. 'Does he work fast or what?'

Joe took his mug of tea from Rod and started reading, momentarily distracted from his worries about Hugo. He skimmed through the story which lay beneath the picture of Mike Martin's first wife. It was full of scorn for Maisie, leaving the reader in little doubt that she had been a hooker who had taken Mike Martin for a fool, catching him at just the right point in his mid-life crisis and persuading him he was still young enough to start a new life with her. The editors had made her words contrast neatly with Martin's statements about how shocked he was to discover Maisie had been involved in crime, and how broken-hearted he was to lose the great love of his life. There were pictures of Martin dabbing tears from his eyes as he talked to reporters.

'He won't get away with this, will he?' Joe asked.

'He may,' Rod said. 'He's got away with worse over the years. But each incident like this brings the possibility of getting to him closer. It means he has one more chink in his armour, one more thing he has to keep covered up and under control. Eventually he'll simply have too many balls in the air at once. He'll drop one and the whole act will fall to pieces.'

'His political friends will have to drop him now, won't they?'

'They'll want to. But do they have any other source of income? I doubt it. Certainly not one quite so bottomless and generous. I think you'll find they'll be able to justify it, assuring themselves and the world that he was just the unfortunate victim of an unscrupulous woman. Don't forget, Martin knows where all their financial skeletons are buried. If they chuck him over too quickly, he might start blabbing about their finances, and I dare say there's a lot they'd like to keep quiet about there.'

Joe put down the papers and let out a deep sigh as he remembered why Rod was there and why he had a lead weight of misery lying in the pit of his stomach.

'What the fuck am I going to do about Hugo?' he asked, his tired eyes filling with tears.

'Cut out the defeatist thinking for a start,' Rod said.

Joe hurriedly blinked back the tears. 'And then what?'

'We keep looking. If we haven't found him by the end of today, then we'll be in bigger trouble. But we have a good few hours to play with before then.'

'Where should we look?'

'If he was going to come to London he would have got to either you or his mother by now.'

'If nobody got to him on the way,' Joe said.

'He's a spunky kid. I doubt it would be easy for anyone to spirit him away.'

'For God's sake, Rod, it happens all the time.'

'Tonight,' Rod held up his hand to stop him, 'if we haven't found him by tonight I'm willing to listen to all that. Not yet.'

'Okay.' Joe nodded. Rod was saying exactly what he wanted to hear, but it didn't lift the feeling of dread from his stomach.

'I suggest we go down to Brighton. I think it's more likely he headed in that direction. I'll drive.'

'Thank you.'

'We're gonna find him, Joe.'

An hour later Joe had showered and Rod had forced some toast into him. They were in the car heading out of London when Joe's phone rang.

'Joe Tye?' a man's voice enquired.

'Speaking.'

'Michael Martin.'

'Oh,' Joe fumbled for something to say, a dreadful thought was beginning to form at the back of his mind at the sound of Martin's voice. 'Good morning.'

'Do I call you Joe Tye, or John Weston?'

'Joe will be fine.' Joe signalled to Rod to pull over into a service station so he could concentrate better. 'How did you get this number?'

Martin ignored the question. 'It seems you knew more about my wife's activities than I did,' he said after a few moments. 'She's killed herself, you know.'

'Yes,' Joe replied, fighting back the fears that were rising inside him, making him want to scream. 'I saw the papers. I'm sorry for your loss.'

'Thank you.' There was another long silence. Joe was determined to wait it out. He had no idea what to say anyway. 'I'd still like to meet with you. I'm anxious to put the record straight as quickly as possible. The press is going to be making up all sorts of lies. I'd like at least one journalist to have the true story. Since you seem to know a lot about it already, you would be the obvious person.'

'I may not be able to make the meeting this evening,' Joe said. 'I have personal problems of my own.'

There was a pause. 'Personal problems?'

'My son's gone missing.' He felt his throat constrict on the words, as if they were trying to throttle him. Something was telling him that this man could be a potential lead to Hugo.

Yet another silence seemed to confirm Joe's suspicions. Joe looked across at Rod who had a puzzled expression on his face, trying to work out what was going on. Joe forced himself not to fill the silence. He had to wait to see what the other man said. It was like a game of poker for the highest stakes imaginable.

'Maybe we can help each other, here,' Martin said, eventually.

'What do you mean?' The knot of dread in Joe's stomach tightened. His hunch had been right. Martin knew something about Hugo. He thought he might be about to be sick, and he had to force his buzzing brain to remain quiet so he could concentrate on what the voice was saying to him down the phone.

'I have a lot of contacts. I might be able to help find your boy for you. Why don't you come round to the house in Wimbledon, so we can talk? I assume you know where I live.'

'I really don't have time right now,' Joe said.

'Have you had any better offers of help?' Martin asked.

'The police are...'

Martin interrupted him with a kindly laugh. 'The police will do whatever they are going to do. It almost certainly won't work. Have you got anything better to do with your time this morning?'

Joe's mind was working at full speed. If Mike Martin knew anything about Hugo's whereabouts, it meant his son was in serious trouble. But Martin hadn't admitted anything that Joe could take to the police. Maybe it was a genuine offer of help. But if he allowed himself to be lured into Martin's house he might never come out. He remembered Len's story about what happened to his son. If that had been true, then Mike Martin was not a man who held any great respect for father-son relationships.

'I'd rather meet in a public place,' he said, making up his mind.

'I've just lost my wife, Joe,' Martin said in a voice so level it was impossible to discern anything from it. 'It would be inappropriate for me to be seen in a hotel bar. Besides, the paparazzi will be following me for days now. Come to the house. I won't eat you. But avoid the front gate, the press are staked out there. There's a small door in the back wall with a bell. None of them know about it. Give three short rings and you'll be let in.' He hung up.

'What was all that about?' Rod asked instantly.

'Are we near Wimbledon?'

'Not far. Why?'

'Mike Martin wants to meet me at his house.'

'Screw that!' Rod said, adamantly.

'He says he might be able to help find Hugo,' Joe said, looking hard into Rod's eyes for a reaction.

'Does he?' Rod appeared to be thinking it through. 'That does change things.'

'He had this number. He could have got it from Hugo. Should we tell the police?'

'Not if you want to see Hugo again.'

Joe gave a sharp intake of breath, and Rod realised he had spoken too carelessly.

'Sorry. But if he does know anything about Hugo's whereabouts he'll want to trade that information. If the police are told he knows something he'll have to deny it. Then it would be impossible to make a deal and he'll get rid of Hugo as quickly as he can. No one would ever be able to prove he knew anything about it.'

'It could be a bluff,' Joe suggested. 'He may just be looking for a way to get me out of the way.'

'Do you want me to come in with you?'

'It would be comforting, but I don't think it would work. I have to take the risk, don't I?'

Rod nodded and put the car into gear.

'Do you know where he lives?' Joe asked.

'Oh, yes.'

'He says go to a back entrance, because the press are out the front.'

They drove in silence, both lost in their own thoughts.

As soon as they turned into the road in Wimbledon they could see the press pack. Dozens of reporters and photographers were camped out on the pavement amidst stepladders and deckchairs, Thermos flasks, take-away coffee cups and camera lenses three feet long. Rod cruised past them and took the first left. The reporters were all too busy talking and laughing amongst themselves to be taking any notice of passing cars.

All the large detached houses of the area seemed to have high walls or clipped hedges to shield them from passing eyes. In contrast to the road at the front, the side street was deserted. Rod slowed to a crawl and the powerful old car rumbled around the next left.

'If this is the back of the property,' Joe said, 'the house must have about two hundred yards of land behind it.'

'It has,' Rod said. 'I spent a good few months on surveillance round here once, when we thought we had him for insider dealing. Remember those days?'

'Christ yes. I didn't know he was involved in that.'

'He was up to his eyes in it. But the fraud squad never managed to pin anything on him.'

'You were in the fraud squad?'

'No,' Rod shook his head. 'They pulled people in from every division to try and nail him. We were watching him round the clock for years, but we never managed to get anything on him.' Rod pulled the car up a few yards away from a gate in a wall. 'That's the one,' he said. 'Give me your phone and I'll programme my number in. If you get into trouble, you just have to press the button and I'll come looking for you.'

'Thanks.' Joe handed him the phone and took some deep breaths as Rod worked, preparing himself for whatever lay ahead.

'Just press zero if you need anything,' Rod said, handing it back to him. 'Good luck.'

Joe took the phone, slipped it into his pocket and climbed out of the car. He walked to the gate without looking back and pressed the bell three times. The gate buzzed and he pushed it open. He found himself walking through a shrubbery into an immaculate garden. The house towered over the neatly mown lawns. A swimming pool stood to one side, with garages on the other. All was suburban tranquillity.

As he walked between the rose beds towards the open French windows, a young woman came out and walked towards him. He had been expecting to be greeted by some muscle-bound minder. This woman looked positively welcoming. She was neatly turned out in an expensive jacket and skirt. Her shoes were discreetly high-heeled and her make-up and hair were immaculate.

'Mr Tye.' She showed the most perfect set of white teeth he had ever seen and shook his hand firmly. 'I'm Christabel, Mr Martin's personal assistant. Mr Martin is looking forward to meeting you. Did you find us all right?'

'No problem,' Joe said, unsure of how to react to such a pleasant greeting from a woman who could just as easily have been welcoming him to a Buckingham Palace garden party.

'I'm sorry about having to ask you to come to the back gate,' she said. 'But we're trying to keep as low a profile as possible at the front. I'm sure you understand. Come in and I'll find you a coffee. Have you had breakfast?'

She led him up the steps to the terrace and through the open doors. Inside, a buffet was laid up, like breakfast in some five-star Caribbean hotel. There were half a dozen people sitting around the room eating and drinking. They were all young and just as well turned out as Christabel. They could have been delegates at a business conference, taking a break from listening to the speakers and using the opportunity for some private business meetings.

'Just a black coffee would be fine,' Joe said. 'I'm in quite a hurry.' He hoped the caffeine would help his tired brain to concentrate. He couldn't afford to make any mistakes with this man or he might never see Hugo again.

'Of course,' she beamed, pouring the coffee. 'We'll be going straight through. Are you sure you wouldn't like some freshly squeezed orange juice?'

'Quite sure,' Joe replied.

'Let's go in then.'

Carrying his coffee for him, Christabel led him through a pair of double doors into a room which must have been originally designed as a ballroom, but which had been converted into a huge working space. A number of people bustled about between the clusters of sofas and desks, all of them young – the men in shirtsleeves, the women in crisply pressed blouses. Computer screens and televisions with the sound turned off flickered all around. Everyone seemed to be talking into telephones in low urgent tones.

A man who Joe assumed must be Mike Martin emerged from the crowd with his hand outstretched. He was physically large and looked strong. He was in shirtsleeves, like all his young workers, and was wearing a black tie and armband. Joe found himself accepting the firm handshake without thinking. The hand was warm and dry and didn't let go of his.

'Neither of us is having a good day today, Joe,' he said with a sad, charming smile. 'Let's hope we can both do something to help one another.'

Joe was too dumbfounded to be able to think what to say. He had been expecting to enter the lair of some Mafia mobster. This was more like being in a fashionable advertising agency or public relations consultancy.

'Come and sit down.' Martin led him to a nest of deep, soft sofas and Christabel ensured that his coffee was standing within easy reach before leaving them together. 'I hear you're a great writer,' Martin said.

'I'm a ghost-writer,' Joe replied, determined to resist being charmed.

'That's what I hear. The best around, I'm told.'

Joe said nothing.

'Maybe we could do something together. I have been wanting to write a book for some time, but the pressures of business and politics...' He shrugged, letting the buzz of activity all around finish his sentence for him.

'At the moment I'm doing a book for one of the girls your wife brought over, filled full of drugs,' Joe said. 'It'll be a good read.'

Martin put his hand to his forehead at the mention of his wife, as if a sudden spasm of pain had passed through his brow. Joe guessed he was supposed to give him more condolences for the loss of Maisie, but somehow he couldn't bring himself to say the words.

'I'd like to help you with that.' Martin had lowered his voice, as if respecting Maisie's memory. 'Obviously I didn't have any idea what she was up to. My own fault. I should have been paying more attention to my marriage. Perhaps if I hadn't been so busy...' He let the thought hang in the air. 'But I might be able to fill you in a little on my wife's character and background. She wasn't all bad, you know.' He lowered his voice still further. 'I loved her so much, Joe. I can hardly believe she's gone.'

'You said you might be able to help me find my son,' Joe changed the subject, placing one of his cards on the invisible poker table which stood between them.

'I've already started on it.' Martin's expression was blank and showed no sign of any emotion – no guilt, no nerves, no aggression. 'I have a number of people working for me. They're all making enquiries. I'm sure we can find the lad for you.'

Now Joe was certain that Martin knew exactly where Hugo was. How could he have possibly started making enquiries when he didn't know what Hugo looked like, or even what age he was? He wanted to leap on top of Martin and punch him until he admitted it, but he knew if he did that he would be destroying all his chances of seeing his son again. He had to force himself to be patient and play the game by Martin's rules. Martin was going to want to trade. Joe had to wait until he knew what the deal was going to be. The effort of self-control was almost physically painful.

'You're an American, aren't you, Joe,' Martin said, settling back with his arms along the back of the sofa.

'That's right.' Joe sat forward on the edge of his seat in an attempt to stop the pace of the conversation from slowing any further. He sipped his coffee, grateful for the rush of caffeine. He had gone through the barrier of tiredness which had threatened to overwhelm him a few hours before. Now everything seemed pin-sharp around him, as if all his senses had been heightened and stretched.

'I wonder if you've noticed something about this country,' Martin drawled. 'They don't like success. People are always looking for ways to bring down anyone who's too successful. Have you noticed that?'

'I've heard it said.'

'The media are the worst. That's why I was a little cagey when you rang the other day. Can you understand that?'

'Sure,' Joe shifted uncomfortably on the luxurious cushions. 'I can understand that.'

'There are a lot of people who would like to see me taken out of political life. It's pure jealousy. They spread rumours and lies about my past in the hope of smearing my name and making it impossible for politicians to work with me. I would like to think that maybe I could rely on you to help me redress the balance a little. Put my side of the story. Tell the truth about me.'

Joe nodded his understanding of this suggestion. Martin's eyes were on his. They seemed not to blink. Joe looked away. It was obvious why Martin had been so successful in life. Saying 'no' to him would be a hard thing to do.

'I think you're a man I can trust,' Martin said, eventually.

'Thank you.' Joe forced his eyes up from his coffee cup to formally acknowledge the compliment.

'If you say you'll support me, I feel sure I can rely on you to keep your word.' Joe took another swallow of the hot coffee as Martin continued. 'Could we talk further once I've recovered a little from the shock of my bereavement?'

'Sure,' Joe said, relieved to have been asked a question which he could answer honestly. In fact, the idea of finding out more about this man was not unappealing. If only half what he had heard about Mike Martin's background was true, he had to be one of the most interesting people around. It would be fascinating to spend some time hearing his own version of his life.

Martin stood up with his hand out, signalling that the interview was over. Joe stood too, unsure what was happening. Where was the deal he was expecting to be offered? Where was Hugo? Was this all Martin wanted of him, a promise of future support? He couldn't leave without something. He couldn't go back to knowing nothing about where his son was. He would have to say something, lay his cards on the table, throw himself on the man's mercy. As he opened his mouth to protest a young man arrived at Martin's side carrying a phone.

'A call for you, Mr Martin.'

Martin took the phone and put it to his ear. He gave a few grunts of acknowledgement, before hanging up.

'It seems your son has been spotted,' he said.

'Where?'

'In Regent Street, asking the way to Hamleys toyshop.'

That was it. Joe knew the deal had been struck. At some time in the future Martin would be calling in this favour, but at that moment he didn't care. Joe didn't wait for Christabel, who was making her way across the room to escort him out. He was already running through the house and into the garden. For a second he couldn't remember where the gate was and stood desperately searching around the tranquil vista of the gardens until he managed to work out which shrubs he had come in through. He ran across to them and found the gate. He yanked open the locks and was in the street. Rod saw him from the waiting car and instantly accelerated to be beside him. Joe jumped into the passenger seat.

'Hamleys in Regent Street,' he said breathlessly. Rod stamped on the accelerator again and the car roared away.

'Hamleys!' Rod exclaimed as he threw the car round a corner. 'Fucking brilliant. Who would ever notice a spare eight year old in there?'

They came north up Regent Street and Rod U-turned across the traffic to bring them to a halt outside the toy shop. Taxis, buses and private cars swerved, stamped on their brakes and hit their horns. Rod and Joe jumped out and ran into the shop. Joe's heart sank. The place was seething with people, mostly tourists by the look of them. The aisles were blocked solid.

'Welcome to Hamleys, sir.' The greeter made him jump. 'Can I be of any assistance to you?'

'I've lost my little boy.' Joe pulled a photograph out of his pocket and thrust it into the woman's face. 'I think he may be in here somewhere. He mustn't be allowed to wander out.'

'Very good, sir.' The woman beckoned over a security officer.

'You start searching,' Rod told Joe. 'I'll stay on the door. Leave me the picture.'

Joe left Rod with the picture, which he started showing to the gathering security staff as Joe pushed his way through the crowd. There was no sign of Hugo on the ground floor. Joe racked his brain, trying to think which section of the shop would be likely to attract his son first. He couldn't think. He started up the escalator. It was crammed with people who weren't moving, just allowing themselves to sail serenely upwards at the speed at which the escalator dictated. Joe pushed his way rudely through, knocking over children and barging their mothers. He was past caring what anyone thought.

The first floor was just as packed as he raced around it, avoiding demonstrators anxious to show him how the latest toys worked.

Another escalator and more people blocking his way. The muscles in his legs, which were still aching from a night spent chasing around the streets of Earls Court and Kensington, were now screaming in protest. He was panting and red in the face. Shoppers were looking at him in alarm, women instinctively pulling their children away from the path of the madman.

Pushing and shoving, gasping for air and forcing his legs to keep running, he reached the top floor. Still there was no sign of Hugo. Joe's body wanted to give up, to lie in a corner and just let the weariness overcome him, to slip away and leave all the pain behind. But his mind wouldn't allow it. He went twice round the top floor, circling every display and carousel, and then started on his way down again.

A large, remote-controlled Formula One racing car screeched across his path. He saw it too late, was moving too fast to stop himself. His foot kicked the car across the floor. It screamed angrily as it spun out of control and hit a pillar in a shower of flying plastic parts.

'Dad, you idiot!' an angry voice shouted and suddenly Hugo was there, right beside him, waving the control box furiously at him. Joe swept the boy up off his feet and held him tightly to his chest. He was unable to get enough breath to scold him, or to tell him how much he loved him, or even to cry. He just clung to him for what seemed, to Hugo, to be hours.

'Get off, Dad,' he protested. 'This is so embarrassing. Can we go to McDonald's for lunch?'

On the ground floor they collected Rod and made their way out into the street.

'Where are we going?' Rod asked.

'Adele's office is just down the street. Let's go there and sort ourselves out.'

'That's not fair,' Hugo protested. 'You promised we could go to McDonald's.'

Joe wasn't listening. He was dialling Fliss' number. Rod scooped Hugo up. 'We'll go,' he said. 'Don't worry.'

'Fliss?' Joe got through. 'I've got him.'

'Where was he?'

'In Hamleys, looking at remote-controlled cars.'

'What made you think of looking there?'

'I just remembered going there with him and took a chance,' Joe lied. 'Do you want to meet us at Adele's office? Hugo wants a McDonald's.'

'Of course. We'll be right there. Is he okay?'

'He's fine. Do you remember the address?'

'Of course.'

'See you in a minute.' He hung up as they piled into the car and turned to face Hugo. 'Where have you been?'

'I went to your flat,' Hugo said, staring out of the window at the passing crowds. 'You weren't there and a friend of yours called Maisie took me for a McDonald's. Then we went to her flat, which was really cool. Then some of her friends turned up and I went to their house, which was cool. They had this shooting range in the cellar and they let me use it. They had these targets which were shaped like people and I shot this man right through the heart. Then they took me to the toyshop, but I lost them.'

'So you had a good time?' Joe asked, as casually as he could manage. 'No problems.'

'Really cool.'

Rod and Joe exchanged looks and Joe blinked away the tears.

Rod parked the car in Soho and they made their way back across the road to Adele's office. They sat round her desk while Adele's secretary made coffee. Fliss and Paolo arrived ten minutes later. Fliss clung to Hugo as tightly as Joe had done.

'Jesus!' Hugo said when she finally let go. 'I thought you two would be really cross with me for running away again.'

'Don't use words like that,' Fliss scolded half-heartedly.

'We are really cross,' Joe said. 'We'll talk about it later. We're just relieved you're safe.'

'Why wouldn't I be safe?' Hugo seemed genuinely puzzled at the idea.

'Where have you been all this time?' Fliss wanted to know.

'With some friends of Dad's,' Hugo said. 'They were really cool.'

'Didn't they think to ring either of us?' Fliss asked Joe.

'Apparently not.' Joe shrugged. 'They aren't people who are exactly used to dealing with kids. Don't make a big thing of it. Just be happy he's here.'

Adele's phone rang and she picked it up.

'Do I have to go back to school?' Hugo asked.

'No!' Joe and Fliss both said together.

'We'll find you somewhere closer to home,' Joe said. 'So we can keep an eye on you ourselves.'

'Joe,' Adele interrupted. 'There's a call for you.'

'On your phone?' Joe was puzzled.

'It's Marion Ray.'

Joe took the phone from her.

'Joe, sweetheart? It's Marion here.' Ray's voice could be clearly heard by all of them. 'Let's do it. My start on the movie has been delayed. I've got a spare week. Can you meet me in LA?'

'Sure,' Joe said. 'No problem.'

'Let your girl work out the details with my people. You can stay at the house.'

'Okay. I'll pass you back to Adele. She'll make all the arrangements. I'm looking forward to working with you. It'll be a great book.'

'Sure it will.'

Having handed back the phone, Joe looked across at Hugo, who was hugging his mother, and staring up into her face. Paolo had his arm around his wife's shoulders and was saying something private into her ear which was making Fliss smile. Joe felt a stab of pain in his chest. The three of them were a family unit which he knew he wasn't part of.

'Hugo,' he said, having to clear his throat to find the words he wanted. 'I've got to go away for a week or two. When I get back we'll go look at a few new schools together, okay?'

Joe looked at Fliss and could see she was avoiding catching his eye. Paolo was also staring into the middle distance and Joe knew that, by the time he got back from Hollywood, they would have made all the arrangements for changing Hugo's school. He felt sick.

'We have to talk about deadlines,' Adele said, having hung up the phone.

'Right.' Joe pulled himself back from the edge of the black hole of depression which had suddenly opened up in front of him. 'There's bound to be a lot of waiting around for Ray. I'll take a laptop with me and start a first draft of the Doris book. When I get back I'll get the rest of Rod's material from him. Then I'll lock myself away in a mountain shack somewhere and get all three written.'

Adele held up her hand to stop his exhausted chatter. 'Not now,' she said. 'Ring me when you've had some sleep and we'll work out a sensible schedule.'

'When you get back,' Rod said quietly as the others talked amongst themselves, 'we'll find a way to bring Mike Martin down once and for all.'

'Just let me sleep, Rod, okay?' Joe protested.

Rod grinned and raised his hands in mock surrender. 'Sure,' he laughed. 'You sleep. Have a holiday with your megastar friend, and then we'll have some more fun and games.'